the *Locket* of DREAMS

BELINDA
MURRELL

RANDOM HOUSE AUSTRALIA

BOOKS BY BELINDA MURRELL

The Locket of Dreams
The Ruby Talisman
The Ivory Rose
The Forgotten Pearl
The River Charm
The Sequin Star

The Sun Sword Trilogy

Book 1: The Quest for the Sun Gem
Book 2: The Voyage of the Owl
Book 3: The Snowy Tower

For Younger Readers

Lulu Bell and the Birthday Unicorn
Lulu Bell and the Fairy Penguin
Lulu Bell and the Cubby Fort
Lulu Bell and the Moon Dragon
Lulu Bell and the Circus Pup
Lulu Bell and the Sea Turtle
Lulu Bell and the Tiger Cub
Lulu Bell and the Pyjama Party
Lulu Bell and the Christmas Elf
Lulu Bell and the Koala Joey
Lulu Bell and the Arabian Nights

For the remarkable Mackenzie women in my family:
My grandmother, 'Nonnie' Joy Mackenzie-Wood
My mother, Gillian Mackenzie Evans
My sister, Kate Forsyth
My daughter, Emily Charlotte Jane Murrell
My niece, Eleanor Joy Mackenzie Forsyth

This project has been assisted by the Australian Government through the Australia Council, its arts funding and advisory body.

A Random House book
Published by Random House Australia Pty Ltd
Level 3, 100 Pacific Highway, North Sydney NSW 2060
www.randomhouse.com.au

First published by Random House Australia in 2009
This edition first published 2015

Addresses for companies within the Random House Group can be found at global.penguinrandomhouse.com

National Library of Australia
Cataloguing-in-Publication Entry

Author: Murrell, Belinda
Title: The locket of dreams / Belinda Murrell
ISBN: 978 0 85798 695 5 (pbk)
Target Audience: For primary school age
Subjects: Adventure – Juvenile fiction
Time travel – Juvenile fiction
Dewey Number: A823.4

Cover design by book design by saso
Cover images © iStockphoto.com
Internal design and typesetting by Midland Typesetters, Australia
Printed in Australia by Griffin Press, an accredited ISO AS/NZS 14001:2004 Environmental Management System printer

Random House Australia uses papers that are natural, renewable and recyclable products and made from wood grown in sustainable forests. The logging and manufacturing processes are expected to conform to the environmental regulations of the country of origin.

Glossary of Scottish Words

Bairn	child
Bannock	flat bread made of oatmeal
Banshee	small fairies with long white hair, which foretell death if seen
Bonnie	beautiful
Brownie	shy household fairyfolk who help humans in return for food
Burn	small river or brook
Changelings	fairy babies left in place of human babies
Crofts	small farms rented by crofters or tenant farmers
Dun	tower or castle
Elfhame	fairyland
Eilean	island
Gae	go
Ghaistie	ghost
Gillie	highland laird's hunting attendant
Glens	valleys
Gorm	blue-green colour of the Scottish hills
Guid	good
Hame	home
Kelpies	fairy water-horses
Ken	know
Knowe	round hillock where fairies dwell
Kirk	church
Selkies	sea-creatures that transform from seals to human form
Sporran	bag, often made of sealskin decorated with silver, worn with a kilt
Trews	tight-fitting traditional Scottish trousers

A fragment of my grandmother Nonnie's favourite poem:

A thing of beauty is a joy for ever:
Its loveliness increases; it will never
Pass into nothingness; but still will keep
A bower quiet for us, and a sleep
Full of sweet dreams, and health, and quiet breathing.

John Keats, 1818

1

Sepia Memories

Sophie and Jessica bent over an old photo album looking at faded sepia photographs of bridal veils, orange blossoms, waxed moustaches and babies in christening gowns that swept the floor. Motes of dust danced up from the black pages and floated in the sunlight streaming through the open window.

Jessica wrinkled her nose at the faint smell of aged, dry paper. She brushed her hand over a photo of a young couple laughing up at the camera. The girls' grandmother, Nonnie, stood beside the antique cedar table pouring tea from a china teapot.

'Nonnie, who are they?' asked Sophie, pointing to the joyful faces.

Nonnie peered at the photograph and a wistful smile crossed her face.

The young woman wore a tailored suit with a fur collar, the straight skirt nearly brushing her ankles. A small hat perched on her neat curls and her face gleamed with fun, lips painted with a dark lipstick. The man, tall and proud, slung one arm protectively around her shoulder while he cradled a pipe in his other hand.

'That is me with your beautiful papa,' Nonnie replied, her voice catching. 'I was twenty and Papa was twenty-two. That photograph was taken a few weeks after we met. I had only known him a short time but we both knew we would marry.'

Sophie and Jessica gazed up at their grandmother, fascinated. Nonnie looked so beautiful and so fragile in the old photograph. They could see the same narrow shoulders and straight back, the same curls, although now streaked with grey, and a hint of the same mischievous smile.

Jessica wriggled beside her sister. 'How did you meet Papa?'

Nonnie laughed as she poured milk from a chubby jug into the fine china teacups.

'I went to a party on a boat with my friends. Actually, I was escorted by a young man whom I had been seeing for some months.' Nonnie pulled a little face. 'Your papa jumped aboard at the last moment, just as we were casting off. He came straight up to sit beside me and seemed so fun and carefree that everyone else seemed dull by comparison.'

Nonnie passed each girl a cup of fragrant milky tea, balanced on a delicate saucer.

'He had no money but so much *joie de vivre* that I couldn't help but love him.' Nonnie blinked rapidly, her eyes shining. 'We were married a few months later, and as they say, the rest is history,' she laughed. 'Your mama was born a year later.'

Nonnie gazed at the photograph fondly, memories crowding the room. The girls' grandfather, Papa, had died the year before, leaving a gaping wound in all their lives.

Sophie jumped up from the sofa, fetched the forgotten rack of toast and carried it over to the table. She and Jessica munched on buttery toast with homemade jam. Two pale faces, lightly sprinkled with freckles, one framed in blonde hair, one dark. Sophie was twelve, Jessica was ten.

Both were staying at their grandmother's apartment for the school holidays and were dressed in their summer best, hair scraped back, bodies scrubbed, their pretty dresses hiding scratched knees and bruised shins from climbing trees.

As Nonnie told them tales of her wedding and youth, they felt as though they were absorbing the air of another era, a softer, more romantic era. An era with no money troubles, no family worries, no school problems.

'Nonnie, who is this?' Sophie asked, pointing to a photograph of a stern-looking matriarch in a stiff lace collar and silk skirts.

'That was my great-grandmother Charlotte Mackenzie, so your great-great-great-grandmother,' Nonnie replied. 'She was the first one of my family to come to Australia, about one hundred and fifty years ago. She was a remarkable woman.'

Nonnie bent and ruffled Sophie's hair.

'She was a bonnie Scot who came to Australia as a young girl about the same age as you, Sophie,' Nonnie continued. 'She was a feisty lass with red hair and green eyes. My mother told me she was considered a real beauty in her day. As a young woman, she had half of Sydney's men madly in love with her.'

Sophie smiled up at her grandmother, imagining herself as a bonnie lassie with half of Sydney at her feet.

'Charlotte Mackenzie eventually fell in love and married a handsome young Welshman called William Thomas and raised a merry tribe of children.'

Jessica and Sophie gazed at the photo of Charlotte Mackenzie, trying to imagine her as a beautiful young girl.

'Actually, Charlotte's story is rather romantic and quite mysterious.' Nonnie settled down at the table, pulling her cup of tea towards her. 'Charlotte Mackenzie was the daughter of a wealthy Scottish laird who owned a beautiful estate on an island off the west coast of Scotland.

'The family had an ancient castle called Dungorm, which was stormed by the English when Bonnie Prince Charlie was hiding there during the Jacobite rebellion. The castle was blown to smithereens but the prince escaped with the help of the Mackenzies.'

Sophie felt a shiver of excitement tingle up her spine. Her family had once owned a ruined Scottish castle. Her family had hidden Bonnie Prince Charlie from the English.

'The family was very wealthy and built a beautiful, grand home on the island, near the ruins of the castle,' Nonnie explained. 'Then a terrible tragedy struck the Mackenzies. No-one really knows what happened because Charlotte would never speak of it, but Charlotte and her sister, Eleanor, were orphaned and sent across the world to Australia to live.

'My mother told me stories of a wicked uncle who deprived the girls of their inheritance. She believed the estate of Dungorm should rightfully have gone to Charlotte.'

Sophie and Jessica glanced at each other, their eyes burning in excitement. Nonnie smiled at their enthusiasm.

'But it was all such a long time ago,' concluded Nonnie. 'No-one cares any more what happened to two young Scottish girls.'

'We care,' retorted Sophie warmly. 'I'd love to know what happened.'

Nonnie was silent for a few moments, her face thoughtful.

'I have a box of Charlotte's things,' Nonnie began. 'Would you like –'

'Yes, yes,' Sophie and Jessica chorused loudly. 'Please, Nonnie,' they added, belatedly remembering their best manners.

Nonnie returned a few minutes later carrying a dark timber box, its lid and sides ornately carved. She set it on the table, gently wiping the dust away.

The box was slightly larger than a shoebox. Its lid was carved with a striking depiction of a stag, its antlers held proudly aloft. A rising full moon circled its head and antlers, while flowers and plants curled around the border.

Words were carved within the border of the lid. Nonnie ran her finger along the words. Across the top was carved *Luceo non Uro* and on the bottom, the English translation.

'*Luceo non Uro*, which is Latin. In English it means "I shine not burn," which is the Mackenzie clan motto.'

'What does that mean?' asked Jessica, wrinkling her brow.

'It means that the Mackenzies try to do their very best in everything they do – to shine, but not to burn out or be consumed,' replied Nonnie. 'It's a worthy aim to have in life. Would you like to open it? I don't think anyone has opened it for fifty years.'

Sophie gently turned the tiny golden key, which grated creakily in the lock. Together the girls lifted the lid and peered inside. A rectangle of faded violet silk lined the box, in which a jumble of different objects nestled together.

One by one the girls lifted the objects out and examined them curiously. A small polished red pebble. A dried and dusty twig. Crumbles of tiny parched brown leaves. A tiny arrowhead shining like freshly burnished silver. A torn swatch of faded green-and-blue tartan. A coil of long, heavy chain and a heart-shaped gold locket.

'That is heather, the national flower of Scotland,' Nonnie explained, pointing to the dried twig. 'In summer the moors of Scotland are covered in a purple haze of heather bells. I think that is probably my favourite colour in the world.'

Nonnie carefully opened the delicate locket to show them the plaited twist of red and black hair. 'It's a love lock. In the old days before photographs, people used to keep a lock of hair inside a locket as a memento of their loved ones.'

'I wonder whose hair's in the locket? Some of it is red – do you think it might be Charlotte's?' wondered Sophie.

'It could be,' agreed Nonnie.

'Why did Charlotte keep a pebble in her treasure box?' cried Jessica, wriggling with enthusiasm. 'What was the tiny arrow used for?'

'Why were Charlotte and her sister sent away?' begged Sophie. 'What happened to their parents?'

'What happened to Castle Dungorm?' Jessica asked, words spilling over themselves. 'Maybe if it really was Charlotte's we could claim the castle for our family!'

Nonnie held up her hands and laughed. 'I told you it was intriguing, but it all happened nearly a hundred and fifty years ago. I'm afraid we'll never truly know the answers to all those questions. It must forever remain a mystery.'

The girls' minds churned with questions that couldn't be answered.

'Come on, girls,' said Nonnie. 'It's a beautiful day. Why don't we go out for a walk?'

That night Sophie lay in bed wearing her long white nightdress embroidered with tiny daisies that Nonnie had given her for Christmas. Sleep eluded her as images of castles and Scottish heather jostled inside her head. These were chased away by thoughts of her home and her own family problems.

No, don't think of that; think of castles, Sophie told herself.

Jessica was asleep in the other bed, breathing deeply and evenly. Sophie tossed and turned, her blonde hair sticking damply to her face and neck.

At last Sophie pulled back the covers and slipped out of bed. She tiptoed to the chest of drawers and opened the dark wooden box with the stag carved on the lid. She could feel the curve of his antlers with her fingertips.

A gleam of light filtered through the partially open door, hardly enough to see by. Using her fingertips she rummaged through the box and found the cool, slippery gold of the old locket chain.

Sophie weighed the heavy chain deliberately in her hand. She traced the engraving on the heart-shaped locket, then quickly, guiltily slipped the chain over her head and inside her nightdress. She didn't know why she felt the urge to wear the old necklace. It just seemed to have a magnetic pull on her.

She wondered about Charlotte and Eleanor Mackenzie. *What was their life like? What did the castle of Dungorm look like?*

Cradling the locket in her palm, Sophie quickly felt sleep sink upon her, snuggling around her like a soft, cozy doona.

She felt her body melting then sliding down a steep tunnel, falling faster and faster, hurtling towards sleep. She shot out of the darkness into a blinding, dazzling vastness of light, with nothing below her. Sophie felt momentarily afraid as she fell but then she realised she was no longer falling but flying, soaring above a deep-green earth.

Far below her she saw two figures moving across the landscape. Her curiosity prickled and she turned her body to swoop towards them. Sophie felt as light as a feather, her body gliding on puffs of breeze.

As she dropped lower she realised the two figures were girls, galloping on ponies, their red hair and long green skirts flying in the wind. It suddenly occurred to Sophie that the two girls, with their veiled hats and full petticoats, looked liked old-fashioned children out of an aged book.

2

Nell's Fall

'Giddy-up, Rosie,' the older girl cried, kicking her heels into the side of her grey mare. 'Race you to the top, Nell!'

Nell responded with a shriek and a flourish of her riding crop. The two girls rode side-saddle, dark-green velvet skirts flapping over their horses' flanks.

The horses galloped down a steep green hill, leaving muddy hoof prints in the spongy turf, their riders whooping with delight. At their heels loped a shaggy black-and-white dog, its tongue lolling, one ear pricked and one flopping over its eye.

At the bottom of the hill, an icy burn tumbled and splashed its way over the grey rocks. The horses barely slowed as they clattered through the shallow water and galloped up the sheer bank on the other side, the dog close behind.

A great clod of mud flew up from Nell's horse's hooves

and struck her sister, Charlotte, on the cheek, splattering her bodice.

Charlotte smeared the clod away with the back of her gloved hand and whispered in Rosie's ear. 'Come on, girl. Let us show them what you can do.'

Nell's horse slowed slightly on the steep slope, sides heaving and clouds of steamy breath snorting from her nostrils. Rosie's ears pricked with excitement and her stride lengthened, gradually outpacing the horse in front of her.

'Whoo hoo,' shrieked Charlotte, crouching over Rosie's neck, her hands tangled in the horse's mane. She leant forward, reins flapping as the wind stung her cheeks and whipped her breath away.

Charlotte felt as if she were flying; the horse's hooves barely seemed to skim the earth.

Over the crest of the hill they galloped, ducking under a low-lying branch, the leaves whipping Charlotte's burning cheeks. At the top, the horses thundered to a stop, their sides heaving and steaming. The black-and-white dog flopped gratefully on the spongy heather.

Over the hill erupted a stunning vista. The girls didn't speak; their eyes roamed the familiar landscape as joy pounded through Charlotte's body. She could never tire of this view.

Rolling hills of emerald-green grass were crisscrossed with grey stone walls and studded with bright-yellow broom and tufts of snowy-white thrift. To the right stretched a steel-grey loch fringed with lichen-spotted rocks, its surface ruffled with the breeze.

A grand mansion of golden stone faced the loch, smoke curling from its many chimneys, its slate-roofed turrets jutting against the sky.

Even further to the right was a small island, quite close to the shore, its surface scattered with the crumbling remains of an ancient stone castle, Castle Dungorm. In the distance the loch opened up to embrace the endless swell of the sea.

'We had better head home, Charlotte,' called Nell, breaking Charlotte's reverie. 'Nanny will be wondering where we are.'

Charlotte nodded reluctantly. It had been a long winter and today was the first spring day the girls had been able to escape the army of people whose sole aim in life seemed to be to keep them indoors at their schoolbooks.

'Come on, Floss,' Charlotte called to the dog. 'Time to go home.'

Floss panted in agreement, her tongue dripping.

In silence they picked their way down the hill, scanning the ground for rabbit holes, enjoying the faint warmth of the sun on their faces and the fresh scents in the air.

Both horses were skittish and edgy after long months in the stable. Rosie pranced and snorted at every imagined threat. As the bank steepened, she started, refusing to move forward. Charlotte held on sternly, calming the mare with her voice and hands.

'Walk on, girl, enough of your nonsense,' Charlotte chided. 'You have been down this way a hundred times before.'

The horse tossed her head sheepishly, sidestepped and cavorted some more, then finally skipped forward. By this time Nell was way in front, cheekily waving at Charlotte from the bottom of the hill.

'See you at home, if you can catch me!' Nell shouted as she urged Bess into a canter.

Scenting home and a warm, dry stable, Nell's horse, Bess, pricked her ears and leapt into a gallop. The flying hooves kicked up thick brown mud, which spattered the horses' flanks and the long velvet skirts trailing behind.

Charlotte's eyes streamed with tears from the freezing wind. Wind whipped her hair, her face burnt and her heart raced with the excitement of the chase, a joyous cry welling from her throat.

Charlotte gained on Nell as they raced around the shore of the loch. Nell glanced over her shoulder, cheering Bess on, but Rosie effortlessly caught up. Neck and neck they galloped, sailing over a dry-stone wall, manes and ringlets flying, leaving Flossie to lope behind.

With an alarmed squawk, a pheasant flitted from its nest right under Bess's hooves. The chestnut reared and bucked in fright, then bolted, flinging Nell to the ground.

Charlotte screamed as Bess galloped away, stirrups and reins flapping wildly. She reined in her own horse, nearly flying over Rosie's head as she slid to a stop.

'Nell, Nell – are you all right?' Below lay the motionless body of her sister crumpled in the grass. Charlotte sobbed as she slithered off her horse. Flossie whined pitifully, licking Nell on the face and pawing her gently.

'Nell, can you hear me?' she begged. 'Nell, please answer me.'

Charlotte's voice rose in panic. The smell of crushed grass and wet mud filled her nostrils, making her stomach heave. She knelt and rolled her sister gently over. Crimson blood welled from the side of Nell's mouth, a stark contrast to the pale white skin. Charlotte stifled a scream.

Her heart in her mouth, Sophie flew closer. Was Nell

dead? She hovered uncertainly, then wondered if she could somehow get help. Perhaps if she followed Bess, the horse would lead her back to the girls' home and she could alert someone to come back with her.

Sophie zoomed away, leaving Charlotte bent over the motionless body of her sister.

Overtaking Bess, Sophie soared through a stone gateway that led to the stable courtyard.

A young stableboy sat rubbing oil into a saddle girth. He jumped to his feet as the sound of galloping hooves echoed through the cobbled gateway. The chestnut pony skittered and shied, hooves slipping on the muddy cobbles.

Sophie flew up to the boy.

'There's been an accident,' Sophie cried. 'Nell's fallen.'

The boy ignored her completely, as if she hadn't spoken, interested only in Bess.

'Duncan. Duncan. Coom quickly,' he yelled. A weather-beaten gillie shuffled from a stall; his plaid and kilt were mud-stained and he had a stiff brush in his hand.

'Och, Bess,' Duncan scolded. The mare looked sheepishly at him and slithered to a stop, thrusting her snorting muzzle into his gentle, gnarled hands. He stroked her, keeping his voice low and soothing.

'Quick, Angus lad. Luiks like the wee lassie has taken a tumble. Saddle up the grey mare for me and call Hamish in. Tell Hamish to fetch me laird and some o' the house lads. And best tell Mary to make ready.'

Young Angus ran to do the old gillie's bidding. Sophie turned to Duncan, and clutched his arm.

'I know where Nell is,' she shouted. 'I can show you.'

Angus shivered as if her touch was cold, but did not answer, stooping to pick up the saddle Angus had abandoned. It was as though Sophie did not exist.

The courtyard was quickly filled with the shouts of running men swiftly saddling horses. Alexander Mackenzie, Laird of Dungorm, strode from the house. Tall and imposing in his blue-and-green kilt, he had the assurance of one used to commanding.

Angus the stable lad stood at the head of a large black gelding as Laird Mackenzie swung his leg into the saddle and signalled his retainers to join him.

A gaggle of stableboys, gardeners and footmen followed, with four dogs excitedly sniffing at their heels. The old gillie, Duncan, set his grey mare to a trot and they headed out of the courtyard, through the chilly tunnel and out into the open countryside.

'Duncan!' Laird Mackenzie called. 'Does anyone know where the lassies were riding today?'

'Well, my laird,' grunted Duncan, 'I am no' exactly sure as the wee lassies saddled the horses wi'out Angus.'

Laird Mackenzie swore. 'When I find those lassies they will feel the back of my strap,' he roared. 'How many times have I told them they must always ride with one of the grooms! Those girls are wild.'

'Och, but wild lassies wi' a guid seat, my laird,' replied Duncan dryly.

'Well, they won't be able to sit on them for a while,' retorted their father, repressing a proud smile. 'Hamish, you take some of the men and head towards the village. Duncan, Angus and I will search to the north, while the others search south. Sound a horn or whistle if you find them. Cameron, you stay here and harness the carriage, ready for when I send for you.'

The horses galloped off in different directions, with the dogs and men running behind. Rain began to fall in white sheets, obliterating the view.

Waving and gesturing, Sophie tried to steer the searchers towards Charlotte and Nell, but they still could not hear or see her so she abandoned them and flew back on her own.

Down below, Sophie could see Charlotte huddled beside Nell, trying to shelter them both under her cloak. Rain was falling in pelting torrents. Sophie alighted beside Nell and took her hand.

Nell shivered violently at the touch, then groaned and rolled over, her right hand clutching her left shoulder.

'Nell, thank God you are alive. Are you hurt badly? Talk to me!' Charlotte pleaded.

Nell groaned again, rolling on the ground. She coughed and spluttered, spitting out blood.

Charlotte knelt by her side, wiping the blood away with the skirt of her petticoat, nearly shaking Nell in her anxiety.

'Please speak to me, Nell,' she commanded. 'Where do you hurt?'

Nell shook her head groggily.

'All . . . over,' she finally whispered. 'My . . . arm hurts . . . and my shoulder.'

Charlotte sighed in relief, then leapt to her feet.

'Come on. We'd better get you home so that Nanny can have a good look at you. Can you stand?'

Nell shook her head.

'No. I . . . feel . . . dreadful.'

'You will be fine,' Charlotte cried. 'I will bring Rosie over to that stump, you climb on and I will lead you home.'

Charlotte grabbed Nell under the armpits to haul her to her feet. Nell screamed as a white pain seared through her arm, her body shaking with tremors. Flossie whined anxiously, trotting around them in a protective circle.

'Oh, I am so sorry. I did not mean to hurt you! What should I do?' Charlotte said, panicking. 'Nell, if I ride back for help, will you be all right until I get back? Flossie will guard you.'

Nell looked up at her with eyes dilated with pain. Charlotte thought for a moment, discarding several plans.

'Nell, I cannot lift you onto Rosie,' Charlotte decided. 'You will have to stay here while I go back for help. I will be as quick as I can, I promise.'

Nell tried to lift her head but nearly swooned with the effort. She bit her lip and nodded slightly.

Charlotte pulled up her skirt, loosened her petticoat and pulled it off. She folded it into a rough pillow and slipped it gently under her sister's head.

'I will fly like the wind,' she promised, stroking Nell's forehead.

Charlotte leapt into the saddle and urged Rosie into the fastest gallop of her life. Through her mind ran images of Nell lying alone and injured, possibly dying.

Sophie felt torn between staying with Nell, or following Charlotte. She stayed beside Nell and Flossie until she heard the distant call of a horn echoing plaintively over the hills and loch. Sophie zoomed towards the sound. She could see Charlotte galloping over the moor, and a horde of horsemen flying towards her.

'Papa, Papa,' Charlotte cried thankfully, nearly tumbling from Rosie's back into her father's arms as they reached each other. 'Nell is badly hurt. Her head is bleeding and I think she may have broken something.'

Laird Mackenzie hugged Charlotte to his chest.

'I pray Nell will be all right, my lovely. Where is she?'

'Near the wall, down by the loch,' Charlotte replied.

'Good. Angus, fetch the carriage. Find blankets and send for the surgeon. We will meet you on the road.'

Nell was lying curled up, whimpering in pain. Her face was white and icy cold. Her dress and hair were saturated.

Alexander Mackenzie leapt from his horse.

'Och, my darling, what have you done?' he whispered softly.

He felt her forehead and ran his hands over her arms and legs, gently feeling for damage. He tenderly lifted her head and removed the petticoat pillow.

'Duncan, do you have your knife?'

'Aye, my laird.'

He used the knife to cut the petticoat into a wide strip to make a sling to immobilise Nell's arm.

Nell winced and shuddered but barely opened her eyes. As her father removed his jacket and covered her, Duncan quickly followed with his rough wool coat.

Charlotte shivered with wet and cold and anxiety. A trickle of water ran into her collar and down her spine.

'Papa, will Nell be all right?' she asked tremulously.

'I think she will survive,' he reassured her. 'Let us get her back home and in front of the fire.'

Laird Mackenzie carefully gathered Nell up into his arms, avoiding her injured side, and strode off towards the road, followed by the subdued and damp riders. They were soon met by Angus bringing the carriage.

While Laird Mackenzie and Duncan struggled to make Nell comfortable, Charlotte went to stand by Angus, burying her cold, wet fingers in the carriage horse's mane.

'Is Bess all right, Angus?' Charlotte asked in a small voice.

'Aye, but 'tis a wonder she was no' hurt as well,' Angus muttered. 'What were ye lassies thinking? And more than likely 'twill be me that gets a licking o'er your antics, no' ye.'

Charlotte looked at him imploringly, her eyes wide with shock.

'I am sorry, Angus. I did not mean for you to be in trouble.'

'Och, Miss Charlotte,' he whispered. 'I were only jesting. Do no' fret, lassie, Miss Eleanor will be fine, ye'll see.'

Laird Mackenzie called to Charlotte impatiently from the carriage, cradling Nell's head in his lap. Charlotte scrambled into the vehicle beside him.

'I am very sorry, Papa,' Charlotte cried impetuously, clutching her father's sleeve with both hands. 'I did not mean for Nell to be injured; and please, please do not punish Angus. He did not know we were going riding. We crept out while he was wheeling the stable waste out to the kitchen garden.'

Laird Mackenzie gazed carefully at his eldest child. He loved her dearly but was sorely worried by her mischievous streak.

'I should punish Angus with a good lashing,' Laird Mackenzie declared. 'One of Angus's jobs is to look after you girls while you go out riding so that you are safe. A thrashing will teach him to remember his responsibilities; and his punishment will remind you to behave as befits your rank.'

Charlotte sobbed, her face pale and streaked with tears.

'Please, no, Papa,' Charlotte begged. 'I promise we will never ride out without Angus again.'

'You are not a crofter's urchin,' Laird Mackenzie continued sternly. 'You are a Mackenzie of Dungorm, and that role brings with it much responsibility. We must look after every person, every animal, every plant and every clod of earth upon this land.'

Charlotte nodded slowly, her face grave.

'I think it is time you learnt about this responsibility,' Laird Mackenzie added. 'Tomorrow you can ride with me around the estate to study what is required of the Mackenzies of Dungorm.'

'Yes, Papa,' murmured Charlotte, her eyes aglow with pleasure at the thought of riding with her beloved papa. 'But what about Angus?'

Laird Mackenzie pulled her to him and kissed her forehead gently. 'Angus will suffer a severe tongue lashing from Duncan, but I trust he will not be harmed.'

Soon after, the carriage trundled into the stable courtyard with Nell inside, wrapped in blankets and held in her father's arms, with Charlotte huddled next to them. The grooms led Rosie and the laird's tall hunter. A flurry of activity greeted their arrival.

An older woman, her grey hair piled under a lace cap,

darted from the front door wringing her hands. 'Where's my puir wee bairn?'

'Here she is, Nanny,' replied Laird Mackenzie soothingly, 'suffering nothing worse than a broken arm, I trust.'

Sophie floated above the scene, watching the bustling activity with interest. No-one seemed to be able to see her. She floated down to the carriage and watched Nell being lifted out and carried up to the house, Charlotte clambering after.

Charlotte turned suddenly and looked up as if she felt the stare of a stranger above her, but she looked right through Sophie as if she were a wisp of mist. Sophie ducked instinctively, shooting behind the carriage and hiding.

Charlotte hurried after her sister, her shoulders hunched with misery. Sophie did not follow but watched in fascination at the activity outside.

Horses were tied to grooming bars, unsaddled, brushed and combed; their hooves were picked; then they were led into the cool darkness of the stables. Sophie could not resist stroking Rosie, her grey flanks wet with sweat. Rosie rolled her eyes in fear and sidled away from Sophie, snorting and shivering.

'Whoa, bonnie girl,' soothed Angus. 'Are ye seeing wee ghaisties again?'

Sophie's attention wandered from the stable yard to the house itself. She decided to explore, her body following her mind's suggestion by zooming through the air, around the corner of the house and round to the front.

The house was grand and huge, a rectangle of warm,

golden stone. Rounded turrets guarded each corner, topped with grey slate roofs. Wide, gracious windows overlooked the expanse of lawns, hedges and flowerbeds rolling down to the grey waters of the loch.

From here, the view of the loch and island was spectacular, the partially ruined keep of the castle soaring against the leaden sky. Sophie flew towards the island, skimming above the water, droplets of salt water soaking her nightdress.

She floated above the tumbledown rocks of the castle ruins, choked with weeds, and spiralled around the tower keep, climbing higher and faster so the golden stones blurred. Then she was speeding up through the grey clouds, the mist damp and clammy in her nostrils, through the black tunnel, back to the warm cocoon of her own bed.

The next morning Sophie woke early, her dream vivid in her memory. She jumped out of bed eager to tell Jessica about it. The locket bumped against her chest. Quickly she took it off and slipped it back inside the wooden chest. Her hands felt sticky and sweaty.

'Jess,' called Sophie softly. 'Are you awake?'

'Mmmm?' answered Jessica sleepily.

'I had an amazing dream last night,' Sophie continued. 'I dreamt about Scotland and Charlotte Mackenzie and the castle of Dungorm.'

Jessica rolled over, her eyes slowly focusing on her sister.

'And Charlotte's sister Nell fell off her pony and broke her arm.'

'Sophie?'

'Yes?'

'What's that all over your nightdress?' asked Jessica, pointing at Sophie.

Sophie looked down where Jessica had pointed. There was a large splash of what looked like dried mud. Sophie picked at it in shock, the mud crumbling off beneath her nail.

'It's mud,' Sophie answered in surprise.

'How did you get mud all over your nightie?'

'I don't know.' Sophie turned her right hand over to examine the dried flakes of dirt.

Then she noticed something else. Her hand was covered in short white hairs. She sniffed her hand. The smell was unmistakeable: salt, sweat and horse. Her hand was sprinkled with fine white horsehairs. Sophie sat down suddenly on the edge of Jessica's bed.

'I dreamt I could fly,' she finished in wonder.

'That's nice,' Jessica muttered, rolling over and pulling the pillow over her dark head. 'But why did you have to wake me up to tell me that?'

3

Eilean Dungorm

All day Sophie kept having flashbacks to her 'dream' of the night before. Had it been a dream? It had seemed so real. Yet she could fly and no-one could see her, as if she were a ghost.

The mud on her nightdress was definitely real, as were the horsehairs on her hand. But they couldn't be; it wasn't possible to travel back in time. *How had it happened? Could it somehow have been the old locket? Was it magic? Could it happen again?*

Nonnie had taken the girls out shopping, then for afternoon tea to her favourite café. Jessica was chattering nonstop, telling Nonnie about her friends at school and a trick they had played on the music teacher.

'Sophie?' asked Nonnie, interrupting Sophie's reverie. 'Are you all right? You've hardly said anything all afternoon, and you haven't eaten a morsel. Are you worrying about your father's job?'

Jessica stopped eating her banana cake, dropping her fork with a clatter.

'No. I mean, yes,' replied Sophie, her mind reluctantly switching back to the present.

Sophie thought of the last few months, when their world had been turned upside down. She didn't really want to think about it. She smiled brightly at Nonnie and Jessica. 'Did Jess tell you she scored an A for her science project, building a boat out of recycled material?'

'I made the hulls out of plastic bottles, lashed with twine, and the sails out of plastic shopping bags,' added Jess, bouncing up and down. 'We had to race the boats across the ocean pool at Manly and mine won by metres. It ran over Lucy's boat and sank it.'

That evening Sophie hurried through her dinner, brushed her teeth, changed into her freshly washed nightdress and kissed Nonnie goodnight.

'Ready for bed already?' laughed Nonnie, hugging her tight. 'That's not like you, Sophie darling. You must be exhausted. What about your usual litany of excuses?'

'I do feel tired tonight,' Sophie fibbed, her heart pounding with excitement.

Nonnie frowned, feeling Sophie's forehead with her hand.

'Do you feel all right, darling? You look a little flushed. I hope you're not coming down with a fever or something.'

'No, I'm not sick. Just a little tired; it's been a busy day,' Sophie assured her grandmother, not wanting her to worry.

Sophie hugged Nonnie again and raced to her room. She opened the chest, took out Charlotte Mackenzie's locket with trembling fingers and slipped it around her neck and inside her nightdress.

She climbed into bed. Jess came racing in after her and bounced up and down on her bed.

'What should we do tomorrow?' begged Jessica. 'Nonnie says we could go and see a movie, and we haven't been to the movies for *months*. We could see that new spy film, or the 3D one, although I think Nonnie would rather see that boring one. What do you think? Or we could go to Chatswood, or the library, or if it's a beautiful day we should really go to the beach.'

Sophie hid her head under the pillow in frustration.

'I'd like to go to sleep, if you would just stop talking,' groaned Sophie impatiently.

'*Sophie*,' complained Jess. 'This is important.'

'Why do you have to be *so* annoying *all* the time?' asked Sophie, glaring at Jess.

'I'm not annoying, I just asked you a simple question about going to the movies,' huffed Jess. 'You're the one who's being annoying.'

'Could you just be *quiet*?' barked Sophie, turning her head to the wall. Jessica threw her pillow at Sophie, hitting her on the back. Sophie threw it back again forcefully, hitting Jess square in the face.

'Yow,' yelled Jess, rubbing her screwed-up face. 'That really hurt.'

'Well, you threw it first,' retorted Sophie, a trifle guiltily. 'If you'd just left me alone, it wouldn't have happened.'

'*Sorry*,' grumbled Jess, turning her back and pulling off her jeans. '*Princess Sophie* needs her *beauty* sleep.'

'Hmmph,' snorted Sophie, rolling over and hitching up the doona.

Sophie tossed and turned, trying to forget her irritating spat with Jessica and make her mind slip into sleep. She thought about Charlotte and Nell, and the contents of the box. *Where did the box come from? Was Nell all right after her fall?*

Of course, sleep took a long time to come. Finally she felt the familiar sensation of her mind slipping and sliding away from consciousness down towards the comforting darkness of slumber.

The light was pale and soft, the sun sailing slowly through a cloud-scudded sky. Down below, Sophie could see a small dinghy being rowed by Angus, the stableboy she recognised from last night, or was it yesterday?

In the boat were a number of passengers, who Sophie recognised as Charlotte, Nell with her arm in a sling, the Laird of Dungorm, Flossie the dog and a striking woman holding a green parasol to shade her pale face. Between them were a huge wicker basket and a pile of tartan rugs.

Sophie swooped down on a gentle breeze and followed the boat, scrutinising each of the passengers in excited curiosity.

Flossie the dog saw Sophie's fluttering white nightdress and barked loudly, leaping to her paws to stand in the stern of the boat, one ear pricked and one ear flopping over her left eye.

'Shh, Flossie,' soothed Charlotte, patting her thick ruff of fur. 'What can you see, a seagull?'

Flossie wagged her tail but continued to stand watch in the boat, her hackles raised. Sophie dropped back a little, not wanting to antagonise the black-and-white dog.

The two girls in the boat wore bonnets trimmed with coloured ribbon, white dresses that reached their mid-calves and had long full sleeves, black stockings and buttoned-up boots. Nell had her arm cradled in a sling but seemed quite recovered from her ordeal.

'Mama, look, a seal,' called Charlotte, pointing into the loch.

A small brown face with twitching whiskers peered at the boat, its brown eyes curious and alert. The seal glided towards the boat, on its side, one flipper raised in the air like a sail. It splashed the water hard with its flipper, sending droplets of water flying towards the boat, then dived under the hull and disappeared.

'I wonder if that's a selkie,' cried Charlotte. 'You know, a sea person hidden in a sealskin. Nanny tells us stories about selkies all the time.'

Alexander Mackenzie snorted in disapproval. 'Nanny fills your head with too many fairytales,' he retorted, but his smile was indulgent.

'Alexander,' reproved the girls' mother gently, 'Nanny is a wonderful woman and a great help.'

'Eliza, the girls are old enough to have a proper governess now,' Alexander replied, obviously repeating a well-worn argument. 'A governess who will not fill their heads with nonsense.'

Eliza sighed, stretching her back.

'We have discussed this before, Alexander,' she said evenly. 'The last governess knew hardly more than the girls do. She taught them nothing but needlework, dance steps and pianoforte.'

Charlotte and Nell rolled their eyes at each other, pulling faces at their shared memory of the governess.

'At least I can teach them most things they need to learn,' Eliza continued. 'It is important in this day and age for girls to be well educated. When they are older, they will go away to school, a good school. But until then I will direct their education myself.'

The Laird of Dungorm smiled at his wife lovingly, admitting defeat.

'Let us not argue about this on such a beautiful and special day,' Eliza said, smiling at Charlotte and squeezing her hand.

'Yes, it is my birthday,' crowed Charlotte, tossing her copper ringlets.

'As if we could have forgotten,' replied Nell, pulling a face. 'You must have mentioned it at least fifty times today.'

'So, for my darling girl's twelfth birthday we will have a delicious picnic on Eilean Dungorm with all your favourite treats, a sail on the loch and a special supper, and have I forgotten something?' asked her father with a mock frown.

'Presents!' squealed Charlotte, pointing to a mysterious bundle partially hidden by the rugs in the bottom of the boat.

'Charlotte, not so wild,' reproved Eliza mildly. 'Remember, you are a lady and should behave like one now you are a very grown-up twelve-year-old.'

'Yes, Mama,' agreed Charlotte dutifully, 'but when can I open my presents?'

Eliza laughed, shrugging her shoulders gracefully. 'After our picnic luncheon, you *enfant terrible*,' she replied, kissing Charlotte on the cheek. 'If you can wait that long.'

Angus the stableboy pulled strongly, riding a small wave up onto the shingle beach of the island, Eilean Dungorm. He held the boat steady while the laird climbed out and solicitously helped out Eliza. Eliza climbed out awkwardly, gathering up her heavy silk skirts.

Sophie flew ahead – her bare feet skimming the top of the waves, the water splashing her toes – then alighted on the beach.

Charlotte and Nell scrambled out, not heeding their father's outstretched arm, and ran up the beach towards the ruins of the castle. Flossie the dog jumped out eagerly, woofing happily, and chased them up the shingle.

Angus pulled out a small anchor and secured the boat, then gathered up the heavy basket, parcel and rugs and slowly followed his master and mistress towards the ruins.

Angus spread one rug over a low stone wall that formed a perfect bench, then flung another over a flat slab that formed a natural low table.

'Thank you, Angus,' Laird Mackenzie said kindly. 'We will not eat for a while. Could you keep a watch on Miss Charlotte and Miss Eleanor, please?'

'Yes, m' laird,' Angus mumbled, bobbing his head, and scampered after the girls. Sophie floated along behind, looking around the island in awe.

Charlotte, Nell and Flossie were exploring the ruins of the castle, climbing over the piles of fallen rocks, brushing past tall pink hollyhocks and crushing yellow buttercups under their boots. Sophie hung back, cautious of Flossie, who turned to stare at her constantly, barking loudly.

'Look, Angus,' Charlotte called, pointing to a bird soaring above the tower. 'A sea eagle.'

Creeping up the side of one wall could be seen the ruin of an old stone staircase. Another staircase wound up inside the stone keep, crumbling and dangerous. The girls ran on towards the shore on the other side of the island, facing towards the west and the loch's narrow opening to the sea.

Angus and Flossie, then Sophie, followed close behind. Angus picked up several flat pebbles and expertly skimmed them across the water, where they jumped six or seven times before sinking into the depths.

'Can you show me how to do that, Angus?' begged Charlotte, as her stones sank without a skip. 'Please?'

Patiently Angus showed the two girls how to skim stones across the water.

'Ye must practise,' he encouraged quietly. ''Tis easy once ye know how.'

Sophie watched the children curiously. She wondered if she could skim a stone too. She bent down and touched a pebble. It felt cool and smooth under her ghostly fingers. Sophie tried to pick it up. Nothing happened. It was as if the tiny pebble weighed a tonne. It was immovable. Sophie gave up in annoyance.

Charlotte squealed and jumped with excitement when one of her pebbles skipped once before sinking.

'Did you see the seal, Angus?' asked Charlotte. 'Do you think it could be a selkie?'

'I do no' know,' Angus answered seriously. 'My mam saw selkies when she was a lass.'

Angus sat down on the shale and stared over the loch as though seeing magical creatures no-one else could see.

'Truly?' asked Nell, plopping down beside him. 'What did they look like? Was she frightened?'

Flossie stretched out with a sigh, while Sophie floated a little closer to listen.

'It was here on Eilean Dungorm, one midsummer eve. She was gathering oysters and cockles for supper when she heard a strange sound o' fighting and wailing.'

The girls leant forward in anticipation. Angus always told a good story. Charlotte wound her hand in the thick fur of Flossie's ruff. Sophie sat down beside them on the shingle.

'Mam crept behind the rocks as quiet as a mouseling,' Angus continued. 'And there on the beach she saw a family o' seals squabbling and fighting. They were so busy crying and wailing that they did no' spy my mam. She crept closer and then she saw the seals using their flippers to peel off their fur coats as easily as you would peel off your own jacket.

'The seals tossed their dark fur coats in a pile and stretched and lolled in the sun. Under their sealskins they looked just like humans, the maids with long black hair and the menfolk strong and lithe, but with no human clothes.'

The girls squirmed in embarrassment at the talk of naked bodies, but Angus continued.

'My mam crept to the pile o' pelts and stretched out to touch one. She said they looked as soft and fine as French velvet. She had heard that if you take the pelt o' a selkie they can ne'er go back to the sea.

'In the old days the fisherfolk used to marry a selkie lass or laddie quite often by stealing their pelts and hiding them so they could no' go back to the sea. I fancy my mam thought she could catch a handsome selkie man and wed him.

'But it all came to naught. One of the selkie women saw my mam and rushed at her, screaming in rage, wielding a branch of driftwood. My mam turned and ran, dropping the pelt.

'The selkie woman hurled the driftwood after her and it struck her on the arm, wounding her sorely. My mam ran on, dripping with blood and dropping her basket o' shellfish.

'She was in sore trouble when she went home, but she could no' resist taking one last look at the beach. All the selkies were gone, with their fine fur pelts too. The only thing left to show was the scar on my mam's arm. She still has it to this day.'

Angus lapsed into silence, signalling the end of his tale. Sophie sighed. Charlotte and Nell were enraptured, gazing out to sea searching for the lost selkies.

'Perhaps it was this very beach,' breathed Nell.

'Did your mam ever see the selkies again?' asked Charlotte.

'No, although there are other folk in the village who have stories o' meeting the selkies,' Angus replied. 'Make no mistake, the selkies and wee folk do no' like to be seen, but they are here all around us.'

Angus was not much older than Charlotte, but he had been earning his own living for several years, which gave him a bearing far more mature than his true age.

'I wonder if we could find some selkies,' Nell exclaimed. 'Come on, Charlotte, let us creep up on the next beach and take a look.'

The girls jumped up and raced to the boulders protecting the next stretch of shale. They tiptoed closer, peering over the boulders hopefully.

The beach was empty. A few seagulls rose screaming from the rocks, frightened by the intrusion. Angus wandered up behind them. Sophie flew, chasing the seagulls and flying with them, high in the sky.

A faint call sounded from the ruins.

''Tis Mama,' Nell cried. 'It is time for luncheon.'

Reluctantly Sophie followed them, torn between the thrill of chasing seagulls and a desire to see what the Mackenzies were doing.

Back at the picnic camp, Eliza was sitting with her charcoals and sketchbook on her lap, shading a sketch of the tower of Dungorm. Laird Mackenzie was reading from a leather-bound book of verse by Robbie Burns.

O My Luve's like a red, red rose,
That's newly sprung in June;
O My Luve's like the melodie
That's sweetly played in tune.

As fair art thou, my bonnie lass,
So deep in luve am I;
And I will luve thee still, my dear,
Till a' the seas gang dry.

Till a' the seas gang dry, my dear,
And the rocks melt wi' the sun;
O I will luve thee still, my dear,
While the sands o' life shall run.

And fare thee weel, my only luve
And fare thee weel awhile!

And I will come again, my luve,
Though it were ten thousand mile.

He bowed with a little flourish and snapped the book shut.

'And I will luve thee still, my dear, while the sands o' life shall run,' he repeated softly.

Charlotte glanced at Nell and rolled her eyes affectionately. They were used to their father lapsing into quotes from his favourite poet. Nell laughed.

'Is it time for luncheon?' Charlotte interrupted.

'Indeed it is, my love,' agreed Eliza with a smile. 'We cannot have the birthday girl fainting from starvation.'

Eliza began to unpack the cane basket, spreading out dishes and platters on the tartan rug. There was a dish of roast chicken portions, flavoured with rosemary and honey. Tiny wedges of sandwiches with various fillings – cucumber, chopped egg and pale pink wafers of ham – were arranged on a silver platter.

Another plate held tiny meat pastries and sausage rolls still warm from the oven, while a glass side dish held a crisp spring salad of cherry tomatoes and cucumbers.

Angus unpacked the silver cutlery and bone china plates, handling them extremely carefully. Eliza served out various dishes for each person. Angus retired to a distant rock, just within earshot, to eat his own rough package of food.

The Laird of Dungorm said a blessing over the meal and they all began to eat.

'What a feast for the birthday girl,' said Alexander, helping himself to a second serving.

After everyone had eaten their fill, Eliza pulled out the

mysterious package, peeling off the checked cloth that had disguised it.

'I think it might be time for a little surprise, Charlotte, what do you think?' Eliza handed the rectangular package over with a smile.

'Oh, thank you, Mama.' Charlotte jiggled with excitement as her fingers eagerly picked at the knotted ribbon. The package was wrapped in pale-blue paper tied with silver ribbon.

The paper fell away, tearing slightly with her impatient fingers. Sophie gasped involuntarily. She recognised the object revealed on Charlotte's lap.

It was a timber box, highly polished and ornately carved with a border of wildflowers. On the lid was carved a beautiful stag, powerful and mysterious, gazing straight out of the wood. Its antlers were held proudly aloft against a round moon.

Charlotte ran her finger along the ridged words carved along the border of the lid.

'*Luceo non Uro* – I shine not burn,' she read softly. 'The Mackenzie clan motto.'

'Once a Mackenzie, always a Mackenzie,' reminded her father.

Charlotte carefully turned the tiny golden key and opened the box, to find it lined with delicate violet silk.

'It is to keep all your treasures safe,' Eliza said. 'And to remind you how much we love you.'

'We asked Dughald the shepherd to carve it for you,' Laird Mackenzie added. 'He worked on it all last winter. He used the ancient oak tree that blew down in the village during the autumn storms.'

His voice dropped to a whisper. 'The box has a secret too. I will show it to you later.'

'Oh, Papa,' Charlotte said, frowning impatiently. 'Show me now!'

'Later.' Her father winked. 'When we are alone and there are no prying eyes. The Mackenzies are good at keeping secrets.' He gestured to Eliza, Nell, Flossie and Angus as if they were a horde of foreign spies.

'Show me too, Papa?' begged Nell. 'Pleeease?'

'No, my love,' answered Laird Mackenzie. 'This particular secret is just for Charlotte, on her birthday. You must wait for your own birthday for your surprise.'

Charlotte, Nell and Eliza laughed happily.

'Thank you, Mama,' cried Charlotte. 'Thank you, Papa. I will treasure my box always.'

Eliza cut the cake, decorated with strawberries and whipped cream, and handed it out on pretty china plates. Angus tidied up the mess, carefully packing everything back into the wicker hamper. The girls ran off to explore the island once more.

'Alexander, can you believe our baby Charlotte is now twelve years old?' asked Eliza, watching the girls play. 'Even little Nell is ten. Where have the years flown?'

'I do not know, but they have been very happy years,' replied Laird Mackenzie, taking his wife's hand and kissing it. 'Let us hope all goes well with this baby too. Perhaps we will be blessed with a boy this time?'

Eliza stroked her belly, with a smile of deep contentment.

'Yes, that would be wonderful.'

Laird Mackenzie stretched out in the sun to rest his eyes.

Eliza picked up her charcoals and sketchbook and began to draw once more. Under her pencil grew the towering ruin of the Castle of Dungorm, guarding the loch, weeds growing in its ramparts and its barbican shattered on the ground.

4

The Star of Serendib

Sophie woke up slowly, a crack of soft, grey light gleaming under the blind. In the other bed, on the other side of the room, she could see a hump under the covers which was her sister Jess, still fast asleep.

Sophie was in her bed at Nonnie's apartment, on the North Shore of Sydney, in her own life in the twenty-first century. A feeling of great excitement welled up inside her.

She looked around at the bedroom, with its cream carpet, yellow-and-white striped wallpaper, white dressing table and framed paintings of pale pink camellias.

Was it all a dream? Or had she really gone back in time and place to the home of Charlotte Mackenzie, in nineteenth-century Scotland? It was too incredible to comprehend.

Sophie remembered the amazing feeling of flying and the secretive feeling of observing the goings-on while no-one except Flossie the dog seemed to be able to see her. It was the greatest adventure she had ever experienced.

If it was all just a dream, it was a dream she really didn't want to wake up from. She felt a strong yearning to be back in Scotland, back in the past, where everything seemed more interesting, more colourful and more alive than her own life here in Sydney with its irritations and worries and sister squabbles.

Perhaps she wouldn't get up today. Perhaps if she stayed in bed for a while, she would go back to sleep and straight back to Scotland. Sophie gently held the gold locket in her hand and curled into a tight ball under the covers. The locket was warm from her skin and gleamed softly in the half-light.

Sophie thought of Scotland and the loch and the ruins of Dungorm. She thought of Charlotte and Nell and Flossie the dog. She thought of Alexander and Eliza Mackenzie and the beautiful gracious house, and she longed to be with them all. What a fascinating life they must have led, a life full of luxury and parties and exquisite treasures.

The servants had been preparing for days. The invitations went out six weeks before on thick white card with Eliza's loopy handwriting. The fine Persian rugs had been rolled back and the parquet floors polished for hours with golden beeswax.

Charlotte and Nell buzzed with excitement. The whole household had been pressed into service cleaning silverware, dusting paintings and ornaments, and moving furniture.

Sophie peered through the windows from the garden, watching all the activity and searching for Charlotte and Nell. She spied them through the kitchen window, and ducked through the back door when a scullery maid went in, carrying flowers from the garden.

The kitchen was a steaming hive of activity with Cook shouting orders, stirring sauces and tasting dishes, her red face streaming with perspiration. Even Nanny had no time for the girls, bustling back and forwards with messages and chores.

Charlotte and Nell watched all the activity in delight. At first Cook had tried to shoo them away in the same way she chased away Marmalade, the fat ginger cat scrounging under the table.

But at their disappointed faces she relented and let them sit in the far corner, licking the china mixing bowls and spoons, and eating crumbly shortbread. Cook had made hundreds of biscuits in pretty shapes: stars, flowers and hearts. Marmalade took refuge at the girls' feet, imperiously licking her paws.

Sally, one of the chambermaids, smiled at the girls, wiping her floury hands on her apron.

''Twill be a merry evening tonight eh, lassies?'

Nanny came scurrying down to find them.

'Come on, lassies, 'tis time for ye both to be coming upstairs to eat your supper and get ready for bed,' Nanny said.

'But Nanny,' pleaded Nell, kicking her black boots against the bench leg, 'it is too early yet.'

'No buts, Miss Nell,' replied Nanny crossly. 'Ye ken your mother, Lady Mackenzie, would like to say guidnight to ye before the guests arrive, and we all have far too much to do to have ye two under our feet.'

Reluctantly the two girls were ushered upstairs to the schoolroom to eat their rice pudding and wash before being escorted to their mother's chamber. Nanny knocked on the door.

'Come in,' sang a soft voice from inside.

Nanny pushed open the door with a curtsey, and Charlotte and Nell ran in towards their mother. Charlotte stopped and stared in awe at the vision of her mother seated at the dressing table. Sophie thought she had never seen anyone look quite so beautiful.

Eliza wore a stunning evening gown of white silk, with a low neck and short puffed sleeves, caught up behind the waist with ruffles and pale blue ribbons. Her dark hair was coaxed up into an elaborate chignon, with a fresh white rose above her left ear.

From her ears dangled heavy chandelier earrings of dazzling diamonds, while a matching necklace glittered and sparkled at her throat.

Sophie crept close. She simply had to stroke that gorgeous dress and see if she could feel the texture of the silk. The material rustled slightly under her fingertips. Sophie jumped backwards before anyone noticed.

'Hello, my darlings,' called Eliza cheerfully to the girls. 'I am nearly ready. What do you think?'

'You look absolutely beautiful,' breathed Nell.

'Stunning,' added Charlotte, smiling. 'I love your new dress.'

'Thank you, my darlings,' Eliza said and smiled in return. She opened her jewellery casket and pulled out a heavy gold ring. It featured a huge cornflower-blue sapphire, which was surrounded by more than a dozen precious diamonds.

Carefully she slipped it onto her left ring finger, over her long white gloves. The cluster of jewels caught the light, flashing blue and white and gold. Sophie caught her breath in awe.

'The Star of Serendib,' sighed Charlotte, staring entranced at the beautiful ring.

Eliza held it up so that the girls could admire it. 'The Star of Serendib,' she agreed. 'Is it not stunning?'

'Tell us the story, Mama,' begged Nell. 'I love this story.'

Eliza glanced at the small clock on her mantelpiece and smiled.

'Very well then, but you must go straight to bed when I have finished.'

The girls nodded vigorously and climbed up on the vast four-poster bed. Sophie floated down beside them, eager to hear the story as well.

'Many years ago, before we were married, your papa went to India with the East India Company to make his fortune,' Eliza began, taking on the singsong tone she used when she was telling a story.

'The Mackenzie family had lost *all* their money from years of poor investments and carelessness. Your papa inherited this land with its ruin of an ancient castle, with nothing else but some tumbledown cottages and a few starving crofters,' Eliza continued, waving her hand towards the window and the lands of Dungorm outside in the shadowy night.

'Alexander gathered what little money he had and sailed to India to work with the merchants who brought the riches of the Far East back to Scotland and England – spices, jewels, gold, cashmere, tea and coffee. At first he struggled, but one day his luck turned.

'He was out riding when he came upon a young native lad and his servant being set upon by ruffians armed with knives and scimitars.' Eliza paused to heighten the suspense.

'Two dead servants lay nearby, covered in blood. The remaining servant had little hope against such a large, well-armed gang, and was losing ground. Your papa did not think twice but galloped into the fray, bellowing with rage and firing his pistol.'

Charlotte and Nell unconsciously shrank together, visualising their beloved father riding into the fight, on his own against a pack of armed, lawless bandits.

'The sight of the big white man firing his pistol and shouting was enough to frighten the bandits into fleeing. It turned out that the young lad was the son of a fabulously wealthy maharajah, an Indian prince, and the bandits were kidnapping him for ransom,' Eliza continued.

'The maharajah was so grateful to him for saving his son that he gave your papa the Star of Serendib, this ring, as a thanksgiving. He helped Alexander with many business opportunities in India so that in a few years he had made his fortune.

'Your papa returned home to Scotland and built this house, furnishing it with treasures from the East. He rebuilt the cottages for the crofters and helped them with their farms so they could make a decent living. Alexander always said that the Star of Serendib was his good-luck talisman. Your father gave the ring to me on our wedding day.'

Nell and Charlotte nodded. They knew all about their parents meeting when they were young and poor; the long, anxious wait while Alexander travelled to the other side of the world and the joyous marriage within weeks of his return – but that was another story.

'The gem is called the Star of Serendib because it has a tiny six-pointed star deep in its heart,' Eliza said, showing the girls the mark in the stone. 'Star sapphires are extremely rare and according to legend are powerful talismans, giving protection to their owners.'

Eliza turned back to the mirror and absent-mindedly squirted a spray of fragrant perfume on her neck and throat.

'I think it is the favourite of all my jewels.' Eliza looked deep into the heart of the gem and smiled. 'Perhaps because it has such a romantic story or because the colour reminds me of the summer sky and cornflowers.

'Anyway, my darlings, time for you to go to bed, and for me to go down to greet our guests.'

The girls sighed, the magic spell broken. Nell yawned and they both reluctantly stood up and came to kiss their mother.

'Goodnight, Mama,' they chorused, breathing in the heady scent of their mother's perfume.

'Goodnight, darlings, sweet dreams,' replied Eliza, giving them both a hug and a kiss. 'I hope our guests do not keep you awake tonight.'

The girls headed to their bedchamber, certain that they could never sleep that night with so much excitement downstairs. Sophie went exploring, skimming along the corridors and peeking over the banisters into the hall below.

The guests started arriving at eight o'clock in carriages pulled by teams of horses, their coats gleaming in the lamplight. Overhead, the full moon was rising, spreading a silvery glow over the countryside.

Men were dressed in formal kilts with ornate sporrans, black jackets, bow ties and white shirts. Women wore billowing, beribboned skirts of delicate silk and white lace, with long white gloves. Most of the ladies wore fashionable crinoline skirts with their stiff cages underneath and had to edge sideways from the carriages to ensure their wide skirts could fit through the doorway.

As the guests arrived and swept up the stone staircase to the front door, they were announced by the butler, who boomed their names into the wide entrance hall.

Alexander and Eliza Mackenzie, Laird and Lady of Dungorm, stood in the entrance hall greeting their guests as they arrived.

The hallway was lit with dozens of candles blazing in the candelabras. A broad marble staircase swept up to the gallery above. The grand reception rooms on the ground floor had fires crackling in the grates and dozens of guests hovering and chattering like fluttering butterflies against the green silk of the walls.

The long drawing room was set up for the dancing, with a band of musicians playing in one corner behind a screen of potted palms. The sitting room and conservatory were set aside for refreshment, conversation and a quieter retreat from the dancing.

Upstairs on the landing crouched three small figures dressed in white nightgowns. Charlotte and Nell had their hair crimped in scraps of white rags to encourage ringlets, while behind them floated the almost transparent figure of Sophie, watching the gaiety below as eagerly as the two sisters.

Gradually the noise below increased as the champagne flowed; the chattering and laughter threatened to drown out the musicians. At a signal from the butler, the musicians struck up the opening chords to a lively dance tune.

The gossiping butterflies gradually parted. Some of the older guests headed eagerly to the tables set up in the library to play cards.

Others headed to the refreshments tables to marvel at the wondrous display of food – cold ham, turkey and chicken, dainty sandwiches, cakes, puddings and biscuits.

As was customary, the host and hostess started the dancing, each choosing a partner for the quadrille. The dancing was elegant and graceful, with swirling skirts and dainty steps.

Nell, Charlotte and Sophie watched entranced as the couples dipped, swayed and promenaded around the room. Everyone laughed and clapped as the tune finished and another began.

'The Honourable Mr and Mrs Roderick Mackenzie,' announced the butler from the hall. The girls strained to catch sight of their uncle and aunt below. The children could not remember meeting their father's younger brother before.

He had lived in London for many years and had recently returned to Scotland, where he had bought a small estate about an hour's ride away and a townhouse in Edinburgh.

Roderick stood in the doorway, looking tall and proud in his black evening jacket and Mackenzie kilt. His wife, Arabella, stood next to him, in her wide crinoline skirt, her face haughty and cold, a tall feather plume nodding on her elaborate black coiffure. They swept into the entrance hallway, causing many to turn and stare.

Alexander stepped forward eagerly, heartily shaking his

brother's hand and bowing to Arabella. Eliza smiled and curtseyed in welcome, murmuring the usual pleasantries.

'Good to see my brother back in the bonnie Scottish highlands,' Alexander said, beaming. 'Are you still a Scot, or have they changed you into a Londoner? And the beautiful Arabella – welcome home.'

'My dear Eliza,' gushed Arabella, kissing the air beside Eliza's cheek. 'How lovely you look . . . and how perfect the Dungorm jewels are with your dress – the diamonds are exquisite. And of course you are wearing the Dungorm sapphire, the Star of Serendib – how utterly divine.'

'Thank you,' replied Eliza graciously. 'You look lovely too.'

'Not the Dungorm jewels,' corrected Alexander, kissing his wife's hand gallantly. 'Simply Eliza's jewels, although my wife's beauty does not really need any adornment at all. She is perfect the way she is.'

Everyone laughed and Eliza blushed, swatting her husband's shoulder with her fan. For the next few minutes the four chatted amiably about the fine autumn weather, the state of the roads and the latest news from London. Then conversation turned to the land and Dungorm and Roderick's new estate.

'The way of the future is sheep,' Roderick exclaimed vehemently. 'The land needs to be cleared of all these rustic farmers, who bring in barely any money, and turned over to more profitable sheep. Except, of course, for some highland moors left wild for deer, grouse and pheasant so we can enjoy our hunting in autumn.'

Arabella nodded regally in agreement, her feather plume bouncing. Eliza frowned, twitching her fan.

'Sheep and cattle are a good investment,' Alexander agreed levelly. 'We have good-sized flocks here at Dungorm and do very well with them. But it is important to diversify for the sake of our tenants.

'Where would the crofters go if we turned them out of their homes? Many of the crofters' families have lived at Dungorm for hundreds, if not thousands, of years. It is their home as much as ours.'

Roderick waved his hand as if brushing away a nuisance fly.

'Pshaw,' Roderick sneered. 'All over the highlands, lairds are evicting tenants and burning down their disease-ridden hovels. Who cares where the vermin go? Probably back to the gutters where they belong.'

Eliza breathed in sharply, her cheeks flushing. 'The crofters at Dungorm are hard-working, honest people,' she retorted warmly. 'As long as I am mistress of Dungorm they will have warm, solid homes to live in, plenty to eat and a good education for their children.'

Alexander squeezed her hand. 'Eliza is right,' he agreed. 'The contract between laird and tenants must go two ways. The crofters till the land and pay their rent, but the laird must also care for his tenants' welfare.'

'Old-fashioned nonsense,' snorted Roderick. 'You always were too soft, Alexander. Next thing I suppose you will be supporting this nonsense of letting the common man vote.'

'Soft or not, Dungorm is my land, and I will manage it as I see fit, so I suppose we must agree to disagree,' allowed Alexander, with a forced smile. 'Now, perhaps you would both like to partake of some refreshment. I have an excellent claret, Roderick, which you might enjoy.'

Alexander steered his brother and sister-in-law towards the refreshments tables. Arabella's eyes appraised the treasures around her: the gilt mirrors, Persian rugs, discreet artworks, polished silverware and fine bone china.

Eliza straightened her shoulders, pasted on a bright smile and went to chat to a couple of dowagers.

'Mama does not look happy with Uncle Roderick and Aunt Arabella, does she?' whispered Nell. 'I do not think she likes them.'

5

The Tale of Jeannie Macdonald

Upstairs on the landing a door opened and Nanny bustled out, a look of mock severity on her face.

'Och, lassies,' she whispered, trying not to attract the attention of the guests below. 'Whate'er are you doing out of your beds at this hour? I have been down helping Cook with the party preparations and when I came up to check, ye were both missing. Now 'tis straight to bed with ye, and no nonsense.'

Nell yawned and scrambled up obediently.

'But Nanny,' argued Charlotte, frowning.

'Do no' Nanny me, young lassie,' Nanny replied sternly. "Tis off ye gae before my Laird and Lady Mackenzie pack me off without a reference to my name.'

Charlotte stood up slowly, a mutinous expression on her face.

Sophie watched the glittering scene below with yearning, but glided after Nell and Charlotte, her curiosity still burning. *What happened to bring Charlotte from this life of bright luxury to the other side of the planet? What terrible tragedy happened to Alexander and Eliza to make the girls orphans at such a young age?*

Sophie caught up with the girls as Nanny opened the door to the large, airy nursery. Flossie the dog flung herself on them all, as though she had been locked up for weeks and expected never to see them again.

Flossie jumped up on Charlotte and Nell, licking their hands and faces exuberantly. She wagged her tail frantically and licked Nanny's fingers, begging not to be banished to the kennels. Then Flossie caught a sense of something or someone else.

Flossie whined and stared at Sophie, then barked sharply. Sophie jumped back, nearly fading through the doorjamb.

'Whate'er is the matter with tha' dog?' Nanny asked in exasperation. 'She has been behaving strangely lately. 'Tis as though she senses the wee folk about. I had best take her downstairs before the whole party hears her barking.'

Flossie turned her back on Sophie and stalked away to her cushion by the fire, her tail between her legs.

'No, no, Nanny,' begged Charlotte. 'Please let her stay. Flossie will not make any more noise, will you, girl?'

Flossie thumped her tail obligingly, her liquid brown eyes staring up at them.

'*Please*, Nanny, could you tell us a story before bed?' added Nell, quickly changing the subject. 'Tell us the one about the water horse and the tailor, or the brownies and the crofter.'

Nanny glanced at the clock on the mantelpiece, hesitating.

'Or perhaps the story of Jeannie Macdonald and the

Fairy Queen?' Nell jumped up onto her high bed and bounced.

'Please, Nanny, I will never be able to sleep after all the excitement,' pleaded Charlotte, scrambling hurriedly into bed and pulling up the sheets, trying to look angelic.

'Well, just a wee one then,' relented Nanny, turning down the lamps and sitting herself in the comfortable armchair by the fire, with her knitting. The click click of the needles set the rhythm for the story, while the fire crackled and spat, adding drama.

The girls cuddled down in their beds, soothed by the dim light and the familiar routine. Sophie floated closer to the fire, even though she could not actually feel its warmth. Flossie raised one eyebrow but did not growl.

'Once upon a time there was a young lassie called Jeannie Macdonald, who lived on the Isle of Skye,' began Nanny, her voice lilting and soft.

'She was a foolish young lass who had a mind to see the fairy folk for herself, which everyone knows is a dangerous wish. Why, if you hear a banshee wailing, someone you love will die soon enough, but if you actually *see* one o' the sprites – perhaps sitting in a branch, all dressed in white, combing its long, fair hair with a silver comb – then ye yourself are not long for this world.'

Charlotte wriggled further under her blankets with a shiver of anticipation. Sophie huddled closer to the comforting blaze of the fire, her bare toes on the tiled hearth.

'Well, there was a fairy knowe near the village where Jeannie Macdonald lived. At full moon, the elves came out o' their underground palace under the hill to dance and sing in the moonlight.

'On these nights the islanders would lock their doors, shiver under their plaids and block their ears from the enchanted music. In the mornings on the hillside, there were often the marks o' round fairy rings or tiny iron elf bolts.

'One full-moon evening, Jeannie decided to hide in the heather to see what she could see. It was a cold, misty night, the clouds hiding the moon's face, when foolish Jeannie watched and waited. She huddled in her plaid, freezing to the core, and the hours crept by as slow as snails.

'At last, Jeannie was ready to give up and gae home to bed, when the clouds parted, revealing the silver moon and flooding the glen with cold, clear light. The moon was straight o'erhead, so Jeannie knew 'twas close to midnight.

'A crack like thunder and the earth itself split open, revealing a doorway underground. Light and unearthly music spilled from the doorway into the darkness, followed by a host o' strange folk, all laughing and chattering.

'Jeannie knew they must be elves – each one was about three feet tall, with pale, pale skin, long pointed ears and flowing hair. Some rode on ponies and some came on foot. Jeannie froze in terror, her heart beating like a wild robin's.'

Nanny paused to unsnag her ball of scarlet wool. The click click of the needles resumed, with the singsong of the story.

'Jeannie Macdonald was just about to run all the way home to her own warm cottage when she saw the Fairy Queen, an elf of incredible beauty. She was dressed all in green, with eyes the same bright colour, and long fair hair, nearly to her knees.

'She rode upon a white horse, shod with pure gold, with golden bells hung all around. Jeannie could not help but exclaim out loud in delight. The queen spied the human lass and beckoned her closer. Jeannie was entranced and her feet moved forward without her command.

'The night passed by in a blur. There was dancing and singing and everything was rich and sumptuous. The fairies invited Jeannie back to their palace, a vast cavern lit with thousands o' scented candles and strewn with unimaginable jewels and treasures.

'Jeannie danced and sang and laughed, besotted with the beauty o' the elven world. There was a feast o' wonderful food and gold pitchers brimming with fragrant wine. Jeannie was passed a plate piled high with delicacies, and a jewelled golden goblet. She was just about to sip the wine when a voice spoke at her elbow.

'"Take care, Jeannie Macdonald. Remember ne'er to taste o' the fairy food or you will be a prisoner o' the elves forever." Jeannie turned around and there was a face she recognised. It was Tam O'Neill, who had been gone this many a long year, sorely missed by his grieving wife and bairns.

'"Do no' make the same mistake I made and now sorely regret," whispered Tam. Jeannie dropped her plate of fairy cakes in horror. There was a loud shriek o' rage from the Queen of Elfhame.

'In the distance Jeannie heard a cock crow to welcome the dawn, and then a deep rumbling as the gate to fairyland began to close. Jeannie ran for her life and slipped through the crack with just seconds to spare.

'Outside, the sun rose and there was no sign that the

fairy feast had e'er been, except in her hand she clutched a tin cup filled with brackish water – a shabby, sorry thing with no jewels or gold.

'Jeannie Macdonald threw it away in disgust and ran all the way home to the village, where she lived a long and happy life, ne'er more to be troubled by a yearning to see the little folk that live underground. On the night o' the full moon, she locks her door tight, and pulls the plaid tight o'er her head, and sleeps all the bright night long.'

Nanny's knitting needles ceased. She rolled her wool up neatly and placed it back in the basket.

'Goodnight, Nanny,' murmured Nell and Charlotte.

'Guidnight, my bairns,' whispered Nanny as she turned out the lamp and tiptoed away. 'Do no' let the wee folk trouble your dreams.'

'Nanny, have you ever seen an elf?' asked Nell sleepily.

'Nae, lassie,' Nanny replied gravely. 'But I do no' yearn for glittering fairy trinkets. Like Jeannie Macdonald, I ken my hame is where my hearth and heart be.'

Sophie felt warm and tired, and she slowly drifted away, up through the ceiling, up through the attic, up through the roof, up through the moonlit night and up through the long, black tunnel, straight into her own snug bed.

When Sophie woke up and stretched for the second time that morning, the sun was now shining brightly. She looked over to the other bed and saw that Jessica was already awake and gone.

With the heavy gold locket warm against her chest, Sophie climbed out of bed. She slipped the necklace off and laid it safely in the faded violet silk of the oak box, which she locked with the tiny key.

Sophie glanced down at her feet, noticing with shock that they were faintly smudged with black and grey. She frowned in puzzlement and tentatively scratched the dirt, sniffing it inquisitively. Her finger smelt smoky. Then it came to her in a flash.

Her heart thumping, Sophie sat down suddenly on the side of her bed. She had just realised that the black marks on her feet were ash and soot from a fire that had been lit on the other side of the world more than a hundred and fifty years ago.

'It's just too weird,' Sophie said out loud. 'It's just not possible.'

Her black, dirty feet peeked back at her from the rug on the floor.

But how could they get so dirty if I spent all night in bed? Sophie wondered. *Perhaps I was sleepwalking. But where did the ash come from? It's summer in Australia with no fires around for kilometres. No-one is allowed to light one in case of bushfires. Perhaps there was a bushfire overnight and I was sleepwalking and stumbled through it? No, that's ridiculous.*

Somehow the idea of sleepwalking through a bushfire in suburban Sydney seemed far more ludicrous than the idea of visiting another country and another century while she slept.

Sophie gathered her clothes and went to the bathroom for a shower to scrub her dirty feet. She cleaned her teeth, brushed her hair and dressed quickly in shorts, T-shirt and runners.

In the kitchen Nonnie was making poached eggs and toast for breakfast, while Jess sipped on a cup of milky tea. There were three places set at the bench, each with neatly placed silver cutlery, teacup and saucer and a freshly ironed linen napkin.

A silver rack held slices of hot toast, while crystal dishes held curly balls of butter, glossy strawberry jam and golden homemade marmalade.

'Good morning, darling,' called Nonnie. 'Did you sleep well? There's tea in the pot if you would like some.'

'Morning, Nonnie,' replied Sophie, taking a seat at the kitchen bench. 'Morning, Jess. Mmmm. Yes, please.'

Nonnie served the steaming eggs on sunny yellow plates, with buttery multi-grain toast. Sophie felt too preoccupied to eat, scenes from the past replaying through her mind.

'Nonnie, how much do you know about Charlotte Mackenzie?' asked Sophie, picking at her food and toying with her fork. 'Where is Dungorm? Why do you think Charlotte would never talk about what happened?'

Nonnie laughed, patting her red-lipsticked mouth with her yellow napkin.

'Still dreaming about Charlotte Mackenzie, Sophie?' Nonnie asked. 'It was all so long ago, so many years before I was even born.'

Sophie flushed a little but she was determined to find out as much as she could. 'Please, Nonnie,' she begged. 'You must remember something more.'

Nonnie smiled at her enthusiasm and sat down.

'Well, Charlotte was born in about 1846 on the west coast of Scotland, north of Glasgow,' Nonnie mused.

'The girls were sent to Australia in 1859, when Charlotte was thirteen and her sister, Nell, was eleven.

Sophie felt a flutter of alarm as she realised that in her visits to the past, Charlotte had already turned twelve, so that whatever took the lives of the girls' parents must happen very soon.

'I don't know why the sisters were sent here, but the nineteenth century was a time of enormous change in Scotland, especially for the tenant farmers. Many rich landowners forced the crofters off the land to make way for highland sheep or red deer. The poor crofters were left homeless and starving so nearly two million people, a quarter of the Scottish population, emigrated to Australia, Canada or America looking for a better life.

'Charlotte and Eleanor were not poor, so their example is not typical. I assume their uncle didn't want to care for them and found someone over here to look after them.'

Sophie nodded, her eyes sparkling.

'I have some old books on Scotland here,' Nonnie added. 'Would you like to look at them and see if you can find out more about the Mackenzies and Dungorm?'

Sophie agreed enthusiastically. The girls finished their breakfast, packed the dishwasher and put the breakfast things away. Nonnie poked her head around the door.

'I have some phone calls to make and bills to pay. Why don't you girls read through those books, then we'll decide what we're going to do today. I know Jess is keen to see a movie this afternoon,' Nonnie suggested.

The books were old, with yellowing pages and a comforting smell. Sophie and Jessica flicked through them, noting maps, tartans, photos of old castles and heather-clad mountains, folk tales and poems. Jess had fun for a while, then wandered away to read her own book, curled up on a chaise longue on the verandah.

Sophie read a brief history of Scotland, from the ancient Celts who lived during the Bronze Age and the fierce Pictish warriors who painted strange blue designs on their faces during battle, through to the Viking invasions and clan wars.

The Scottish were a warring bunch, constantly fighting over land and power. It was a cruel and violent history, a prime example being when the Campbell clan tricked their way into the homes of the Macdonald clan at Glencoe, then after sharing their hospitality, forced the Macdonalds, including women, children and the elderly, out into the bitter snow, murdering them indiscriminately.

Sophie read on, intrigued by the tales of the Jacobite rebellion in the eighteenth century, when Bonnie Prince Charlie raised an army to try to claim the Scottish throne. At first, he was successful, capturing Edinburgh and routing the English, but finally the Jacobites were massacred in the battle at Culloden.

It was a romantic story, with Jacobite sympathisers hiding the young prince in secret cubbyholes and wild hills for months. At last, in 1746, a Scottish noblewoman called Flora Macdonald helped the prince to escape by dressing him as a woman and rowing him across to the Isle of Skye. A fortune in gold is believed to be buried somewhere in the Scottish highlands awaiting Prince Charlie's return.

The English retaliated by banning all things Scottish, including bagpipes, kilts and the Gaelic language. By the 1850s, though – when Charlotte was living at Dungorm –

Queen Victoria loved Scotland, so everything Scottish was highly fashionable.

Sophie moved on to read a book of Scottish fairytales with stories about all the many magic fairy folk who inhabited the Scottish landscape. The water spirits included kelpies, the handsome water horses who lived in the lochs and brooks; selkies, the mysterious seal people; and sea trowes, naughty spirits living under the sea.

Household spirits included brownies, who loved helping humans in return for gifts of food or milk; and bogles, mischievous creatures creating mess and mayhem, mostly just to annoy humans. Banshees foretold death. A changeling was the fractious baby of elves, placed in the cradle of a stolen human baby to trick the parents.

Sophie loved the folk tales but none moved her quite as much as the story of Jeannie Macdonald told by Nanny in her singsong Scottish voice.

Finally Sophie found a book on Scottish clans. She learnt that the Mackenzies were one of the great families of north-west Scotland. Their lands had once stretched from the west coast near the Isle of Skye to the north of Ullapool and east to the Black Isle, near Inverness.

The Mackenzie tartan was a green, blue and black check with an overlay of red and white. Like all the clans, they had feuded with their neighbours and their history was a violent one of wars, battles, curses and tragedies. Yet there was no mention of Dungorm or Alexander and Eliza Mackenzie.

At last Nonnie came back and Sophie closed the book with a sigh. She wasn't sure if her reading had really helped her understand more about Charlotte Mackenzie, but at least it was a start.

'Come on, Sophie and Jess,' called Nonnie. 'You've been reading all morning. Let's go and get some fresh air and put the roses back in your cheeks. You're looking a little peaky, Sophie.'

Thoughts of Scotland, the Mackenzies and Castle Dungorm floated through Sophie's head all day. Nonnie took them to see the spy movie in the afternoon, but not even this could distract her from thoughts of the Mackenzies.

'Did you enjoy the movie, Sophie?' asked Nonnie. 'You're very quiet. Is there anything bothering you?'

'No,' Sophie answered with a quick grin. 'Just thinking.'

'Don't think too much or you'll wear your brain out,' teased Jess, flicking Sophie's hair.

'Ha, ha! You can talk! At least I have a brain to wear out!' retorted Sophie.

She made an effort to be chatty as they played cards after dinner. But she couldn't help glancing frequently at her watch, waiting for the slow-moving hands to make it around to bedtime, when she could clean her teeth, pull on her nightie, hide the locket around her neck and climb under the doona. *How did Alexander and Eliza die? How did the girls become orphans? Sleep, sleep – oh when would it ever come?*

6

The Voyage of the Eliza Mackenzie

This time, the light was different in Scotland when Sophie floated above the house of Dungorm. It was grey and flat and dreary. Squalls of rain beat against the windows and soaked Sophie's nightdress.

As quickly as she could, Sophie faded through an upstairs attic window and into the house. She searched the house, looking for Charlotte and Nell.

Sophie floated down the back stairs, dodging a chamber-maid carrying up a load of coal. On the ground floor she checked the sitting room and the conservatory; then she heard the sound of low voices coming from the drawing room.

Cautiously she glided through the door and into the room. A fire was blazing on the hearth, but it did little to disperse the chill, so everyone was wearing thick, warm clothes.

She seemed to have come in on a family discussion of some seriousness, judging by the sombre expressions on Eliza's and Alexander's faces. Sophie felt momentarily guilty to be eavesdropping on a private conversation.

It's too late for that, she thought. *I've been eavesdropping on private conversations for nights now. And maybe I'll find out something useful.*

Charlotte and Nell sat quietly on stools near the fire, with Flossie at their feet. Flossie noticed Sophie and sat up, her ears pricked, but for the first time she didn't bark or growl. She thumped her tail in greeting then lay down once more.

'But Alexander, what business could be so urgent that you need to travel by ship at this time of year?' Eliza argued, jumping up from her armchair and dropping a small linen cloth she was embroidering. 'Why not take a little longer and go by road?'

'The roads are dreadful at this time of year too, and I need to get to Glasgow urgently to sign some papers,' Alexander replied patiently, patting her on the arm. 'If I take the ship, I need only be away for a matter of days, and then I can be back here with you and the girls all the sooner.'

He smiled over at Charlotte and Nell, who smiled tentatively back.

'It will be fine, Eliza,' continued Alexander. 'You know we have done this trip dozens of times. *Eliza Mackenzie* is a sturdy, safe ship and is standing by in the harbour ready to go. My valet is packing, so I can leave as soon as the carriage is ready.'

Eliza sighed, admitting defeat, and dropped back into her chair, her embroidery forgotten.

'I do not like it at all,' she finished anxiously, twisting the Star of Serendib ring on her finger.

Alexander smiled and quoted his favourite poet, Robbie Burns, with a voice thrumming with mock drama, and with exaggerated hand gestures. It was a poem he knew by heart.

'From thee, Eliza, I must go,
And from my native shore;
The cruel fates between us throw
A boundless ocean's roar:
But boundless oceans, roaring wide,
Between my love and me,
They never, never can divide
My heart and soul from thee.

'Farewell, farewell, Eliza dear,
The maid that I adore . . .'

Alexander trailed off laughing, as Eliza threw a green velvet cushion at his head.

'Not very ladylike, my Lady Mackenzie,' he chided with false severity.

'But you are *not* leaving your native shore or crossing a boundless ocean, my Laird Mackenzie,' Eliza retorted.

'Exactly, so I will be fine, my love,' Alexander reassured her. 'Now, what pretty trifles can I fetch my three beautiful girls in Glasgow – silks, lace, ribbon?'

'Presents!' cried Nell in glee.

'Books,' added Charlotte. 'We need some new books.'

'I shall bring plenty,' agreed Alexander dotingly. 'I should be back by Wednesday week so tell Cook to plan a fitting dinner for the laird of the house.'

A discreet knock sounded at the door.

'M' laird, the carriage is ready,' announced the butler.

'Thank you, Wilson. I shall be there in a moment.'

Alexander swept each of the girls up off the floor and into his arms for a bear hug and a rain of kisses.

'Be good for your mama while I'm away, you mischievous lassies, or there will be no presents for anyone,' Alexander teased, dropping Nell down gently on the floor.

Then he picked up Eliza's hand and kissed it gently.

'Farewell, farewell Eliza dear, the maid that I adore,' he whispered. 'I will be home soon, my love, never fear.'

Eliza stood up to hug him wordlessly. Alexander kissed her hard then walked quickly through the door, keen to finish the scene of farewell. The girls ran to the door to watch Wilson hand Alexander his hat and coat and hold the front door open. Alexander blew them one more kiss, and then he was gone.

Eliza sank back into her chair, then smiled brightly at the girls.

'Well, the journey should only take a few days,' Eliza said. 'And I wonder what presents Papa will choose for us. I hope he remembers to bring the velvet for your new dresses; you are both growing so much.'

'I hope he finds me a pretty blue velvet,' said Nell.

Eliza stooped to pick up the dropped linen and Sophie noticed she moved a bit awkwardly. When Eliza leant back into the armchair and wedged a cushion behind her back, Sophie realised that Eliza's pregnancy was now very obvious.

Outside, the wind howled, lashing the rain against the windows. Charlotte and Nell sat on the floor playing spillikins, while Eliza stared into the fire, her sewing forgotten. Sophie curled up on the window seat. Marmalade, the fat ginger cat, stalked over and sniffed her suspiciously, then ignored her.

Sophie felt exhausted but fought sleep, frightened she would slip back to her own time if she slept. She watched patiently as Eliza and the girls went up to bed. A servant banked the fire for the night and extinguished the candles, leaving Sophie in pitch darkness.

When the house was quiet, Sophie found a candle on the mantelpiece and, concentrating with all her might, tried to lift it up. She fumbled and knocked it and dropped it.

It seemed so strange that something as simple as picking up a candle was so difficult, yet she could fly and be invisible and dissolve through solid walls, all of which were totally impossible in her own life.

At last Sophie was able to pick up the candle, with trembling fingers. She held the wick against the red coals of the fire until it burst into flame. Now she had light.

Sophie wandered around the drawing room checking the portraits on the wall, the knick-knacks on the piano and the Indian curios on the mantelpiece by the candle's flickering light.

A huge gilt mirror was hung over the fireplace in the drawing room. Sophie stared in the mirror at her reflection. She was not there, only the candle floating mysteriously by itself in midair, the drawing room reflected behind it. It gave her a fright: did she really exist any more?

Sophie took the candle and wandered through the ground floor, exploring. She could go into only the rooms where the doors were left ajar, as she could not fade through the doorways carrying the candle.

The clock chimed the quarter hour. The house was asleep. Only Marmalade the ginger cat remained to keep her company, strolling at her heels.

The storm outside gradually intensified until it was shaking the very foundations of the house. The wind buffeted the windows and rattled the doors and the shutters. The clock on the mantelpiece struck one o'clock.

A clatter sounded from the driveway. A horse galloped up the gravel, its hoof beats hardly audible over the storm. A crash sounded on the front door – a banging of fists –and then came an indecipherable shout. Sophie froze, her heart in her mouth.

With sudden clarity she knew what that terrible banging meant. She knew what dreadful news was on the other side of that door. In slow motion, she heard the stirrings in the house. Sophie blew out the candle flame and floated towards the front door.

Wilson the butler, wearing a jacket over his nightclothes, hurried down the back stairs and into the hall, carrying a hastily lit lantern. Nanny bustled after him, a thin wrapper over her nightclothes, her hair covered by a mob-cap. She was followed by two chambermaids, who were clutching each other nervously.

Wilson unbolted the big front door, which slowly swung open. A saturated fisherman fell into the hallway, shedding puddles from his sou-wester.

'My God, man!' Wilson exclaimed. 'Whatever has happened?'

'Storm,' panted the fisherman, breathless from his breakneck ride. 'Ship hit the rocks near Kyle of Lochalsh. *Eliza Mackenzie* sank without trace. We saved two mates.

We fear the crew and the laird of Dungorm are lost.'

A faint sob came from the top of the marble staircase.

'Alexander? No. No. Please God, not my Alexander.'

Eliza stood like a ghost in her long white nightgown, a crimson shawl thrown over her shoulders and her long hair tumbling down her back. One of the chambermaids shrieked.

'My lady,' cried Nanny, running up the stairs. But Nanny was too late. Eliza crumpled to the floor and slid down the stairs, her head banging on the hard marble.

'Noooooo,' screamed Sophie and found herself whooshing up the stairs, past the gaping servants, past Nanny and up to Eliza's tumbling body. When Sophie reached her, a moment later, Eliza had fallen only a couple of steps.

Sophie was as frail as tissue paper. She could see right through her own hand to the rich Persian carpet below. Yet somehow her panic gave her strength. She skimmed up the stairs and met Eliza's falling body with her own transparent ghostly one.

Sophie concentrated with all her mind. *Save Eliza. Stop her falling.*

Somehow, like a mother who manages to lift an impossibly heavy car off the body of her fallen child, Sophie managed to break Eliza's fall and stop her on the third step. In a moment Nanny was there fussing over Eliza, cradling her head in her lap and murmuring soothing noises, while fat, salty tears fell from her eyes.

Downstairs the chambermaids sobbed in shock and fear. Wilson the butler shouted orders, sending for smelling salts, wet cloths, towels for the fisherman, hot tea.

All the servants were now gathered in the hall and leapt

to his command, tending Eliza, fetching items, rubbing down and stabling the shivering horse, towelling the fisherman dry and leading him to the kitchen for hot tea and rum.

Sophie collapsed on the stairs, trembling violently with the effort of saving Eliza, overwhelmed with both relief and grief. Sally the chambermaid stepped right through Sophie's ghostly body as she ran up the stairs.

Nanny carefully checked Eliza's head, neck and back before supervising two footmen who carried her back to bed. The chambermaid hurried in with the smelling salts and wet cloths.

Nanny looked at Eliza's wan face. It seemed cruel to wake her up, to make her face this nightmare. Nanny took a deep breath, then waved the pungent smelling salts under Eliza's nose.

Eliza coughed and choked. She woke up, her eyelids fluttering open. She took in Nanny, the smelling salts, her vicious headache and the feeling that her insides had been ripped open by a knife. Consciousness flooded back.

'Alexander, oh, Alexander,' Eliza moaned. Sophie floated near the dressing table, tears spilling down her cheeks. She wondered where Charlotte and Nell were. Was it possible they had slept through all this commotion?

'Where are my girls?' begged Eliza. 'Do they know? Are they awake?'

Nanny shook her head, trying to speak. 'I sent one o' the kitchen maids to check on them . . . the bonnie lassies were sleeping like bairns. I could no' bear to wake them up, and I wanted to make sure ye were all right first.'

'Thank you, Nanny,' whispered Eliza. 'You did well. I do not want to scare them unnecessarily. Hopefully by morning we will have found him.' She paused, her voice cracking.

'I am quite well now, thank you, Nanny,' Eliza continued in a stronger voice. 'I want all the servants dressed warmly and ready to ride to Kyle of Lochalsh. You of course must stay here to look after my bairns.

'I will go with the servants to organise the search party for the survivors. We will hunt all night and all day if we have to. Can you please ask the servants to lay out my riding habit and saddle my horse?'

Eliza fell back, exhausted from the energy expended in this speech. Nanny cried openly now, sobs wracking her rounded frame.

'Nanny, we have to be strong now,' Eliza continued, touching Nanny gently on the arm. 'We have to do everything we can. It is not time yet to grieve him.'

Nanny pulled herself together.

'My lady, ye' canna ride to Lochalsh in this storm,' Nanny said firmly. 'Ye will kill the wee bairn. Let the men gae and search. Ye should stay and rest. 'Tis an absolute miracle ye were no' killed just now when ye fell down the stairs.'

Eliza touched her belly for reassurance and nodded.

'All right,' Eliza conceded. 'Please send my wishes to the men. We will just have to wait and pray and hope.' She turned her face away so Nanny wouldn't see the tears welling just below the surface.

Nanny curtseyed and bustled off. Eliza climbed clumsily out of bed and stumbled to her daughters' room.

Charlotte and Nell were sleeping peacefully, oblivious to the drama around them.

Eliza gazed down at each child in turn, and gently tucked in their covers. Charlotte stirred, then awoke. It took a moment for her to focus.

'Mama?'

'Oh, my darling,' Eliza sobbed. 'We are going to have to be very brave.'

Nell woke and, seeing her mother's face so strange and swollen, began to cry in fear. Charlotte jumped out of bed and flung herself into her mother's arms. 'Mama, what is wrong?'

Eliza said only one word. 'Papa.'

Eliza spent the day reading to the girls from *Pride and Prejudice*.

Sophie too had listened, drawing comfort from the words. It was strange. Sophie had never met Alexander and he had certainly never even seen her, yet her grief felt as though it was for a member of her own family, which she supposed he actually was.

Eliza checked the window every few pages, searching for a glimpse of the returning servants bringing with them either her salvation or life sentence. At last, many hours later, when it was almost dark again, she glimpsed the cavalcade from the nursery window. She called frantically for Nanny to watch the girls and keep them away.

The servants walked slowly into the stable yard, their horses hanging their heads in exhaustion. Behind them bumped a rickety old farm cart, with a blanket-shrouded shape lying on the back.

Eliza flew down the staircase and met the returning servants as they carried the scarlet-draped body into the hall. The men, grey with weariness, carried their hats in their hands, refusing to meet Eliza's gaze.

'My lady,' blurted Wilson, 'I am so sorry. We found my laird's body this afternoon, washed up on the shore of Lochalsh. We brought it straight home; we thought you would want to know as soon as possible.'

'Thank you, Wilson,' murmured Eliza. As if of its own accord, her hand reached out and gently, softly stroked the draped body. 'Could you please carry him in here? I want to look after him myself.'

Alexander's body was laid out on a table in the sitting room and Eliza closed the door, locking everyone out. The servants scurried around, watching the door nervously.

At last Eliza emerged and wordlessly climbed the stairs to the nursery to comfort her daughters.

'Darlings, your papa is dead. There is no doubt now.' Eliza slumped, all the fight gone from her, and hugged Charlotte and Nell closely. 'It is just us now.'

Charlotte buried her head in her mother's skirt but somehow she had already known the worst. Nell just stared uncomprehendingly. How could their larger-than-life, laughing father be gone?

Sophie could not bear to watch Eliza, Charlotte and Nell's grief. She turned away and swooped up through the window and up through the clouds, back to her own world.

Sophie woke with an aching head, her pillow wet with tears. She took the locket off and held it in her hand, feeling its weight. Should she put the locket away in its oak box? Did she really want to know the rest of Charlotte's story?

But could she bear not to know? Could she bear never to go back to the past?

Sophie thought of her own family's problems. She had tried to ignore these for months but learning about Charlotte's family dramas had made her realise her own troubles were not going to go away.

Her dad, Jack, had lost his marketing job six months ago, when his company had gone bankrupt. At first he had been cheery and optimistic, telling the girls that it would not take him long to find another job. He had dressed in his suit every day and read the newspaper, circling all the jobs he would apply for.

He had visited headhunters (apparently these were people who helped you find jobs, not cannibals) and made hundreds of phone calls. He had attended interview after interview, only to be told he was over-qualified for the job and the economy was depressed.

Sophie's mum, Karen, had worked part-time as a graphic artist, but was now working full-time to pay the mortgage and bills and buy the groceries. There was not enough money to pay for everything, so the family had to *economise.* First went the ballet and piano lessons, then over time, more and more changes had to be made.

Karen made lots of different meals with cheap mince, and one Sophie and Jess jokingly called 'dead vegetable soup', made from the weekly leftovers. There was no money for treats such as going to the movies, buying new clothes or books or even takeaway.

As the months sped by, Jack had fallen into a deep depression. He spent half the day in his pyjamas and had taken to reading the sport and comics in the newspaper, instead of the business and jobs pages. The highlight of his day was watching mindless programs on television and he had started to yell at the children, making everyone feel miserable.

The decision had been made that after the holidays, Sophie and Jess would have to leave their expensive private school and go to the local public school, leaving all their friends. Sophie's stomach filled with butterflies whenever she thought about it. But that wasn't the worst of it.

Last week she had heard her parents fighting over the credit card bills. Her mother suggested they should sell their home and rent somewhere cheaper until Jack found another job. Jack had shouted back, then stormed out of the house. He had returned hours later, quiet and withdrawn.

Karen had decided it might be nicer for the girls to stay with Nonnie for two weeks, to give them all a break. Sophie was scared of what was happening at home. She worried they might lose their home; she worried her parents might break up; she worried her dad was so sick and sad that her old cheerful, happy dad would never come back.

Sophie put the locket back on, pulled the covers over her head and thought of Charlotte losing her father, Alexander Mackenzie.

When Sophie returned, it was five days after Alexander's death. His brother, Roderick, and sister-in-law, Arabella, had come to stay for the funeral.

Eliza had washed and dressed her husband's body in a white sleeping gown and he lay in the drawing room. For five days, Eliza had sat with her husband, keeping a vigil. Around her the servants crept anxiously, attending to all the many duties of a house in mourning.

There were letters to write, cards of condolence to open, messages to be sent to the far corners of Britain, the funeral to organise, mourning clothes to be ordered.

At last Eliza left her husband's side. She wandered down the hall into Alexander's study, to find Roderick rifling through the papers on the desk. Eliza froze with indignation.

'Ah, Eliza,' Roderick said, quickly covering up a letter he had been reading. 'How are you, my dear?'

'Roderick, I would greatly appreciate it if you could try to keep your long nose out of my husband's private papers,' snapped Eliza.

'My dear Eliza, I'm only trying to help,' retorted Roderick. 'At a time like this you need all the support you can get, and of course it's too much to expect you to grasp Alexander's complex business affairs.'

'Why? Because I am a woman?' asked Eliza, dangerously polite.

'Well, yes, of course,' replied Roderick smugly. 'It's much too complicated for your delicate sensibilities at this time.'

'It is too much for my delicate sensibilities to have you pawing through my dead husband's things, so I would greatly appreciate it if you could leave me alone for a few moments.'

Roderick could do nothing but agree, albeit with bad grace, and leave the room.

Eliza picked up the paper Roderick had been reading. It was one of the crofter's tenancy contracts. Next time Roderick surreptitiously tried the study door, he found it firmly locked.

That evening at dinner, Eliza toyed with her food, hardly eating anything. Arabella chatted cheerily, ostentatiously flaunting the brand-new black of her mourning gown. The black silk dramatically emphasised her pale skin, black hair and slim figure.

Sophie floated restlessly around the dining room, causing the candles to flicker and gutter.

'There seems to be a terrible *draught* in this room, Eliza,' complained Arabella. 'I do not know how you can bear it.'

Eliza also wore head-to-toe dull black, as was expected of a widow. The dressmaker and her assistants had spent days and nights sewing the required mourning gowns for Eliza, Charlotte and Nell. While adults wore black for mourning, children usually wore white.

The girls sat quietly, joining the adults for dinner but saying very little.

'I wonder, my dear Eliza, what you will do now with the girls,' quizzed Arabella, her black feather headdress bobbing. 'I suppose you will be sending them to boarding school. I know an excellent boarding school in Edinburgh that is marvellous for teaching dancing and deportment.

'Goodness knows, Charlotte and Nell could do with some help there,' she continued. 'They will never find a husband unless they learn to walk like ladies.' She trilled with laughter.

Eliza flushed with mortification. One of the candles on the mantelpiece flickered and went out.

'No thank you, Arabella,' replied Eliza with difficulty. 'Charlotte and Nell will stay here at home with me.'

'Oh, I wonder if you do not die of boredom, here in the middle of nowhere,' Arabella said. 'Well, of course, as a widow you will not be able to go to parties or balls for a year.

'I suppose you will want to move to Glasgow or Edinburgh. You may meet some eligible older gentlemen there. After all, you are not so *very* old now, and I am sure you would wish to remarry in time.'

Charlotte clenched her fists under the table with fury and Nell gasped with shock, tears welling. Sophie floated behind Charlotte and Nell, stunned by how insensitive and insufferable Arabella was. She longed to touch the girls on the shoulder or the back to comfort them.

'Thank you, Arabella, for thinking of me,' answered Eliza through clenched teeth. 'But as my husband has only just *died* and is not yet *buried*, I had not planned so far ahead quite yet.'

Arabella blushed at the rebuke and fell silent.

'I have been meaning to talk to you, Eliza,' began Roderick, his fork picking over his fish.

'Yes, Roderick?'

'It is about the Dungorm jewels,' Roderick continued. 'Of course, as a widow you will not wear any jewels for a very long time, and I believe they would be much safer stored away in a bank vault. I know an excellent bank in Edinburgh and could happily arrange their safekeeping there.'

Arabella nearly purred with pleasure. Eliza's head jerked up in shock.

'Of course, you could always send for them when you are ready to start wearing them again,' added Roderick hurriedly.

Eliza breathed deeply and evenly before replying. Sophie hovered behind Eliza's chair wondering how Eliza would react.

'My husband brought me my jewels as a wedding present.'

'Exactly,' Roderick replied. 'Which is why we want to keep them safely in the bank.'

'I do not want . . .' Eliza paused, took a breath and then continued. 'I do not want the jewels my husband gave me as a gift of his love to moulder away in a bank vault, nor to be worn by your wife to fancy Edinburgh soirees.

'I am quite happy to keep them here where they belong, so at least if I cannot wear them, I can be delighted by their beauty to remind me of what once was.'

'Quite,' Roderick responded. Arabella deflated rapidly, shooting a poisonous look at her husband.

Eliza rose to her feet, her napkin dropping to the floor.

'If you will excuse me, Charlotte and Nell, I find I have a migraine coming on.'

Charlotte and Nell glanced at each other in concern. Their mother never had migraines.

Sophie smiled to herself. She felt Eliza had come out the best from her encounters with Roderick and Arabella Mackenzie. Sophie felt a moment of wickedness come over her, and she carefully tugged gently at the plate of salmon placed in front of Arabella.

At first nothing happened. Sophie tried harder. The plate teetered for a moment on the edge of the table. Sophie concentrated really hard and smash, the plate tumbled into Arabella's lap, basting her in dripping fish juices and lumps of flesh.

'Something touched me!' Arabella shrieked loudly. 'Something knocked my plate down. Oh, my gown!'

Sophie swooped in glee and floated up to the ceiling.

Charlotte and Nell giggled audibly then coughed loudly into their napkins. They had not smiled for what seemed a very long time.

'There now, Arabella,' soothed her husband. 'I think you are a little overwrought. Why don't you go upstairs and have a rest?'

7

Staying Longer

Sophie knew that if she fell asleep wearing the gold locket in her own world, she fell down through a tunnel of sleep into Charlotte's world. In the past she had simply swooped up again, like flying in a dream, through the tunnel and back to her own bed.

But several nights had gone by and Sophie sensed that there was much more to Charlotte's story. Sophie decided she would try not to go home to the future, to Australia, to Nonnie's apartment. Instead she would see how long she could stay in Charlotte's world, in nineteenth-century Scotland.

Time seemed to run differently in the different worlds. The first night, her visit had been very short, perhaps an hour or so. Her later visits had been progressively longer.

With each visit she had seemed to grow more substantial in the past world. Instead of merely being a misty onlooker, now she could actually make things happen if she concentrated hard enough.

She had saved Eliza from falling down the stairs and tipped Arabella's dinner in her lap. Perhaps, if she tried through force of will, she could stay longer in the past and learn all there was to learn about Charlotte Mackenzie of Dungorm.

The next day was the hardest of all: the funeral.

Once more the day dawned grey and drizzly, as most days did in Scotland in late autumn. All was black and grey. It was hard to believe that it was only a little less than a week since Alexander had been alive and well and making jokes at the breakfast table.

The carriage came around to the front door, its black paintwork gleaming and speckled with raindrops. Two other wagons stood ready, both draped in black crepe.

All the horses had been brushed until they shone, with black ribbon plaited into their manes and tails, and long black feather plumes attached to their bridles. The drivers, dressed in frockcoats and top hats, stood at the horses' heads, soothing them.

The servants, dressed in black, lined the steps, forming a guard of honour. Four servants carried the timber coffin out of the house and down the stairs, and carefully arranged it on the back of the first wagon. Uncle Roderick followed and climbed into the carriage behind.

As was custom, the women did not attend the funeral ceremony but stayed at home to grieve in private. Charlotte watched the sombre cavalcade from the window of her mother's bedroom, tears rolling down her face. Eliza stood beside Charlotte, twisting her handkerchief into sodden knots.

Nell sat in a chair, staring into the fire, her face swollen and tear stained. She could not bear to watch the coffin being taken away.

Sophie hovered anxiously, helpless to do anything to alleviate the overwhelming grief of the family. Charlotte turned suddenly and glanced sharply at the space where Sophie was, but, seeing nothing, turned her eyes back to the window, to watch the servants outside file over to the last wagon and climb up.

The cavalcade set off, clopping sedately down the gravel drive. Sophie decided to follow it, to escape into the fresh air and see what happened.

Sophie slipped out through the wall and flew over the iron-grey loch, whipped by the wind into small white-capped waves. She saw the majestic ruins of Castle Dungorm on its tiny island, seabirds swooping around its shattered keep and tumbled stones.

The carriage trundled on past the rolling green pastures, dotted with black-faced sheep huddled against the cold, and the hills where Nell and Charlotte had raced their ponies last spring.

The horses clopped further, their heads bobbing up and down, through a set of ornate wrought-iron gates flanked by tall sandstone pillars, with a small gatehouse on the left. Sophie floated behind.

The road twisted to the right towards the village, but the cavalcade stopped at the small stone kirk, with its ancient stained-glass windows and higgledy-piggledy graveyard.

Despite the steadily falling rain, the kirkyard was filled with local villagers, fishermen, crofters and tradesmen, all dressed in their Sunday best. A number of carriages and horses were tethered in the meadow across the road, indicating that more people were inside the building.

A villager dressed in a kilt and tam-o'-shanter stood to the side of the kirk door playing a lament on the bagpipes. The haunting, mournful music wafted out over the kirkyard, through the rain and up over the hills, sending shivers up Sophie's spine.

The coffin was ceremoniously carried into the kirk, followed by Roderick Mackenzie. Once he was seated, the villagers came crowding in to stand at the back and sides of the small kirk. Sophie gazed about her intently, trying to guess the occupations of the locals by their dress and demeanour.

The service was long and wordy, punctuated by muffled coughs and sniffs. Then it was over and the coffin was carried out once more, followed by the subdued congregation.

At the end of the kirkyard, under a huge old oak tree, a marble crypt had been built. The piper played a sombre tune as Alexander's coffin was carried into the crypt and laid to rest on a stone plinth.

An ornate headstone behind the coffin had words freshly carved into one half of the stone.

Alexander James Mackenzie, Laird of Dungorm
Born 2.8.1816
Died 7.10.1857

Beloved husband of Eliza Mackenzie
Beloved father of Charlotte and Eleanor

But boundless oceans, roaring wide,
Between my love and me,

They never, never can divide
My heart and soul from thee.

Luceo non Uro

A stone carving of an angel guarded the grave, her wings spread protectively behind her back.

The other half of the stone was chillingly bare, and below it was the empty half of the plinth, waiting for another coffin to fill it. Sophie shivered in the cold, dark air of the crypt. She flew outside to escape the last of the service, followed by the haunting song of the bagpipe, and swiftly soared back to Charlotte and Dungorm.

Charlotte was woken by a scream, which was quickly cut short. It clawed through the exhausted, miserable fug of her brain and brought her to instant wakefulness. She slithered out of bed, pulled a shawl around her white nightdress and slipped her feet into the slippers by her bed.

Sophie was instantly alert, her heart pounding.

Charlotte tiptoed out of their room, careful not to wake the still-sleeping Nell, and down the brightly lit hallway. A muffled cry came from a room further down the hall.

Charlotte crept down the hallway, past several closed doors, paintings and portraits and the top of the sweeping staircase. Unbeknownst to Charlotte, Sophie followed right behind her, her bare feet nearly skimming the carpet.

Her heart like a stone at the bottom of her stomach, Charlotte paused outside her mother's room and listened at the door. She could hear odd, muffled noises and a small cry of distress. She turned the knob and flung the door open, almost falling in her haste.

Eliza was in bed, in her long nightgown, the covers tumbled and knotted. Her hair was tangled and her face shone with moisture. Nanny sat beside the bed, bathing Eliza's face with a damp cloth and murmuring soothing words.

Eliza clutched Nanny's left hand so tightly both their fingers were bloodless and white.

'I will ring for the surgeon –' Nanny began.

'No,' Eliza retorted forcefully. Then she let go of Nanny's hand, collapsing back against the pillows.

Charlotte sprang forward with a cry of horror, Sophie beside her.

'Hello, darling,' panted Eliza breathlessly. 'Do not worry. Mama is not feeling very well but Nanny is looking after me, so you can go back to sleep. I am sure I will be much better in the morning.'

Charlotte looked at Nanny for confirmation. Nanny nodded, but swiftly glanced away.

'Give me a kiss, darling, and go back to bed,' Eliza continued. She gave Charlotte a strained smile as Charlotte kissed her on the cheek.

'I love you, darling,' Eliza said. 'Do not worry; everything will be fine.'

Charlotte stepped away from the bed, looking back uncertainly at her mother. Nanny stood up and followed her to the door, shooing her out gently. Nanny and Sophie followed Charlotte into the hall.

'Miss Charlotte, dear,' Nanny whispered, 'I wonder if

ye could do me a wee favour and ring the bell for Wilson. I want ye to ask him to send one o' the lads riding at once to the mainland for the surgeon. Lady Dungorm is no' well, and I am thinking it would be best if the surgeon came quickly.'

Nanny's voice seemed calm but Charlotte, who had known Nanny her whole life, could sense the suppressed panic beneath the surface.

'Of course, Nanny,' Charlotte replied quickly, her voice cracking with fear.

'There ye are, my bonnie lassie,' Nanny replied. 'Ring for Wilson, then gae straight back to bed.'

Nanny did not wait for Charlotte to reply but hurried back into Eliza's chamber. Charlotte heard another low moan of pain from behind the closed door. Her mind was made up in a flash.

Charlotte ran down the marble staircase, her padding feet making no noise in her cotton slippers. She drew back the bolts on the back door, slipped out into the night and ran to the stables. Sophie swooped beside her. What was Charlotte going to do?

In the tack room Charlotte lit a lamp and found a bridle, a carrot and an old mackintosh, which she shrugged over her nightgown. Then she walked slowly down the corridor of the stables, talking softly to the horses.

She stopped, quietly and calmly, at the stall of her father's favourite hunter, Tamburlaine, the fastest horse on the estate. He was a massive eighteen hands high, much taller than her own pony, Rosie.

Sophie stayed well back, not wanting to spook the horse with her proximity.

Tamburlaine accepted the withered carrot happily, with a whickering hurrumph and a tickling breath on Charlotte's cheek.

Cautiously, Charlotte slipped the bridle over Tamburlaine's head while he still had it down low, and buckled the strap. Her cold hands fumbled with the unfamiliar task, then she led him out of the stall, down the corridor and out into the stable yard.

There was still one more difficult task, which was to actually mount the huge horse. Charlotte led him past the mounting block and over to the water butt which caught the rainwater from the roof. She scrambled up onto the water butt, then onto Tamburlaine's broad, bare back.

The time for slowness was over. Charlotte gathered the reins, wrapping her fingers in Tamburlaine's mane, and kicked her slippered feet into Tamburlaine's sides. The hunter caught her panic and leapt into a gallop.

Charlotte hunched right over his neck, clinging on for her very life. Her slippers did not even last until the stable-yard arch, dropping away into the mud. Charlotte prayed she could guide him. Her weight and strength were nothing compared to Alexander's.

The intelligent horse seemed to sense her need and flew out of the stable yard and along the pale glimmer of the road leading to the village. They clattered through the small village and out the other side, heading to the ferry-man's cottage.

Sophie skimmed alongside, well away from the horse.

The island was separated from the mainland by a narrow loch, crossed by barge. Charlotte rode Tamburlaine right to the ferryman's front door and rang the bell furiously.

'Who is there at this time o' the night?' cried the ferryman, sticking his head out the window.

''Tis Charlotte Mackenzie. An emergency – my mother – the surgeon – please hurry.'

The ferryman flung open the door and rushed down to the loch, pulling on his jacket as he ran.

'Do no' fret, lassie,' he called back, untying the rope securing his barge. 'I will fetch the sawbones. 'Twill be quicker. Ye wait inside with my wife, and I will take ye back to Dungorm when I return.'

Charlotte nodded wearily and watched as the competent ferryman took the oars and was speedily swallowed by the darkness. But Charlotte did not go inside and wait with the ferryman's wife. Instead she turned Tamburlaine's head and cantered for home, Sophie flying beside her.

Once Tamburlaine was safely returned to his stall, rubbed down and fed a bucket of oats, Charlotte raced to the house, the sharp gravel bruising and cutting her feet.

Lights blazed in the back of the house and servants hurried back and forth, from the kitchen, to the laundry, to the back servants' staircase, carrying pails of boiling water and piles of linen.

Charlotte dashed upstairs to her mother's chamber. Once more she threw open the door without knocking and rushed into the room. Her mother lay limp – her long hair now brushed and plaited, her skin as pale as the white nightgown and sheets – but still gently breathing.

Sophie heaved a silent sigh of relief. They were not too late.

Nanny was in the corner folding some towels, her face creased with grief.

'Och, Miss Charlotte,' Nanny whispered. 'Your mother's sleeping. I think 'tis best if ye gae to bed.'

'No, I am not sleeping, Nanny,' replied Eliza from the bed, her voice weary. 'I want to talk to Miss Charlotte for a few moments. Would you mind leaving us? I would appreciate it if you could ensure no-one disturbs us. Thank you, Nanny.'

Nanny looked inclined to argue, but years of working for great families had ingrained a sense of unquestioning obedience. She nodded and left the room, closing the door behind her. Sophie was torn: should she go too, or should she stay and listen? Curiosity won and Sophie stayed.

Eliza lay back exhausted after her short speech. She gathered her strength and her thoughts then patted the bed beside her. Charlotte sat down on the eiderdown, confused and anxious.

'You had a little brother, Charlotte,' Eliza whispered. 'He did not last long in this world, but I did get to hold him for a few minutes. I called him Alexander James. He came too early – impatient like his father. The baby died a short while ago.'

Eliza stopped and closed her eyes. Charlotte stared at her with round frightened eyes, uncomprehending.

'Charlotte, I want to give you something, just in case,' Eliza continued. 'Could you fetch me my jewel casket from my dressing table?'

Charlotte brought over the small gilt box with trembling hands and laid it on the bed. This was where her mother kept the jewellery she wore every day. The other jewels – the priceless diamonds, pearls and emeralds – were kept locked away in a safe in Alexander's dressing room.

'Charlotte, if anything were to happen to me . . .'

Charlotte froze, her mind refusing to accept her mother's words. She felt as though she was in a terrible nightmare and she longed to wake up, so everything could be as it was before.

'Of course, everything I own would be yours and Nell's,' Eliza continued.

'No.'

'Listen to me please, Charlotte; this is important. I want you to be strong.'

Charlotte listened carefully, although she could not see through the hot tears running down her face. Sophie sobbed too.

'*If* something ever happened to me, I would like you to have my wedding ring, the Star of Serendib, which Papa brought me back from India. I want you to take it now and look after it until I am better.'

Eliza rubbed the sparkling sapphire with her thin fingers then tucked it inside Charlotte's palm.

'My gold bangle will be for Nell and I want you to have my gold locket so I can be close to you when you wear it. Put them somewhere safe until I need them again.' Eliza paused once more, breathing raggedly for a few moments.

'Darling, I do not know what the future holds for any of us, but one thing I do know is that I will always love you both so much. If I cannot be there, please look after Nell for me. Remember, I will always watch over you . . .'

Eliza closed her eyes and seemed to fall into a half sleep. Charlotte waited for a moment, then quietly returned the jewel casket to the dressing table and tiptoed back to the bed. She kissed her mother gently on the forehead, like a mother would kiss a sleeping child.

'I love you,' Charlotte whispered. Eliza smiled softly but did not open her eyes.

Down below, Charlotte heard the commotion of the surgeon arriving. She slipped away to her room and hid the jewellery in her carved oak treasure box.

Charlotte knelt beside her bed, her eyes shut tightly and her hands clasped together in prayer.

'Please God, do not let Mama die. Please save her,' she murmured her prayer over and over.

Sophie sat beside her, longing to comfort Charlotte with a hug and be comforted by her in turn.

Half an hour later, Nanny came in to fetch the girls. She did not speak but gently shook Nell awake and beckoned them to follow her down the hall to their mother's room. Charlotte helped the sleepy Nell out of bed. Sophie followed the girls down the hallway, feeling as frightened as the girls looked.

The surgeon was just leaving their mother's chamber, carrying a small bag.

'Miss Charlotte, Miss Nell,' he said. 'I'm so sorry but there was nothing I could do. Lady Mackenzie lost too much blood. Your mother is . . . dead. I thought perhaps you might like to see her –'

Nell screamed and fell to the floor, her body crumpled like a rag doll. Charlotte sucked in her breath, too shocked to speak. The doctor glanced imploringly at Nanny then hurried away down the corridor.

Gently, Nanny coaxed Nell to her feet and half carried her into Eliza's darkened bedroom, with Charlotte and Sophie stumbling behind.

Eliza lay on the bed as if she were sleeping peacefully,

her dark hair spread on the white pillows. The girls rushed to her bedside and fell to their knees on the floor

'Mama,' sobbed Nell. 'Mama, please come back.'

A flicker of white caught Sophie's eye. In the corner of the room floated an apparition, a woman dressed in a long white gown. In her arms she held a small wrapped bundle.

With a start Sophie realised the apparition was Eliza Mackenzie, Lady of Dungorm, and in her arms was her newborn son. Eliza floated over to Charlotte and Nell and kissed each one on top of their heads. The girls seemed oblivious to her misty embrace. Eliza turned and smiled at Sophie.

'Look after my girls.' A muted whisper sounded in Sophie's ear. 'Help them if you can.'

The apparition wavered and faded and disappeared.

Sophie flew after her. 'Stop. No, Eliza, wait,' she cried.

Charlotte looked up suddenly and stared sharply at the corner where Sophie floated. Sophie melted away through the wall into the dressing room, leaving the girls to their grief.

So that was how it happened that Eliza and her baby son, Alexander, were buried in the Mackenzie crypt so soon after her husband, leaving two orphaned girls, all alone in the world.

8

The Burning Papers

When Sophie next visited Scotland, it was only a few days after Eliza's death, but Sophie noticed many changes at Dungorm.

Roderick and Arabella Mackenzie had arrived to stay. This time they brought their son and heir, Roddy, a thin, pasty boy who had little interest in his white-clad cousins.

The three children spent a lot of time together eating their meals in the schoolroom and doing lessons there with Nanny. Aunt Arabella did not believe that losing both your parents in the space of a few weeks was a good enough excuse to miss lessons.

She also disapproved strongly of Eliza's opinions on education for girls, believing that deportment, embroidery, music and dancing were far more important than science, mathematics and languages.

Roddy did not enjoy lessons and thought it was much more fun to pinch Nell's arm, throw pencils at Charlotte, spill ink on the girls' dictation or put earwigs in Nanny's tea. Nanny was given a book of useless facts that the children were supposed to memorise, such as the length of the Nile River and the height of the tallest mountain in Scotland.

Aunt Arabella also believed in plain food for children: gruels, porridge, rice pudding, bread-and-butter pudding, boiled mutton and boiled potatoes. Anything more was difficult for delicate stomachs to digest, she said. So mealtimes were miserable affairs, where Nell and Charlotte ate little and Roddy amused himself by flicking raisins from the pudding at the girls.

Flossie was banned from the house, living out in the kennels with the farm dogs. The girls could sometimes hear her howling during their lessons, a sound Charlotte hated.

As soon as the dinner bell rang downstairs and she knew her aunt and uncle were occupied, Charlotte would slip down the servants' stairs to the kennels and untie Flossie. Flossie would go crazy with excitement, jumping and licking and wagging her tail.

But as soon as they came to the back door, the dog knew she had to be quiet. Charlotte would sneak Flossie up the back stairs and hide her in the nursery for the night, then take her back down again at breakfast time. Most of the servants knew about Flossie's illicit bedtime visits but none of them would ever dream of giving away the girls' secret.

These were not the only changes implemented by Uncle Roderick and Aunt Arabella that affected the bewildered sisters. Sophie's heart ached for them.

Usually the girls had plenty of time for reading, helping

themselves to their favourite authors such as the Brontë sisters, Jane Austen and Sir Walter Scott. However, Aunt Arabella did not approve, instead choosing some illuminating moral tracts and religious essays that the girls should read.

Charlotte slipped down the back stairs to the library. She simply had to read a decent book or she felt she would go mad. She wanted to lose herself in another world, in someone else's story, so she could forget her own misery for a short time. As usual, Sophie followed Charlotte closely.

While standing outside the library door, Charlotte heard her uncle speaking to Wilson inside.

In a split second she decided to hide. She simply did not want to meet her uncle or explain why she was going to the library. There was a door on her left, leading to her father's study.

Charlotte turned the doorknob and ducked inside. She listened carefully, but to her horror, heard her uncle finish his instructions to Wilson right outside the study door. He was coming in.

In a panic, Charlotte glanced around. Her uncle would be furious to find her here in the study.

Charlotte saw the deep velvet couch, where her father used to read, in front of the bookshelf. She crawled in behind it and hoped her uncle would not discover her.

Invisible Sophie did not need to hide, but waited by the door, listening.

Uncle Roderick strode to the desk, covered in piles of paper, and sat down. He scanned the letters, contracts and circulars in the pile nearest him. Charlotte grew stiff and uncomfortable, cramped in a crouch.

Sophie peered over Roderick's shoulder to see what he was reading. They all seemed to be boring business letters so Sophie floated over to look out the window.

Charlotte crawled to the end of the couch, where she could peek around the edge and watch what her uncle was doing.

When Uncle Roderick had finished sorting one pile, he started on another. Charlotte's foot had gone to sleep and was tingling with pain, but she dared not move it.

Uncle Roderick sighed with impatience, crumpling another letter and tossing it in the waste-paper basket. Others he placed on one of three piles on the desk, sorting them carefully.

At last, Roderick found something that it seemed he had been looking for. He stood up quickly and looked around. He hurried to the door and carefully locked it, then, using the lamp on the desk, warily read the document in his hands.

Sophie moved closer to see what it was. Roderick seemed to sense her presence and moved away. Sophie only had a quick glimpse of the document, but it looked like something official, written on thick parchment in Alexander's handwriting.

When Uncle Roderick had finished reading, he held the document in his hands for a moment as though weighing up its contents, then crumpled it and threw it on the fire.

Roderick used the poker to push the ball of paper deep into the heart of the flame. The flame licked the paper ball and flared high, greedily consuming the parchment until it was a pile of flaky ashes.

Roderick replaced the fire guard and left the room.

There was an ominous clunk and Charlotte realised she had been locked in. She stretched her aching muscles and rubbed her blood-deprived feet. When a few minutes had elapsed she carefully listened at the door. It was silent outside. Cautiously she tried the knob, but the door was indeed locked.

Sophie faded out through the door, hoping to unlock it for Charlotte, but the key was gone. She shimmered back through the door into the study.

Charlotte was checking the fireplace, but there was nothing left of the mysterious document her uncle had burnt. She turned to the papers on the desk. One pile seemed to be correspondence from acquaintances; another was bills; while another held business letters.

Carefully Charlotte uncrumpled a paper from the waste bin. It was a letter from one of Papa's clubs in Glasgow, informing him of an upcoming lecture. No clues here.

There was only one thing she found that interested Charlotte and that was her father's battered old book of Robert Burns' poems. She slipped it into the pocket of her pinafore. Now she had to get out of the study before her uncle returned. She checked the top drawer of Alexander's desk where he used to keep his keys. They were gone.

Next she tried the window, which was locked from the inside with a simple catch. It only took a moment to unlatch it, lift the window and slither through the opening onto the outside sill. Sophie slipped through while the window was open, just before Charlotte banged it down.

Charlotte leapt from the ledge across the garden bed onto the lawn, to avoid leaving telltale footprints in the soil. A moment later she was heading for the back door, near the kitchens, to sneak up the servants' stairs to the schoolroom. Her aunt and uncle were rarely seen in the back quarters of the house.

Charlotte slipped past Sally the chambermaid, who was carrying buckets of coal upstairs to fuel the schoolroom fire, and gave her a conspiratorial smile.

'Cook said to tell you she is making gingerbread, if you and Miss Eleanor want to come down to the kitchen now,' Sally whispered.

'Thank you, Sally,' Charlotte replied politely, even though she had little appetite. She did not want to hurt dear, kind Cook's feelings. 'I will find Nell.'

The kitchen was the usual warm bustle, with servants working and Cook directing the preparation of several dishes at once. On one wall was the large wood-fired stove with small ovens set on the side and several saucepans on top. Copper pots and bunches of herbs hung from the mantelpiece.

Scullery maids chopped vegetables and kneaded dough at the scrubbed table in the centre of the room. Marmalade occupied his usual place under the table, licking his paws and washing his face.

Cook smiled a hearty welcome when Charlotte and Nell entered, Sophie behind them.

'Just in time!' Cook cried. 'The gingerbread is ready to come out o' the oven, and I made lemon tarts, meringues and chocolate cake. 'Tis such a chilly day, I thought ye might like hot chocolate as well.'

Neither Charlotte nor Nell had eaten anything much since their mother's death, as Cook very well knew, so she had gone to a lot of trouble to make some of their favourite treats.

Cook had set a little table in the corner of the kitchen, next to the bench where the girls usually sat. It was covered in a white linen tablecloth, silver cutlery and china plates, with a blue-and-white jug in the centre filled with an arrangement of autumn berries.

Best of all was the food: a large cake covered in chocolate icing, a platter of delicate white meringues, a crystal bowl of whipped cream and a plate of crumbly lemon tarts.

Charlotte felt a prickle of tears against her eyelids but blinked them away.

'Thank you, Cook,' she said warmly, as the girls took their seats. To their surprise, both Charlotte and Nell found they did have an appetite after all, especially when Cook opened the oven door and the kitchen filled with the spicy aroma of hot gingerbread. The smell made Sophie's mouth water, as she squeezed onto the end of the bench.

The girls tried a little of everything and then a little bit more.

Cook carried over two tall mugs of foaming hot chocolate. Charlotte and Nell sipped appreciatively, not talking, just listening to the comforting babble of voices washing over them. They had not felt this warm and safe since their parents died. They felt almost happy.

The servants lapsed back into the strong Scots dialect that they spoke amongst themselves, a mixture of Gaelic words and heavily accented English. It would be impossible for most English speakers to understand them, but the girls had been hearing it all their lives. Sophie found she could also understand most of the conversation.

The servants talked about village gossip – who was getting married in the spring, who was expecting a bairn –

the weather and the crops. It was feared the potato crop might fail again.

'Ailsa says the wee folk have bewitched her cow – the butter will no' churn and the milk is sour,' one maid said. 'She tried rubbing the beast with a blue bonnet to break the spell, but the magic was too strong.'

'Och, Ailsa must scour the milking buckets and the butter churn and scald them with boiling water,' snorted Cook. 'Tha' should fix the wee folk's magic.'

The others nodded in agreement.

Sally burst in the door, her face flushed, carrying a tray covered in dishes and a teapot.

'Tha' woman is impossible!' she cried. 'My *ladyship* said the cake was too dry and the tea too strong and Cook would need a new job if her cooking did no' improve.'

Cook flushed and bit her lip. She felt the cake in the cake tin; it was fresh and moist.

'She probably left it sitting too long,' Cook grumbled. 'I think she is trying to remind us who is the lady o' the house now.'

The servants rolled their eyes and nodded. All of them had some different experience of the new regime to complain or gossip about.

'Hamish said the new master wants to sell most o' the horses and let the stable lads go,' cried one.

Charlotte and Nell had stopped eating and were listening avidly, not daring to move in case the servants remembered they were there. Charlotte worried about their friend Angus the stableboy. He would be destitute if he lost his job.

'She told Mr Wilson tha' she wanted to economise on candles and coal in the schoolroom and servants' quarters,' added another. ''Twill be a long, cold winter for us in the attics if we are no' to have enough fuel and light.'

'The steward said the master was checking through the books and moaning about the crofters' rents. He said too much o' the estate was cropped with oats, potatoes and barley, and no' enough with sheep. Do ye think he is meaning to send the crofters off the land like so many lairds are doing in the highlands?'

'Can he do tha'? I ken he is the lassies' guardian, but surely the estate belongs to them now and should be run the way 'tis until they are old enough to decide?'

'Aye, but my laird's will has no' been found. Thomas heard the master telling the minister when he called around t'other day. There is only a very auld will, made before the lassies were e'en born. But the minister said my laird made a new will which should be in the study. So 'tis all a bit vague.'

'Still, my laird and lady are barely cold in their graves and the puir lassies have had no time to grieve . . . 'tis just no' right.'

Suddenly Cook remembered the lassies were sitting right here in her kitchen and coughed loudly with embarrassment. She hoped the lassies hadn't understood the conversation.

'Now, Miss Charlotte and Miss Eleanor, was tha' nice? Perhaps ye'd best be getting back to the schoolroom before your aunt notices ye are no' there.'

The servants all looked guilty and busily returned to the various chores that they were supposed to be doing.

'Thank you for the afternoon tea, Cook,' Charlotte said with a small smile. 'It was the best food I have eaten in ages.'

''Tis a pleasure, my lassie,' Cook answered. 'Any time either o' ye are hungry, just come down to my kitchen. There will always be food for ye here. I know ye do no' much like rice pudding.'

Nell nodded but didn't speak. She had not had much to say the last few weeks.

As the girls climbed the stairs, Charlotte turned over the gossip they had heard in the kitchen.

Selling the horses, clearing the crofts, letting staff go. Such big changes. Charlotte thought back to the papers Uncle Roderick had burnt that morning and wondered if it could be the missing will – the document that set out who her father wanted to leave his property to after his death.

That evening Charlotte was just about to sneak downstairs to fetch Flossie from the kennel when she bumped into Aunt Arabella, dressed for dinner in a low-cut black dress with a wide crinoline skirt. To Charlotte's horror, Arabella was wearing the diamond necklace and chandelier earrings that her mother had worn on special occasions.

'Oh, Charlotte, where are you going?' Arabella asked impatiently. 'Should you not be in the schoolroom eating your supper?'

'I . . . I am going . . . to the –' stuttered Charlotte guiltily.

'Oh, never mind,' Arabella cut her off. 'I have been meaning to ask you. I have searched and searched through the Dungorm jewels but I cannot find the Star of Serendib. It is a very valuable ring and should be locked in the safe. Do you have any idea where it might be?'

Charlotte's heart skipped in fright. She was sure if Arabella ever found the Star of Serendib, she would take it for herself.

'It . . . I . . . My mother always wore that ring. It was her favourite.'

'Yes, I know that, but where is it now?' Arabella raised her voice with irritation. 'There were other things missing also. I suppose one of the servants must have taken them. I must call the constable.'

Arabella is a loathsome woman, thought Sophie in disgust. *How could she be so cruel?*

'No!' Charlotte cried. 'The servants would never steal from my mother. They loved her. My mother gave me some of her things just before she died – her locket and a bracelet for Nell. My mother said all her jewellery was to be ours.'

'Well,' sniffed Arabella, protectively clutching the priceless diamonds she wore around her neck, 'I do not know that it was your mother's to give away so easily; they are the Dungorm jewels. Hmmm, well, I mean, perhaps when you are older . . . Anyway, run along, child. I will be late for supper.'

Charlotte was absolutely certain that her aunt would stop at nothing to get her hands on the Star of Serendib.

It was something in her glittering eyes when she spoke of it. It was revealed by the way she clutched her mother's diamonds as if they were the most precious thing in the world to her, more precious than husband, son or nieces. It was pure avarice.

I will never, ever let that woman take the Star of Serendib, thought Charlotte with determination. *My mother gave me her talisman and I will cherish it my whole life.*

9

The Moors

The next morning dawned fair and crisp, a golden autumn morning and possibly one of the last fair mornings for many months. Nanny had left the girls while she ran some errands, and Roddy was in bed with a chill.

The outdoors called to Charlotte, whispering of sunshine, rolling moors, emerald hillsides, fresh air and a breeze in her hair. It was hard to be miserable all of the time. Would the whole of the rest of her life be this long dull ache of despair?

Charlotte whispered to Nell and led her down the back stairs to the stables. They let Flossie free and saddled and bridled their ponies. In a few minutes they were riding out the archway of the stable yard and heading for the moors, with Flossie lolloping happily at their heels, her tongue lolling.

Angus the stableboy saw them and quickly saddled another pony and set off after them. He soon caught up with them. Charlotte was glad of the company. Nell hardly said a word these days.

It was wonderful to be on horseback again. The horses were fresh, just as tired of their containment in the stables as the girls were of their enforced inactivity in the schoolroom.

Charlotte let Rosie have her head and she stretched out in a wild gallop, Nell and Angus following close behind. Black-faced sheep scattered from their flight, startled from their endless grazing. Sophie flew along, keeping pace with the others, relieved to be outside in the sunshine as much as the girls.

When Rosie tired, they slowed to a walk. The air was fresh and cold and clear. It felt like a draught of new life itself.

On the moor, Rosie cantered, following the stock trails through the heather, swinging through its rhythmic bends and turns. In summer this was a vast sea of purple heather bells as far as the horizon. In winter it was a vast white sea of snow. A sudden fallen log was cleared in a flying leap and still they cantered on, horse and girl as one.

Charlotte headed towards her favourite hill, where she could see the whole Dungorm estate laid out at her feet like a map: the house, the loch, the castle ruins on the island, the fields and moors, the village and kirk, the roads, and in the distance, the great ocean.

At the top they all halted, letting the ponies crop the grass. Angus said nothing, allowing the girls the peace of their own thoughts. The faraway sun felt warm on their backs and bathed the world in a golden glow.

Flossie lay down panting, happy to be with her favourite

people once more. Sophie sat on the grass beside the dog and twined her cold fingers in Flossie's thick fur.

Charlotte drank in the view. This was her home, her land, her people. She loved it with a passion.

They walked slowly down the hill and back to the shore of the loch. Rusty-red weed lay along the round grey stones of the shore. The water, as usual, was grey and cold, with white-capped waves skimming across the top with the breeze. They trotted past the island and the castle, and then at last headed for home.

The beauty of the morning was quickly destroyed when they returned, for Aunt Arabella had discovered them missing. They were summoned to meet her and Uncle Roderick in the sitting room. With trepidation, Sophie went too.

'What is the meaning of this?' bellowed Uncle Roderick. 'Where have you been?'

'It was a beautiful morning – probably the last one for the year – so we went riding,' answered Charlotte. 'It was lovely.'

'You went riding? Alone? On the moors?' Uncle Roderick blustered.

'We were not alone,' Charlotte maintained. 'Angus accompanied us, and we had Flossie too.'

'A dog and a stableboy are not fit companions for the ladies of Dungorm. This is simply not seemly behaviour.'

'Well, who else should we have ridden with? Papa always said we should ride with Angus so we were safe.'

'This is what comes of not having a proper governess,' Roderick pronounced. 'Your nanny is obviously not able to control you.'

Arabella nodded vigorously. Nell hung her head. Sophie fumed.

'Fortunately I have already taken steps to remedy this situation,' Roderick continued. 'I have engaged a governess and she will be arriving very shortly. You have been allowed to be wilful and spoilt, indulged by your parents. But no more. A strict governess will tame this wild behaviour and mould you into the young ladies we expect.'

Charlotte trembled with fury and irritation, thoughts tumbling through her mind. Not allowed to ride? A strange governess? What would happen to Nanny? What right had Uncle Roderick to come in and change everything? It was not fair. Nothing was fair.

Weeks of misery and frustration and anger at the world bubbled up in Charlotte and she flew into a wild rage, shouting and storming and crying.

'How dare you? What right do you have? You cannot just come here and ruin everything. You cannot just take everything that was ours! It is just not fair! I hate you. I hate you. We all hate you.'

Roderick rang the bell furiously so Wilson and the footman came running.

'Why did you burn my father's papers?' accused Charlotte. 'I saw you! Was it his will? How can you ruin our lives?'

'Take Miss Charlotte upstairs and lock her in her room,' Roderick ordered. 'She is hysterical and raving nonsense. Tell Cook that Miss Charlotte will not require any food today.'

'Yes, my laird,' replied Wilson stiffly. He gently took Charlotte by the arm and led her away to the nursery. Nell followed silently, her head bowed.

A few moments later, Uncle Roderick came to the door.

'Eleanor, you are to go next door to the schoolroom and return to your lessons,' Roderick ordered. 'Do not contact your sister or bring her any food, or you will share her punishment, is that understood?'

Nell nodded once, her head still facing the floor, and shuffled out the door.

'You will apologise in the morning, or your confinement will continue until you do. I will not tolerate this behaviour. Think carefully about your actions.'

Roderick left. Charlotte did think. She worried about her sister Nell. The life and spirit seemed to have been crushed out of her. She was a different child to her old, sweet self. Charlotte worried about the staff, especially Nanny and Angus. Uncle Roderick might punish them, or they could even lose their jobs. She yearned to fight her uncle and aunt with every bone in her body. But what would happen to her sister and friends if she did?

Sophie flitted between Charlotte and Nell, checking on them in their punishment. By mid-afternoon Charlotte was hungry, but no-one came near. In the evening the door was unlocked and Nell came in, looking pale and sick. The door was locked immediately behind her.

'I am sorry,' Nell murmured, her face miserable. 'I could not bring you any food. Aunt Arabella watched me to make sure I did not hide any away. I could not eat anything anyway. How could I eat when you were hungry?'

Charlotte gave her sister a hug. 'It is all right. We will be all right. At least we have each other and Flossie and the ponies.'

Charlotte's stomach was rumbling. She prowled around

the room, looking out the window into the darkness and in the cupboards. She tried the door once more, rattling the knob.

As Charlotte passed the window again, a thought came to her. Outside the window were the broad branches of an oak tree, barely visible in the gloom. Sophie could see Charlotte's pale face reflected in the window panes.

A blast of cold air froze her face and hands as Charlotte opened the window.

Charlotte estimated the distance from the windowsill to the nearest branch, and the distance to the ground if she fell. Could it take her weight? Could she jump that far? Hunger won out over nerves.

'Nell, I am going to climb down the tree, to find some food in the kitchen. You stay here and I will be back shortly.'

'No, Charlotte!' cried Nell, clutching Charlotte's arm. 'It is too dangerous. You might fall.'

Charlotte squeezed Nell's hand.

'I will be fine. It is not that far.'

'If you are going down the tree, I am coming too,' insisted Nell. 'We can look out for each other.'

'No, Nell. If we get caught . . .'

'If you go, I am coming too. Besides, I had no supper either.'

'Come on then,' invited Charlotte with a smile.

Charlotte went first, swinging herself onto the windowsill and lowering herself down onto the branch. Nell tentatively followed. Bough by bough, branch by branch, they clambered down the tree to the ground, listening for the sound of anyone who might discover them.

Sophie floated down quickly and scouted around the dark garden. There was no-one there.

The lighted window of the servants' parlour showed the servants chatting after their supper. Charlotte and Nell crept to the kitchen door and cautiously turned the doorknob. It was still unlocked.

The door creaked open. There was no-one there. Charlotte, Nell and Sophie prowled around the kitchen, which was still warm from the day's cooking. The only sign of life was Marmalade curled up on a cushion on the bench, miaowing in welcome.

Nell glanced around nervously, jumping as a log settled in the grate. Sophie blew on the coals to make the flames leap higher.

'Do not worry,' Charlotte reassured Nell, reading her thoughts. 'Uncle Roderick and Aunt Arabella would never condescend to come into the kitchen, so we are safe. And if any of the servants come in they would never give us away to *them*.'

In the pantry Charlotte discovered a welcome sight: the remains of a chicken-and-ham pie, a fruitcake, a bowl of freshly picked berries from the garden and an old lamb bone.

Charlotte and Nell set two places at the long kitchen table and laid out the food they had found. Charlotte slipped out the back door and raced over to the kennels to untie Flossie and bring her inside.

They sat down together to enjoy their illicit late-night feast, with Marmalade sitting between them, delicately accepting offerings of shredded chicken and ham. Flossie noisily chewed the lamb bone under the table and licked her mistresses' bare hands.

'This is really good,' said Nell, licking crumbs from her top lip. 'I have not had Cook's fruitcake for so long.'

Charlotte's heart filled with gladness. Nell had hardly spoken since their father's death. It was good to see a small spark of the old Nell back.

Sophie risked stealing a titbit of fruitcake to taste it. She wondered how it would look to the girls, a crumbly morsel flying through the air. *Will it disappear when I swallow it, or will they see it still floating there in midair in my tummy?* Sophie thought.

The fruitcake was completely tasteless to Sophie; it was very disappointing. It looked so good. The girls did not seem to notice the flying crumb.

'I am sure Cook would not mind us helping ourselves to food,' added Charlotte. 'She did tell us to come down to the kitchen if ever we were hungry. More ham, puss?'

'Miaow,' agreed Marmalade, uncurling her pink tongue.

They had seconds of everything, then sat back feeling replete and happier. Charlotte rubbed her feet on Flossie's shaggy back. Flossie shivered with happiness.

'I suppose we should clean up, take Flossie back to the kennels then climb back up to bed,' Charlotte suggested with a sigh. Nell nodded and they set to work packing away the food.

In a few minutes, Flossie was returned to her kennel, whining piteously, and Charlotte and Nell had climbed back up the oak tree to their bedroom window. Sophie watched the girls climb in the window, then scooted up through the sky, back to her own bed.

10

The Coming of Miss Crowe

Charlotte and Nell were sitting in the schoolroom, their heads nodding over their workbooks, when a ruckus sounded below in the stable yard, with dogs barking and grooms calling.

Charlotte and Nell ran to the window, Sophie floating right behind them. Roddy ignored them, digging the top of the desk with his penknife. The family carriage had pulled up and a tall, thin middle-aged woman dressed in black disembarked.

'Who could it be?' wondered Charlotte. 'She looks like a crow.'

Nell giggled. 'And look at that hat! It looks like the nest on top of the bird. I wonder if there are any chicks in there?'

Charlotte chuckled in turn, her face alight.

Sophie giggled too. The woman had an enormous black bonnet perched upon a riot of tightly curled mousy-brown ringlets.

Then both sisters stopped smiling. At the same time they realised that it was the first joke they had shared together in ages, which reminded them of why they didn't share jokes any more, and both felt immediately enveloped by a thick fug of misery. Listlessly they turned from the window and returned to the school table.

Aunt Arabella shortly entered, followed by the unknown woman.

'Ah, Charlotte, Eleanor and darling Roddy,' Aunt Arabella gushed, 'I would like to introduce you to your new governess, Miss Crowe.'

On closer inspection, Miss Crowe bore an even greater similarity to her namesake, with a sharp beaky nose and small beady eyes. Charlotte and Nell glanced at each other, their eyes alight with mischief and their lips twitching.

It was hard to repress the giggle that came bubbling up their throats completely uninvited. Charlotte coughed and stepped forward with a curtsey.

Sophie could only think of the crows in Australia, which could peck out the eyes of young lambs. A shiver ran up her spine. Sophie did not like this woman at all.

'Good morning, Master Roddy, Miss Charlotte, Miss Eleanor,' squeaked Miss Crowe, clutching her umbrella rather fiercely. 'I pray we shall get on famously.'

'Good morning, Miss Crowe,' Charlotte and Nell chorused. Roddy nodded rather sullenly after a prod from his mother.

'Now, Miss Crowe is my second cousin, and she has kindly agreed to teach you girls needlework, pianoforte, dancing, posture and, most of all, *decorum*,' Aunt Arabella explained.

Charlotte and Nell glanced at each other in consternation. *Decorum?*

'Miss Crowe will oversee Roddy's education until his tutor arrives,' Aunt Arabella continued. 'My darling, your papa has engaged one of the best tutors in England to supervise your studies until you go away to school.'

Roddy smirked at his cousins, then pulled a face when his mother turned away.

'But Aunt Arabella!' Charlotte exclaimed. 'What about the rest of our studies – French and German, botany, mathematics, composition? Mama –'

'Your uncle and I have decided that such studies are quite unnecessary for young ladies,' interrupted Aunt Arabella. 'Your education should provide you with the accomplishments to attract a suitable offer of marriage.'

Aunt Arabella glanced fondly at her son Roddy, who was picking some dirt from his fingernails.

Charlotte glared at them both in horror.

'But I loathe needlework,' Charlotte protested. 'And I do not want to get married.'

'Charlotte, that is enough,' rebuked Aunt Arabella. 'You must learn to hold your tongue. Miss Crowe, you understand that your most compelling duty is to train my nieces to behave in a fitting manner, to beat them into submission if need be. My husband and I do not believe in sparing the rod and spoiling the child, as my poor sister-in-law unfortunately did. They must be taught to behave.'

Miss Crowe clutched her umbrella even tighter. Charlotte flushed with rage and mortification. Nell stood with her head hanging, her spirit crushed.

'Now, children,' Aunt Arabella said and smiled sweetly,

'I will leave you to get acquainted with Miss Crowe. Perhaps needlework would be a good place to start? You may have the rest of the morning off, Roddy. Perhaps you would like to go riding with the stableboy?'

Aunt Arabella bustled off, followed by a gleeful Roddy, who pinched Nell hard on the shoulder as he strolled by. Sophie pushed a chair in front of Roddy as he passed, causing him to trip.

'How did that get there?' blustered Roddy to his mother as he followed her out the door. 'That chair was not there a moment ago.'

'Let us get started with embroidery,' trilled Miss Crow. 'I thought a sampler would be suitable, so you can practise your alphabet and numbers.'

Charlotte gazed at Nell in despair. Obediently they went to fetch their needles, thimbles, embroidery silk and material, and then they sat and sewed and sewed while the clock on the schoolroom mantelpiece crawled slowly around.

Sophie felt her eyes burning with tiredness. She yawned widely, then pinched herself to stay awake. She decided to slip through the wall and fly down to the stables to visit the horses and Flossie. That would be much more interesting than sitting here watching the girls do their embroidery.

Finally the girls were released from their needlework. They listlessly picked at their cold, stodgy rice pudding, and were sent down to say goodnight to their aunt and uncle.

Sophie followed them closely, swooping over the staircase banister and free-falling down into the hallway below.

Sophie felt totally at home now in her invisible, ghostly, floating self, and celebrated by scooting back up and around the chandelier, making the candle flames tremble, then plunging once more down to the floor below.

In the sitting room, Aunt Arabella closely scrutinised the needlework they had completed that day, holding it close to the lamplight and sighing in dismay at Charlotte's untidy stitches.

'I trust you will work better tomorrow, Charlotte,' Arabella scolded. 'Now you girls may be excused to retire to your bedchamber. Roddy, you may stay down here for a while. Good evening, girls.'

Aunt Arabella offered her cheek for a kiss. Charlotte and Nell said goodnight and silently climbed up the stairs to their bedroom, Sophie shimmering behind them.

Charlotte opened the door to find Miss Crowe starting guiltily, bending over Charlotte's bed. In her hands was Charlotte's birthday box with the lid open and the contents strewn over the bedcover.

There was the golden locket Eliza had given her, Nell's gold bangle, Charlotte's journal and the copy of her father's poems of Robbie Burns. Miss Crowe hurriedly dropped the box on the bed.

A scarlet rage swept through Charlotte like a wildfire.

'How dare you touch my things!' shouted Charlotte. 'How dare you open my special box! It was locked. I will tell my uncle and you will be dismissed. How dare you?'

Miss Crowe flushed guiltily.

'Your – your aunt requested that – that I search your room,' Miss Crowe stuttered. 'Arabella told me that some valuable pieces of jewellery were missing and she thought you may have taken them to play with. I thought the box was an obvious place to keep jewels and found the key in your dresser.'

'How dare she!' shrieked Charlotte, sobbing now with rage and frustration.

Nell came and tried to comfort her with a hug.

'Charlotte, that is enough,' admonished Aunt Arabella from the doorway. 'Your behaviour is atrocious. I will not have you speaking to Miss Crowe in such a manner. Perhaps a caning will teach you some manners.'

Aunt Arabella strode to the bed and sorted through the items scattered on the eiderdown. She picked up the bangle and the locket, and curled her fingers around them protectively.

'These are too valuable for a child to have,' she explained haughtily. 'You will only lose them. I will keep them safe until you are older.'

Arabella turned to Miss Crowe. 'Any sign of the sapphire?' Miss Crowe shook her head. 'Did you look under the mattress and behind the shoes?'

'I looked everywhere you suggested, Arabella, and there was no sign of it,' Miss Crowe confirmed, carefully avoiding looking at Charlotte.

Aunt Arabella snorted with displeasure. She grabbed Charlotte by the arm and squeezed her tightly.

'Where is the Star of Serendib?' Arabella said threateningly. 'I know you have it hidden somewhere. Your mother's maid said the ring was definitely in the jewel casket just before your mother died. Not even the threat of the constables could make her change her story. I am convinced you know where it is.'

Charlotte flushed, then went pale, her thoughts churning with anger, fear and grief.

'If my mother had given me the Star of Serendib,' Charlotte finally replied, staring at her aunt with blazing eyes, 'I would rather throw it into the loch than give it to you.'

Aunt Arabella was speechless with fury. She released Charlotte's arm and stalked to the door, her silken skirts crackling and swishing as if venting her anger. At the door, she turned and glared at the subdued group behind her.

'Miss Crowe, I believe Miss Charlotte would benefit from a severe caning,' Arabella ordered. 'Perhaps *that* would improve her manners and her memory.' Then she dangled the gold locket and bangle from her fingertips, watching them glitter and glow in the lamplight. 'Meanwhile, I will go and find somewhere safe to keep these trinkets.'

Miss Crowe nodded grimly and followed Arabella from the room. In a moment, Miss Crowe returned with a long, thin cane, which she bent experimentally between her hands.

When she released the thin end, the cane whooshed through the air and vibrated menacingly. Charlotte swallowed fearfully. Miss Crowe turned the key in the lock behind her and pocketed the key.

'I am sorry, Charlotte,' Miss Crowe announced, looking not the least bit sorry at all. 'Your aunt has asked me to punish you, which I am sure will hurt me a lot more than it will hurt you. Could you oblige me by holding out your hand? I think ten blows should be sufficient.'

'Please, no!' Nell cried, huddling closer to Charlotte.

Charlotte hesitated and stepped back, her eyes flitting to the door and the window, but there was no escape there. Sophie fluttered anxiously up near the ceiling. She could not believe that Miss Crowe would actually hit Charlotte.

'Come now, Charlotte,' Miss Crowe admonished. 'We do not have all evening, and it is better to co-operate now or it will be twenty blows, and a good deal harder than if you just held out your hand now.'

Charlotte thought for a moment. There seemed no other option, so she held out her hand with the palm facing upwards. It trembled slightly. Charlotte bit the inside of her lip and waited for the blows.

Nell caught Miss Crowe's arm. 'Please do not hit her,' she begged.

Miss Crowe pushed Nell away roughly.

Sophie felt anger boiling up inside her. Charlotte and Nell had done nothing to deserve punishment.

The cane swished up and down viciously, over and over again. The thin end of the cane bit into the soft flesh of Charlotte's palm, her wrist, the sensitive tips of her fingers. Charlotte clenched her teeth and refused to cry.

When the cane had swiped down three times, Miss Crowe paused, the cane raised above her shoulder. Charlotte's palm was striped with ugly welts, oozing crimson blood. Nell was crying loudly. Sophie was itching to do something, anything, to stop this barbaric punishment.

'Do you have anything to tell me about the Star of Serendib?' Miss Crowe asked, raising her eyebrow.

Charlotte shook her head vehemently. Miss Crowe tutted disbelievingly and resumed her thrashing with the cane, swishing down upon Charlotte's hand with greater force.

'No!' shouted Nell, throwing herself in front of Miss Crowe's arm, and the rapidly descending cane. 'Please stop.' The cane thrashed down on Nell's shoulder and back, cutting her cruelly.

Sophie rushed forward at the same moment, furious at the brutal beating that poor Charlotte and now Nell were receiving. Sophie knew that a strong emotion such as fear, grief or anger somehow made her ethereal presence in this past world more substantial.

Sophie snatched the cane from Miss Crowe's unsuspecting fist. She grasped both ends of the cane and snapped them together, splintering the cane.

Three pairs of frightened eyes stared directly at Sophie standing there in her embroidered white nightdress, with bare feet, pale face and tumbled fair hair. Sophie snapped the cane back the other way, breaking it in two.

'Don't you ever do that again,' Sophie threatened Miss Crowe. Sophie felt her strength wavering and her form shimmering and thinning. She floated to the fire and threw the broken cane onto the flames, where it smouldered and flared.

'Wha' . . . was . . . that?' squeaked Miss Crowe, her body quaking with shock.

'A guardian angel sent by my mother to make sure you never harm my sister again,' retorted Nell strongly. 'Come on, Charlotte. Sit down and I will fetch wet bandages and ointment.'

Miss Crowe scuttled for the door as if all the hounds of hell were on her tail. Nell followed quickly behind her, running to the kitchen.

Sophie sat down next to Charlotte. Sophie felt weak and

insubstantial, but she wanted to wait with Charlotte until Nell returned to look after her.

'Who are you?' asked Charlotte, directing the question towards the fireplace. 'Are you a kindly spirit? Are you a guardian angel, as my sister said, or a malevolent ghost sent to trouble us?'

Charlotte obviously could no longer see Sophie but could somehow still sense her presence.

'I'm a friend,' answered Sophie softly, but she could not tell if Charlotte could hear her.

Sophie felt woozy and exhausted and desperately needed to sleep after the strain of her exertions. She floated gently off the bed, up towards the ceiling, then up into the cloudy dark sky way above and up, up to her own snug bed at Nonnie's apartment.

Charlotte was left sitting on the bed wondering if she might have been dreaming. Yet when she checked, she could clearly see the charred remains of the cane in the grate. Had she seen a ghost or an angel or a fairy sprite? Whatever it was, Charlotte was very grateful she had appeared.

11

Uncle Roderick's News

It was late when Sophie finally awoke the next morning. The sun blazed through the window, revealing a deep-blue sky. Jess's bed was empty and Sophie could hear the muted hum of voices from the kitchen. Sophie stretched long and hard, her muscles stiff and sore.

A feeling of great sadness washed over her as she remembered the deaths of Alexander and Eliza and baby James. What a terrible thing for Charlotte and Eliza to experience: the loss of all their family. Sophie thought of her own mother and father and little Will. What if she lost her own family?

At last she climbed out of bed and padded to the window, cradling the gold locket in her hand. Outside was a stately gum tree, its strong branches reaching for the sky. Its bark was streaked white and grey and brown and red, its leaves silvery-green against the sky. A cheeky kookaburra sat on a branch and laughed at her, its familiar chortle echoing through the garden.

The bushy green suburbs rolled away below, and in the far distance she could see the sparkling blue smudge of the harbour and the glittering office towers of Sydney. Nonnie's apartment seemed a million miles away from the misty lochs and rolling heather of Scotland in the 1850s.

Sophie shook herself mentally, carefully placed the locket in the carved wooden box and headed to the bathroom for a long hot shower, images of Charlotte Mackenzie and Dungorm rolling through her head.

Did Charlotte really throw the Star of Serendib in the loch? How did she manage to get back the locket from Aunt Arabella? How did Charlotte and Nell come to escape awful Aunt Arabella and Uncle Roderick, and come out to Australia all alone?

'Good morning, darling,' Nonnie greeted Sophie as she entered the kitchen. 'You had such a long sleep, I thought you might be ill. Your mum rang this morning to talk to you both, but she said she'd ring back later this morning.'

Nonnie, as usual, was dressed immaculately, in a tweed suit, pearl brooch, stockings and high-heeled pumps, her mouth slicked with red lipstick, her hair styled and curled. Sophie smiled wanly and gave her grandmother a good morning hug and kiss.

'Mum said that Sammy is really missing us,' Jess added, bouncing over to the table. 'She's been sleeping curled up at Mum's feet and keeps getting up to check our room to see if we're home yet. Will checked under our doonas this morning, sure that we *must* be home by now.'

Sophie smiled to think of their big black dog and baby brother, Will, searching the house looking for them. She missed Sammy too, and the cats and Mum and Dad and Will, now that she thought about it, but there hadn't been much room for thoughts of home lately.

Sophie helped herself to a piece of toast, while Nonnie made her some tea. Tea was something they were rarely allowed to drink at home, but Nonnie always made them a milky cup with breakfast, served in a pretty china teacup and saucer.

'Thanks, Nonnie,' Sophie said, and smiled.

The phone rang just then and Nonnie suggested that Sophie answer it, as it was probably her mother.

'Hi, darling,' came her mother's cheery, familiar voice. 'How are you? Are you feeling all right? Nonnie said you slept for hours this morning and that you've been very quiet the last few days.'

'No, I'm fine, Mum,' replied Sophie. 'Just tired. It's been a busy term at school.'

'I know, but if you aren't feeling well you can always come home. Are you worrying about changing schools?'

'Mum, I said I'm fine,' reiterated Sophie firmly. 'I'm not worrying about school or anything else.'

'Now, I hope you and Jess aren't fighting, are you? Remember, you promised me?'

Sophie paused, thinking guiltily of the whispered battle she and Jess had had over the washing-up last night.

'No, Mum,' responded Sophie. 'We're not fighting. Well, not really. How's Dad? How's Will?'

'Will's fine, up to his usual mischief,' replied Sophie's mum. 'Your father's a little better the last couple of days, I think. He took Will for a walk in the pram this morning, it's such a gorgeous day.'

'That's good,' Sophie replied. 'I hope Dad is feeling better. How's work?'

Sophie's mum chattered on about the latest news from home.

'Mum, Nonnie showed us a beautiful old box which belonged to her great-grandmother Charlotte Mackenzie,' Sophie offered.

'Mmmm, I remember the one. There was some intriguing mystery about my great-great-grandmother. I've forgotten what it was all about – wicked uncles and stolen inheritances, I think. Now, darling, I'm sorry I have to go, but I've heaps of work to do.'

'That's okay, Mum,' replied Sophie, disappointed that her mother had no light to shed on the box.

'I'll see you next week. I can't wait. I'm really missing you both dreadfully; so are Daddy and Will. It's far too quiet around here without you!'

'Miss you too, Mum.'

'I love you, darling. Don't forget to call me and I'll come and get you if you want to come home.'

'No, it's fine, Mum.' Sophie paused and thought about Charlotte and Eliza, and that terrible night when Eliza had died with baby Alexander.

'I love you too, Mum,' Sophie finished, with a choke in her voice. 'Look after yourself and baby Will.'

Her mother sounded puzzled. 'I'll try, sweetie. Bye.'

'Bye, Mum.'

Sophie hung up and went back to the table. Her toast was cold and she found she had no appetite for it after all. She pushed it away and sipped on her tea, listening to Jess and Nonnie chat about the plans for the day: a long walk, a trip to the park and some shopping in the afternoon.

'You didn't eat your toast, Sophie,' said Nonnie with concern. 'Would you like a fresh piece?'

'No thanks, Nonnie,' replied Sophie hurriedly, clearing the table. 'I'm not really hungry this morning.'

Nonnie looked a bit worried but said nothing more.

It was with a great feeling of trepidation that Sophie prepared for bed that night after dinner. She waited until Jessica was out of the room, then surreptitiously put the heavy gold locket around her neck, and climbed under the covers.

She tried to read her book, but the words danced maddeningly in front of her eyes and her thoughts kept drifting to another time and place, a more exciting time and place: a land of rolling mist, steel-grey lochs and emerald hills. *How did the girls come to leave Dungorm? Why were they sent to Australia?*

In a moment, Sophie could see them. A thick bank of mist rolled in from the sea, blanketing the loch and swirling around the old castle keep of Dungorm. Black-faced highland sheep dotted the deep-green hills. Grey smoke drifted from the golden chimneys of the great house of Dungorm. Sophie swooped towards the house, heading to the windows of the schoolroom on the upper floor.

Sophie found Charlotte and Nell downstairs at the dining table. They were dressed in what looked like their Sunday best – white woollen mourning dresses with ruffled petticoats below, thick black stockings and buttoned-up boots – and their hair was tied neatly back with white velvet ribbons.

Roddy wore a white-and-navy sailor suit, with a jaunty tie and wide square lapels to his collar. He was currently kicking Nell under the table trying to make her cry out. Nell ignored him. Aunt Arabella sat opposite, with Uncle Roderick at the head of the table carving the beef.

A serving maid passed around a platter of potatoes while another served the buttered carrots and boiled cabbage. When the food was served and the servants had retired, Uncle Roderick said grace and everyone began to eat.

Uncle Roderick chewed his mouthful of beef and gravy, swallowed and cleared his throat loudly.

'Charlotte and Eleanor, I have some important news to share with you,' Uncle Roderick announced, glancing quickly at his wife, who nodded sagely.

'Some time ago, your aunt and I received a letter from a relative of your mother's, a certain Mrs McLaughlin, who currently resides in the colony of New South Wales.'

Sophie held her breath. This must be it: this was the Australian connection.

Charlotte and Nell glanced at each other. Annie McLaughlin was Eliza's cousin who had migrated to Australia fourteen years before with her husband. Eliza and Annie had been very close friends all their lives and had regularly written letters to each other after their separation.

Eliza had often read them interesting snippets of Annie's letters describing life in that faraway country of Australia. Charlotte wondered why Uncle Roderick was interested in Eliza's cousin, Annie McLaughlin.

'Mrs McLaughlin wrote to say that she had thought of your mother as a sister, so if there was anything she could do for you girls, we should let her know,' Uncle Roderick continued chattily, however he did not meet the girls' eyes.

'Consequently, I wrote to her several months ago to see if she would consent to have you girls go and live with her and her family.'

Sophie sighed. Charlotte breathed in sharply, hardly believing her ears. Uncle Roderick could not be serious.

'We received a reply last week agreeing to the suggestion, and have written to Mrs McLaughlin telling her to expect you on the next ship to Australia,' Uncle Roderick continued calmly, helping himself to another pile of potatoes.

'Your berths are booked on a clipper called *Commodore Perry* which leaves Liverpool in two weeks. I have informed the servants to prepare your things for the journey, so I expect your full co-operation.'

Uncle Roderick resumed eating his roast beef. Aunt Arabella smiled triumphantly at her husband, then at the girls. Roddy gave Charlotte a sharp kick under the table and grinned at her, poking out his tongue.

Charlotte's mind whirled, refusing to absorb this earth-shattering news. Nell sat silently, tears streaming down her face.

'But – but Uncle,' stuttered Charlotte. 'We have never even met Mrs McLaughlin or her family. They live thousands of miles away, on the other side of the earth. We cannot possibly go and live with them.'

Charlotte swallowed a huge lump in her throat, fighting the tears that threatened to spill, trying to keep her tone calm and reasonable. 'Dungorm is our home. Dungorm was our parents' home,' she continued, her voice breaking. 'Please do not send us away.'

'Now, Charlotte, stop making such a fuss,' Uncle Roderick huffed in annoyance. 'It's all decided, the tickets booked and paid for. The letter has been sent to Mrs McLaughlin letting her know when to expect you, and I have arranged for money to be sent for your upkeep. It cannot be changed now.'

Aunt Arabella nodded vehemently. 'It is impossible for you to stay here,' she added. 'My poor nerves cannot cope with so many children in the house. It is too much work and worry.'

Charlotte thought in disbelief of the army of servants at Dungorm whose sole purpose in life was to make sure that Aunt Arabella never had to lift a finger, even to dress herself.

'My poor cousin Miss Crowe barely lasted a week and had to leave, her nerves completely shot,' Aunt Arabella continued forcefully. 'Apparently you girls frightened her with some nonsense about ghosts in the house.'

Sophie caused the candles in the centre of the table to sputter.

Charlotte and Nell glanced at the candles, then at each other, remembering the horrible Miss Crowe packing her bags in hysterics and demanding to be conveyed at once to the nearest railway station.

'Besides, your uncle and I find this country life far too quiet, so we plan to move back to Edinburgh, and our house there is too small for extra children.'

'We could stay here,' Charlotte began eagerly. 'Nanny and Cook could look after us. We would be fine.'

Nell nodded hopefully, her eyes round and wide. Uncle Roderick scowled and thumped the table with his flattened palm, making the crystal glasses chink.

'That is enough, Charlotte,' he roared. 'It's far too expensive to keep staff on in an unused house. Of course we will let most of the staff go, and just bring in servants when we return for the autumn hunting season.

'Now, if you have finished your meal,' he continued, forcing himself to be calm, 'you may go and start planning what to take. Your trunks must be packed ready to go by the end of this week.'

Charlotte stood up, her fists clenched. Nell rose slowly to her feet.

'You cannot do this,' shouted Charlotte, staring at her aunt and uncle in disbelief. She wanted to shake Uncle Roderick, shake him until he changed his mind. 'We are not going. Dungorm is our home. Just because you burnt my father's will does not mean you can turn us out. You cannot send us away.'

'Charlotte, *enough*,' roared Uncle Roderick. 'What nonsense. How dare you suggest I burnt your father's will. There was no will, but that makes no difference. I am the laird of Dungorm now. You are just children. *I* am your legal guardian and *I* decide what is best for you both. Now, go to your room before I call Wilson to drag you.'

Without a word, Charlotte stormed from the room and up the stairs, Nell running behind her. Through the open door of their bedroom, they heard a familiar voice raised in indignation.

It was Sally the chambermaid.

'It is criminal, that's wha' it is,' Sally objected. 'Those wee precious bairns bein' sent to the other side o' the world to that horrible place in New South Wales, just so he can take their home and fortune.'

'My puir darling lassies,' agreed Nanny with a sob. 'He is a hard man. Who could e'er believe he was the brother of our own puir Laird Mackenzie, God bless his soul. Lady Mackenzie would be furious.'

'They say those immigrant ships are disease-ridden coffin ships,' Sally added with relish. 'On one ship last year, there was a measles epidemic and dozens o' children died. Four years ago, one ship went down in a storm less than twenty-four hours after leaving Liverpool and everyone on board, three hundred and eighty souls, lost their lives.'

Nanny sobbed again loudly, burying her face in her apron.

'They say there are murderous highwaymen in Australia that kill honest folk just minding their own business, bloodthirsty natives and all manner o' strange beasts and monsters,' Sally continued. ''Tis a death sentence he is giving those bairns, as certain as anything.'

Nell gave a frightened sob, pushing her fist into her mouth to muffle it.

'Quiet, Sally,' Nanny ordered hurriedly. ''Tis the young lassies coming up. Ye canna mention any o' your fanciful tales to Miss Charlotte and Miss Nell. If we lose our jobs at Dungorm, as Wilson fears, we may well be following the bairns out to the colonies looking for work.'

Charlotte took a deep breath, then pushed the door open and walked in. Nanny was sitting on the bed, overcome with emotion, while Sally bent over two large trunks in the middle of the floor.

'Good evening, Nanny. Good evening, Sally,' Charlotte said. 'I see you have heard that my uncle is sending us to Australia.'

Nanny burst into a fresh fit of crying, wiping her eyes on her apron. 'My puir wee bairns. My puir wee bairns,' she sobbed repeatedly.

Charlotte and Nell ran to Nanny and were enveloped in a big, warm, wet hug.

'I wish I could come with ye to keep ye safe.'

Sally and Sophie hovered nearby, helpless to comfort them. The three cried together for many long minutes, until Charlotte finally pulled herself together.

'It will be all right,' Charlotte announced shakily. 'Someone must be able to convince my uncle to let us stay. I will speak to the minister tomorrow. We cannot be cast out of our own home so easily.'

'Do you think the minister could convince our uncle?' asked Nell, hopefully. 'Someone must be able to make him change his mind.'

Sophie knew that nothing would change Roderick's mind so easily, but she had to admire Charlotte for fighting.

''Tis a brave lassie ye are, Miss Charlotte,' Nanny said approvingly, drying her eyes. 'You are so like your father sometimes.'

Nanny helped the girls change into their nightdresses and nightcaps, while Sally went downstairs to fetch a special treat from Cook: two foaming mugs of hot milky chocolate and a plate of her famous crumbly shortbread.

The girls were too exhausted to eat but sipped appreciatively at the hot chocolate, which somehow made them feel a little better. They soon fell into a troubled sleep, filled with troubled dreams.

Charlotte tried. She surreptitiously rode her pony to the village the next morning and explained everything to the minister of the village kirk. He looked grave and nodded frequently, absorbing the details of the story. She told him about the papers she saw Roderick burning in her father's study, and how Arabella had taken all her mother's jewels.

Later that morning, the minister called at Dungorm House and spent an hour closeted in the study with Uncle Roderick. Sophie knew it was useless – nothing would make Uncle Roderick change his mind. The minister finally left, looking graver than when he arrived. Uncle Roderick waited until the front door had been closed behind his unexpected guest, then turned to face the stairs.

'Charlotte Eliza Mackenzie, come down here now,' Uncle Roderick roared.

Charlotte and Nell had been waiting desperately in the schoolroom and dashed down the stairs to hear the result of the meeting.

'How dare you discuss our family business with anyone outside this house! You are going to Australia and that is final. Now, go to your room and start sorting your belongings. I do not want to hear another word about it.'

The study door slammed loudly and Charlotte, Nell and Sophie crept back up to their room.

As if to taunt them, the weather that week was glorious. It was now June, and early summer. The hills were swathed with wildflowers and the sun shone warmly. It was perfect weather for riding on the hills, sailing to the island or walking around the shaly beaches of the loch. Yet the girls had no time for this.

'Nell, I simply have to get out,' cried Charlotte, striding up and down, looking out the window at the dazzling day. 'I feel as if I am going mad. I simply must ride over the hills of Dungorm one last time.'

Sophie knew exactly how she felt.

'Uncle Roderick will not let us,' replied Nell flatly.

'Uncle Roderick will not let us do anything, ever,' agreed Charlotte, turning to look at Nell. 'We might get mud on our dresses and disgrace the Mackenzie name. I have a plan.'

Nell looked up from sorting through her old dolls.

'What plan?'

'Tonight is a full moon,' explained Charlotte, her face alight. 'We could climb down the oak tree and go riding. We could have a moonlight canter on the moors. It will be our only chance.'

'If Uncle Roderick finds out, we will get in the most dreadful trouble,' Nell said, and frowned.

'What will he do to us? Send us to Australia? He cannot do anything worse to us!' argued Charlotte. 'Please, Nell. If you will not come with me, I shall go anyway.'

'You cannot go by yourself,' replied Nell. 'What if you fall? Oh, all right then. I will come too.'

That evening, Nell fell asleep in her bed, but Charlotte sat on the floor by the fire reading a book with a candle. Sophie read over her shoulder.

When the grandfather clock in the schoolroom struck half past ten, Charlotte gently woke Nell.

Silently the pair dressed themselves, climbed down the oak tree, then slipped from shadow to shadow through the garden. Sophie floated ahead of them, carefully watching out for anyone about. There was no-one.

Lights were still on in the drawing room, where they could see Uncle Roderick and Aunt Arabella sitting by the fire.

At the kennels they freed Flossie, then they bridled their ponies, Rosie and Bess, in the stables. The horses were glad to see them, despite the lateness of the hour, and whinnied a snuffly welcome. The girls did not bother with saddles as they did not want the creak of leather or the clank of a stirrup to give them away.

They led the horses outside, mounted and, keeping to the shadows on this moonlit night, headed out the archway and into the night. Sophie soared along beside them, enjoying flying in the silvery moonlight.

Despite all their care, it was impossible to fetch the horses, tack up and ride off without making some slight noise.

Half a mile from the house, they heard a clatter of horse's hooves behind them. Sophie swung around ready to protect the girls from any danger. Charlotte and Nell stiffened in fear.

It was Angus the stableboy, riding one of the ponies. He lifted his hat, with a cheeky grin.

'And where might ye be gaeing in the middle o' a full moon night, me bonnie lassies?'

'Oh Angus, you frightened me,' Charlotte replied. 'We just had to get out. Our aunt and uncle will not let us ride and they keep us cooped up in the schoolroom all the time, so we thought we might have a canter on the moors . . . one last time.'

Angus smiled to himself. He had heard many tales from the servant hall about what had been happening to the young ladies of the grand house.

'Well, ye are no' planning on dancing with the elves are ye, now?' he asked.

The idea occurred to Charlotte that perhaps it would be better to be captured by fairies than sent to Australia.

'No, of course not,' Charlotte replied. 'Do not be ridiculous. We just want to ride.'

Up on the high moors, the three horses cantered, the riders carefully watching for rabbit holes in the half-light. They slowed to a safer walk, Sophie flying behind.

Flossie snuffled the ground with her nose, sniffing around in a rough circle, following a couple of scent trails through the heather. She stopped at an interesting odour in a patch of ferns and barked sharply.

Charlotte ignored her. Flossie again barked insistently, then ran to Rosie and rounded her up as if she were a recalcitrant sheep, and herded her towards the scent.

'All right, Flossie, all right. I am coming,' laughed Charlotte, dismounting from Rosie.

Flossie ran ahead happily and thrust her nose deep into the undergrowth. Charlotte knelt and parted the ferns where Flossie pointed. Something glinted in the moonlight.

Charlotte picked it up. On her palm lay a tiny piece of sparkling silver fashioned into the shape of an arrowhead. A short, broken shaft of timber jutted from the base. She held the miniature arrowhead up to the growing light and examined it carefully.

'Oh my goodness,' whispered Charlotte. 'Oh Flossie, you clever girl. Look, Nell. Flossie found an elf bolt.'

Charlotte stroked Flossie's shaggy head and her floppy left ear.

Nell, Sophie and Angus crowded around, exclaiming over Flossie's find.

'Finding an elf bolt is very guid luck,' exclaimed Angus, fingering the silver arrowhead.

'Nell and I could do with some good luck,' replied Charlotte. 'Maybe Uncle Roderick will change his mind and let us stay after all.'

'Nae, tha' man has a heart o' iron,' pronounced Angus, shaking his head.

It was lucky that the girls had ridden out that night, for the next morning a man arrived to take away many of Dungorm's horses, including Rosie and Bess. This was nearly more than the girls could bear. Nell would not even go to the stables to say goodbye to Bess, but lay in her bed, her face turned to the wall.

Charlotte hurried down to the stables to spend her last moments with her beloved pony. Charlotte clung to Rosie's mane in the darkness of her stall, weeping hopelessly onto her warm neck.

Rosie snorted comfortingly and shook her mane, tickling Charlotte's nose. Charlotte breathed in the familiar scent of horse. All too soon Angus arrived to gently lead Rosie away.

'I truly am sorry, Miss Charlotte,' he whispered gruffly. 'I must take her now. I wish I could do something for ye.'

Charlotte nodded and smiled a watery smile at Angus. 'Thank you, Angus. I appreciate your kindness.'

Charlotte patted Rosie one last time and kissed her on her velvety nose. 'Look after yourself, my darling girl. I will miss you sorely.'

Rosie hurrumphed her farewell into Charlotte's hair as though communicating her love and sorrow, then reluctantly followed Angus out into the light.

Charlotte dropped down into the muddy straw of the stall, all the strength gone from her legs. She could not watch the horses being led away. Sophie lay beside her, her heart like lead.

Flossie found Charlotte there, and pushed her nose into Charlotte's hand, licking her fingers. They huddled together for hours, giving each other some comfort, until Angus came to tell Charlotte she was wanted in the house.

12

Preparations for the Journey

In the afternoon, a box arrived from Glasgow with items for the girls' journey, including new boots, stockings, shawls, cloaks, handkerchiefs, chemises, nightgowns, caps, bonnets and yards of white cotton, flannel and woollen material to make up into dresses.

Nanny and the chambermaids Sally and Molly spent hours measuring and making new dresses, petticoats and underclothes with plenty of extra material in the seams to allow for growth. The trunks gradually filled with the neatly folded and ironed garments.

Charlotte and Nell had to sort through their books and toys and decide which they would take. The trunks filled all too quickly and there was not enough room to take everything they wished.

The girls had cried until they could cry no more. Now they both walked around mechanically, in a fug of misery, doing as they were told, eating little, speaking little, watching the last few days of their life at Dungorm fly before their eyes.

In a daze, they learnt the details of their journey. Uncle Roderick would accompany them for the first part of their trip. They would be taken by carriage to catch the ferry over to the mainland. A coach would take them to the nearest railway station, where they would catch a train via Glasgow down to Liverpool, in northern England.

In Liverpool, Uncle Roderick would leave them and return to Dungorm, and Charlotte and Nell would be placed under the protection of the ship's captain and the stewardesses.

The ship would sail on the high tide and travel ever southwards, through the Irish Sea, down the coast of Europe, past the exotic lands of Africa and the East, over the equator, around the very bottom of the Cape of Good Hope; then it would be blown by the fierce trade winds around the bottom of Australia to Port Phillip Bay, in the colony of Victoria.

There they would change ships to a coastal steamer, which would take them up to the town of Sydney. Another steamer would take them to a small country town called Easthaven, where the McLaughlins would send someone to meet them. The whole journey would take more than three months.

Charlotte's head reeled with the enormity of the journey. They had never travelled further than Edinburgh or Glasgow for occasional shopping and theatre expeditions.

Their parents had sometimes travelled to London, but they had always left the girls at Dungorm in the excellent care of Nanny and the servants. Charlotte could not imagine a journey of so many thousands of miles.

Nell had retreated into a silent shell. She hardly spoke or ate, but wandered in a grief-stricken daze, much like the first days after her parents' deaths.

On the last day before their planned departure, Aunt Arabella organised a farewell dinner.

The girls could barely eat and barely speak, but Aunt Arabella chattered about the many interesting things the girls would see on their journey. Roddy munched his way through several courses and was so kind as to refrain from pinching or kicking the girls during their final meal at Dungorm.

Uncle Roderick seemed nervous and jumpy, and finally excused himself, saying he had some urgent business to attend to in his study. Charlotte suspected it was probably a pipe that needed to be smoked.

Charlotte took the opportunity to excuse herself and Nell, saying they were tired and needed an early night before their departure tomorrow. Charlotte escorted Nell quickly up to their room.

Upstairs she found Nanny grumbling as she carefully repacked all the trunks and carpetbags.

'Why are you repacking the trunks, Nanny?' Charlotte asked. 'I thought you had finished.'

Nanny rolled her eyes to heaven, as she folded one of Nell's white dresses.

'Your aunt came in and rummaged through all your things,' explained Nanny, shaking her head. 'She said she wanted to make sure you had no' forgotten anything, but I suspect she was looking for something in particular.

She even looked right through that bonnie box of yours. Whate'er it was, she dinna find it.'

Nanny smiled at Charlotte conspiratorially. Charlotte thought she had a very good idea of exactly what her aunt had been searching for: the Star of Serendib. A plan came to Charlotte's mind.

'You have a little rest, Nell,' Charlotte suggested to her sister. 'There is something I need to do before we leave.'

Charlotte, with Sophie following, slipped into her parents' old bedchamber, which was now used by Aunt Arabella and Uncle Roderick. The room looked strange littered with their belongings.

It smelt peculiar too, of Aunt Arabella's heavy floral scent, instead of Eliza's more delicate perfume. It made Charlotte's heart lurch with sadness.

Charlotte touched the silver-backed brushes and cosmetic pots on her mother's dressing table, but there was little of her mother left here.

On the dressing table was a small golden jewellery box. Charlotte had hoped to find her mother's locket and bangle and retrieve them quietly. She felt too frightened to directly ask her aunt and uncle to return them, as she was sure they would refuse her. But when she tried the casket it was securely locked.

Charlotte felt sick with nerves, but fear of leaving Dungorm without her mother's jewellery spurred her on. She rummaged through the drawers of the dresser looking for the key. It was nowhere to be found.

A slight noise outside warned her that someone was coming. Charlotte quickly closed the dressing table drawers, returned the casket to its place and ran through the door into the adjoining dressing room.

The room was lined with hanging dresses: silks and velvets in blues, greens, whites, violets and black. Below were neat rows of shoes, buttoned boots and dancing slippers.

Charlotte and Sophie could hear the sound of someone moving around in the room next door, then coming closer. Charlotte pressed back into the row of dresses, terrified that Arabella would discover her hiding there.

Sophie slipped through the door into the bedroom, looking for a diversion to help Charlotte. Arabella was walking towards the dressing room, hand outstretched to open the door.

Sophie swooped to the dressing table. Concentrating with all her energy, she picked up a heavy crystal perfume bottle and threw it across the room. The bottle smashed against the wall; the room filled with an overpowering reek and perfume dripped down the silk wall-hangings.

Aunt Arabella turned with a cry, her hand to her mouth in shock.

Charlotte heard the smash and ran to the door at the other end of the dressing room that led to the tiny maid's room. Hopefully Suzette would be downstairs. Suzette had been Eliza's maid and was now lady's maid for Arabella.

Charlotte opened the door quietly. The room appeared to be empty. Charlotte tiptoed carefully across the floor towards the door that opened into the corridor.

'Bon soir, ma petite,' came a soft French voice in greeting.

Charlotte turned in sudden fright, her heart beating wildly.

Suzette was seated by the window, carefully repairing one of Aunt Arabella's gowns by the warm light of the window.

'*Bon soir*, Suzette,' replied Charlotte nervously, glancing over her shoulder towards Aunt Arabella's room. 'Suzette, *please* do not tell my aunt you saw me here.'

Suzette smiled comfortingly, shaking her head. '*Mais non, ma petite.*'

'*Merci beaucoup*, Suzette,' Charlotte replied gratefully. '*Au revoir.*'

'*Au revoir et bonne chance.*'

'Suzette, come here now,' screeched Arabella from her room.

'*Oui, madame*,' called Suzette, winking at Charlotte and rising to her feet.

Charlotte did not return to her room, but slipped away into the garden to walk and think and say goodbye to her homeland, with her faithful black-and-white dog, Flossie, at her heels.

Flossie sensed Charlotte's sadness, pushing her nose into Charlotte's hand whenever she paused in her rambling. Charlotte scratched her on the head and whispered comfortingly to Flossie. Sophie wandered with them, keeping them company.

It was a beautiful midsummer evening, the night of the summer solstice, on June 21. The sun would not set until nearly 11 pm.

The two gardeners were busy watering flowerbeds and weeding edges. They doffed their caps at Charlotte but did not disturb her reverie. The air was filled with the delicious scents of roses and honeysuckle.

She wandered over the arched stone bridge across the icy burn that tumbled and burbled down towards the loch. Colourful wildflowers grew between the cracks in the stone: crimson valerian, pink hollyhocks and white daisies. Yellow buttercups and blue forget-me-nots grew in a tangled profusion along the burn's bank, together with feathery green bracken.

A hedge grew to her right, marking the boundary of the field. Pale-pink dog roses bobbed in the evening breeze, caressing her cheek with their soft petals.

It was far too early yet for Charlotte's favourite flower, the purple bells of heather, which clothed all the hills in a deep-purple mantle. The hills were still deep emerald green dotted with the fluffy white bodies of the black-faced sheep and their lambs. The shepherds had not yet brought them into their hurdles for the night.

In the field next to her, shaggy russet-red calves tussled and chased each other, skipping around their placid mothers who grazed peacefully.

At last Charlotte reached the grey shaly beach of the loch. Small waves rolled at her feet, filling the air with their soothing lap, lap, lap. The ruined tower of Castle Dungorm was bathed in a golden glow and there were flocks of seabirds wheeling and screeching around the island.

Far out in the loch she could see the sleek brown bodies of two seals playing in the waves. It reminded her sharply of her birthday picnic on Eilean Dungorm, when the seal had smiled at her with its whiskery face and she had dreamt of selkies playing on the island's shores.

It was one of the most beautiful summer evenings Charlotte could remember. She wished her parents were here to share its golden beauty. Knowing it was her last evening at Dungorm, she tried to memorise every detail, every scent, every sound.

She wandered along the shore of the loch. In the distance she could see the great blue swell of the ocean, the ocean that was going to carry her to the other side of the world. She stooped down and picked up a round rusty-red pebble worn smooth by the tumbling of the loch water. She clutched it tightly in her hand and wandered on.

Sophie looked down at the pebbles. She suddenly remembered where she had seen one just like them.

Flossie picked up the scent of a rabbit or deer and scampered on ahead, her tail wagging enthusiastically. Then she remembered her sad mistress and came lolloping back, her tongue hanging out, one ear pricked and one ear floppy.

Charlotte gave a cry of surprise. Just ahead she spied a small splash of deep purple. Stooping down she discovered a tiny patch of blossoming heather, the very first blooms sheltered in a warm south-facing crevice.

Carefully Charlotte picked two sprays of delicate purple heather bells. It seemed like a blessing, a lucky omen. She tucked them away in her pocket, together with the pebble she had collected on the beach.

Sophie had never seen blooming heather before and was delighted with the discovery. She stooped and fingered the tiny purple bells sheltered in the cranny. Sophie felt thrilled, realising for the first time the significance of the red pebble and the sprigs of heather in Charlotte's treasure box.

At last Charlotte turned back towards the golden walls of Dungorm, glowing pink in the evening rays of the sun.

Sophie's excitement made her feel stronger and less

ethereal. She felt an overwhelming desire to talk to Charlotte, to touch her, to be seen by Charlotte. Sophie concentrated as hard as she could. She felt her gauzy limbs thicken and quicken and strengthen.

Sophie floated down onto the path in front of Charlotte. She was not sure what she expected to happen. Would Charlotte walk right through her? Would Charlotte be able to see her? Could they communicate?

Flossie saw her first. The dog did not bark or growl, but simply ran up to Sophie and tried to lick her transparent hand. Charlotte was watching Flossie distractedly, then caught a glimpse of something unusual, a shimmer of light, a thrill of energy.

Sophie concentrated harder. Her form wavered and flickered. Charlotte gasped. She saw a figure, the figure of a girl dressed in a long white gown, with bare feet and shimmering gold hair shining in the evening sun.

'What are you?' begged Charlotte, stepping backwards. 'A ghost? An angel? Or an elf?'

Sophie considered these options carefully. Could she even reply?

'Not a ghost,' Sophie assured Charlotte, trying her hardest to be heard. 'Not an elf either, just a friend. My name is Sophie.'

'A friend?' Charlotte smiled bravely. 'A spirit friend. Why are you here? What do you want?'

Sophie paused, wondering exactly what she did want to say to Charlotte, on the eve of Charlotte leaving behind everything she had ever known.

'I wanted to tell you that everything will be all right, Charlotte,' Sophie began hesitantly, remembering Nonnie's stories of Charlotte's later life. 'You and Nell will get to Australia safely. It's a very beautiful place. I think you will be happy there.'

Charlotte frowned. 'I hope so,' she replied at last.

Sophie felt dizzy with the effort of speaking and being visible. Her form began to waver and disappear.

'Wait,' commanded Charlotte, reaching out to Sophie. 'Tell me more. Will I ever come home to Dungorm? Will we ever . . .?' But Sophie had disappeared, exhausted by her few moments of visibility.

Charlotte shook her head and gently pinched her skin, to check she was awake and not dreaming this strange apparition. Charlotte felt the pinch clearly and hurried home to Nell, her head in a whirl.

Up in their room, Charlotte found Nell lying in her bed, crying. Charlotte sat down next to Nell on the bed and Flossie flopped down on the floor, her nose snuffling Nell's face.

'Nell, I brought you a present,' Charlotte said gently, taking the sprig of blooming heather from her pocket. Nell sat up slowly, her face red, swollen and tear stained.

'The heather has bloomed early this year, just for us,' Charlotte explained. 'It is beautiful. Come and look out the window. Dungorm has given us the gift of a glorious evening, to say farewell to us.'

Nell smiled wanly at the sight of the heather and obediently struggled to the window, her legs feeling weak and shaky. Sophie joined them, wondering if this would be her last view of Dungorm too.

Outside the window was the most magnificent view of the golden sun sinking to the west, the picturesque ruins of Dungorm castle rising from the burnished waters of the loch, the flourishing gardens, and in the distance the blue-gold smudge of the sea.

'It is so beautiful, Charlotte,' murmured Nell. 'How are we ever to live away from Dungorm, from Scotland, from our home?'

'We will come back, Nell,' insisted Charlotte. 'Do not worry. One day we will come back to Dungorm. Surely he cannot mean for us to go forever.'

Nell nodded wearily and sighed.

'Do you think Aunt Arabella will give us back Mama's locket and bangle?' Nell asked eventually.

'Not readily,' Charlotte conceded. 'But I have a plan.'

Together the girls sat on the bed with their arms entwined and Flossie at their feet. They stared out the window, watching the sun slowly sink into the horizon and the sky change colour to yellow, peach, crimson, blood red and, lastly, deepest purple.

Sally lugged in some buckets of hot water, and Nanny helped them bathe in the tin hip bath in front of the fire. Then she helped them change into their nightdresses and nightcaps.

'Time for bed now, lassies,' ordered Nanny, turning down the blankets.

'Please, Nanny,' begged Charlotte, 'we just want to watch our last sunset at Dungorm. We may never see it again.'

'All right, my bairns,' agreed Nanny with misty eyes. 'But do no' stay up all night long.' Nanny did not even try to put Flossie outside in the kennels for the night, allowing them one last night together.

The sun finally sank into the sea at about 11 pm and the sky grew darker, but still they watched, not wanting to miss a moment of their last evening at Dungorm. At last, Charlotte, Nell and Sophie all fell asleep on the same bed, dreaming of seas and sailing ships and strange faraway places.

13

The Visit of the Poltergeist

Nanny came in early the next morning with a jug of hot water. The girls were sleepy after their late night and were reluctant to get up. Flossie seemed subdued and worried, sensing her world was about to be destroyed.

'Och, lassies,' scolded Nanny gently. 'Ye canna be lazy this morning or ye will miss the train.'

Charlotte felt a flutter of fear in her stomach, like a flock of flittering butterflies. She climbed out of bed obediently and washed her face and hands in the steaming water.

Nanny helped her to dress in the usual layers of drawers, stockings, chemise, petticoats and warm dress. Even in the height of summer, Scottish weather was cool and changeable, switching from sunshine to rain to frosty winds and sleet in the space of minutes. Nanny brushed Charlotte's hair vigorously and tied it back with a white velvet ribbon.

When Charlotte was dressed, Nanny gently coaxed Nell from her bed and dressed her, as she used to when

Nell was but a small, helpless child. The trunks were locked and standing by the door ready to be carried down to the carriage. Each girl had a small carpetbag packed with the clothes and necessities for the journey to Liverpool.

Charlotte tucked the sprig of blooming heather inside her father's book of Robbie Burns' poetry to dry.

Next to her bed she had a pair of silver-framed portraits of her parents. Carefully she folded these together and buried them deep in her carpetbag, safely wrapped in a shawl.

Unlocking the carved timber box that had been her birthday present from her parents, Charlotte carefully placed inside it the book and red pebble she had found on the beach. The box, containing all her most precious possessions in the world, was carefully locked and packed away in the top of Charlotte's carpetbag.

Nanny fussed around and brought the girls some tea and toast, and all too soon there was the sound of the carriage drawing up at the front door and a discreet knock on the door. Four of the serving lads took the girls' luggage down to the carriage.

'Well, my lassies,' sighed Nanny, twitching their skirts and straightening the ribbons on their bonnets. 'Come downstairs and say guidbye to your aunt and uncle. Say guidbye to Flossie first, there is nae time to be lost.'

Charlotte felt a pain in her stomach as strong as a blow. She and Nell dropped to the floor and hugged their dog with all their hearts, rubbing her black-and-white fur, stroking her soft ears, whispering gentle words of love and farewell.

'Come on, lassies,' Nanny urged. ''Tis time to be gaeing. Waiting will no' make it any easier.'

Nanny scrubbed their tear-streaked faces with a handkerchief and hustled Charlotte and Nell up, out the door and down the stairs. In the hallway, all the servants were waiting respectfully.

Charlotte and Nell closely followed Nanny – rustling in their starched white dresses, stiff bonnets and squeaky new boots – and murmured their farewells. The serving girls bobbed curtseys, a couple wiping away tears, while the men nodded awkwardly, mumbling a few messages that hid the depth of their feeling.

It cannot be real, thought Charlotte. She was leaving the people she had known her whole life and now might never see again.

Charlotte felt as though she should be weeping or screaming. Yet she felt a total sense of disbelief, a sense of displacement as though she were a dispassionate bystander, just watching herself say goodbye to her friends, her home, her life.

Aunt Arabella and Uncle Roderick swept down the stairs, followed by the girls' cousin, Roddy.

'*Adieu et bon voyage*, Charlotte and Eleanor,' said Arabella, pecking each girl on the cheek.

'Come on, girls,' urged Uncle Roderick, looking shamefaced. 'Say your farewells quickly. We must not be late for the train.'

Charlotte took a deep breath. She had a plan that had come to her last night during her walk.

'Before we go, I must ask a favour,' Charlotte said quickly, in a loud voice which carried to many of the servants standing around. 'When my mother was on her deathbed, she gave me her gold locket and a bangle for Nell.'

Aunt Arabella moved forward as if to interrupt but Charlotte hurried on, the words spilling out like a torrent.

'Mama said I must always wear the locket so I could feel she was watching over me,' Charlotte continued. 'Aunt Arabella took the locket and bangle for safekeeping, but now that we are leaving our home, probably forever, I would like to have Mama's things returned to us.'

Aunt Arabella gasped in outrage. Uncle Roderick went pale, then pink, a slight sweat breaking out on his forehead. He glanced quickly around at the large crowd of servants gathered in the hall, who were now watching with great interest for his response. He desperately glanced at Aunt Arabella, who glared back at him meaningfully.

Charlotte held her breath in anticipation. Nell looked up at her uncle with wide round eyes, her face wan.

'Well,' blurted Uncle Roderick, 'well . . . they are very valuable . . .'

Sophie could not believe it. Uncle Roderick was going to refuse to honour his sister-in-law's dying wish. Was it not enough to take the house, the ponies, their home?

Sophie felt the familiar sense of anger and frustration welling up inside. She summoned up all her strength and swooped through the hallway like a rush of wind, making the curtains billow, the candles flicker and the candelabra swing wildly.

Sally the chambermaid screamed. Nanny grabbed Charlotte and Nell and held them tightly by the shoulders. Uncle Roderick jumped, his face white. Sophie rushed past him, tweaking his cravat.

'Of course you may have your mother's locket and bangle,' Uncle Roderick said quickly, smoothing down the dishevelled cravat. 'Suzette, fetch them from my wife's jewel casket. Arabella, give her the key. It is time we left or we really will miss our train.'

Aunt Arabella fumbled in her reticule, her lips tightly set with fury. Wordlessly she handed Suzette the small gold key, and Suzette ran upstairs to fetch the items.

Charlotte took the locket on its chain with a sense of triumph. She slipped it over her head and hid the locket inside the collar of her dress. The bangle was still too large for Nell's slender wrist so Nanny helped her tuck it away safely in the carpetbag.

'Thank you, Uncle Roderick,' said Charlotte quietly. 'My mother would appreciate you looking after us.'

Uncle Roderick coughed once more.

'Yes,' he agreed. 'Of course. Anything I can do to help. Roddy, say goodbye to your cousins.'

Roddy smiled warmly at his cousins for the first time since coming to Dungorm. He gave each one a brief hug.

'Well done outwitting my mother,' Roddy whispered to Charlotte. 'Not many people can do that, especially not my father.'

Lastly, Charlotte and Nell said goodbye to Nanny, their beloved Nanny who had looked after them since birth. She hugged them both fiercely.

'God bless ye, my wee bairns,' Nanny choked. 'Miss Charlotte, ye must look after Miss Nell and keep her safe. Please write to us and let us ken how ye fare?'

'I do not want to go to Australia,' wailed Nell, flinging her arms around Nanny.

'I ken, my sweet,' Nanny replied gently. 'But wha' canna be changed must be endured.'

There was one last hug. Sophie brushed Nanny on the arm to say goodbye, and Nanny shivered.

'Goodbye, Nanny, thank you for everything,' Sophie whispered, knowing that Nanny couldn't hear but needing to say goodbye anyway.

'Fare-ye-well, lassies. Fare-ye-well.'

Uncle Roderick shooed the girls out in front of him, bundling them out to the driveway and into the carriage.

Sophie swooped through the carriage door at the last moment and squeezed into the small space next to Charlotte. Charlotte glanced at the space beside her, a quizzical look on her face.

The carriage jolted forward and slowly rolled out of the driveway. The driver clicked loudly and flicked his whip. The horses broke into a trot and clattered onto the roadway, their necks arched proudly.

'Thank you,' whispered Charlotte softly to the space on the seat beside her.

'Pardon?' asked Uncle Roderick brusquely.

'Oh. I said thank you for returning Mama's locket,' replied Charlotte.

'Humph,' snorted Uncle Roderick, opening his newspaper.

The carriage thundered past the kirk and through the crofters' village. Charlotte stared out the window, watching the beloved landscape of Dungorm slip away in the hazy June sunshine.

She turned and looked out the back window. A flicker of movement from behind caught Charlotte's eye.

On the road leading from Dungorm came a flash of black

and white, a shadow of movement. Charlotte's heart leapt into her mouth.

'Wait,' she called urgently. 'It is Flossie, chasing us.'

Nell and Sophie turned to look. Flossie was loping behind, her ears flopping and tongue panting.

'Stop,' shouted Charlotte. 'Stop the carriage. It is Flossie.'

The driver checked the horses. Uncle Roderick leant out the window.

'Drive on . . . at full speed,' Uncle Roderick yelled. The driver responded with a crack of his whip. The horses broke into a canter.

Charlotte and Nell stared out the back window of the carriage, tears streaming down their faces, watching Flossie drop further and further behind, getting smaller and smaller, until she disappeared altogether. Charlotte thought her heart had finally broken into hundreds of tiny pieces.

Sophie suddenly felt exhausted. She could not bear any more.

She fled, away from the scene of Charlotte and Nell yearning for their dog, up and away from the shiny black horsedrawn carriage, the kirk, the loch and the rolling green hills of Dungorm. She drifted up and away to the dark tunnel of sleep.

14

Misery

Sophie woke up feeling exhausted, with a pounding headache. From the living room, she could hear the sound of the radio playing, and Nonnie and Jess laughing together as they washed up.

Sophie lifted the locket over her head and slipped it under her pillow. She pulled the covers over her head and tried to go back to sleep. But sleep eluded her.

Why did everything have to be so difficult? Why did Eliza and Alexander have to die? Why did Charlotte and Nell have to lose everything they loved?

Sophie curled herself into a ball and wept. She cried until there were no tears left. She cried for Eliza and Alexander and James, for Charlotte and Nell. She cried for her own parents, and for herself and Jess and Will.

At last she stopped crying and crept from her bedroom to the bathroom to fetch some tissues. As she crept silently past Nonnie's room, she heard her grandmother on the phone.

'I'm really worried about her, Karen,' explained Nonnie. 'Sophie has hardly eaten anything since she came here. She's fading away to a shadow. She's pale, with big dark circles under her eyes, and when I went to wake her this morning she was crying as though her heart would break. I don't know what to do.'

Nonnie paused to listen to Sophie's mother's response. 'Do you think she might be anorexic? I know lots of girls these days seem to get anorexia and stop eating.' She listened again. 'Should I take her to a doctor?' . . . 'Do you think she's worrying about Jack's retrenchment?' . . . 'Do you need me to lend you some money?' . . . 'No, that's what families are for, darling.' . . . 'Talk to Jack.'

Sophie crept away, feeling devastated. Her grandmother thought she might be anorexic. Everyone was worried about her, as if they didn't all have enough to worry about.

She climbed back into bed, her face to the wall. She did not want to face Nonnie or her life.

Think of something else – Charlotte and Nell on their long, dangerous journey. Her hand found the locket under the pillow and pulled it back over her head.

Sophie whooshed down through the tunnel of darkness into a stormy sky. She could see a vast, tossing ocean, and in the middle bobbed a tiny ship, its sails furled tightly and masts heeling over. Charlotte and Nell must be on that ship.

Sophie found them in one of the cabins.

Nell tossed and turned in her lower bunk, a bucket beside her bed. She had been in bed all day.

'Charlotte, I feel terrible,' Nell moaned. 'My head aches, my throat's sore and my stomach's roiling.'

'I know, Nell. You will feel better in a day or so,' soothed Charlotte.

A chilly wind continued to blow from the north. The waves grew stronger and higher, urging the ship ever southwards.

Waves slapped on the hull, sailors called, timbers groaned, sails flapped and the ship pitched and rolled, heeled and surged.

Charlotte listened anxiously to the wind in the rigging and the sails flapping.

She remembered the horror stories she had overheard Sally telling Nanny about the ship that had been wrecked in a wild storm less than a day's sail from Liverpool, when every person on board had drowned.

Thoughts crowded her mind, of the terrible wreck of the *Eliza Mackenzie* at Kyle of Lochalsh, where her own strong father had lost his life.

'Come on, Nell,' coaxed Charlotte. 'We should go up to the saloon, where there are other people. Perhaps we will find out what is going on. It must be better than this tiny airless cabin.'

Charlotte supported Nell as they walked through the corridor, fighting the pitch and roll of the ship.

They heard frightened cries and moans coming from the crowded steerage hold, and smelt the faint waft of vomit and unwashed bodies.

In the saloon, Charlotte and Nell found a place on one of the long benches.

'Shall we play backgammon, Nell?' suggested Charlotte.

'It will take your mind off the storm and the illness.'

Nell played listlessly, distracted by the frightening sounds and motion.

A sudden lurch tossed a teapot, cups, saucer and milk jug to the floor. A woman carrying her baby crashed heavily as she lost her footing. The baby wailed in fright.

Nell and Charlotte clung to each other to avoid being pitched to the floor as well.

They sat in miserable silence, fighting the unpredictable wallowing of the ship and the waves of fear engulfing them. Sophie huddled beside them feeling as much trepidation as the passengers.

Babies screamed. Children cried. Ladies moaned. Gentlemen made hearty jokes which did little to alleviate the fear.

One by one, passengers succumbed to seasickness, hurrying away to their cabins looking pale and clammy. One of the smaller children vomited in the saloon, filling the air with its putrid stink. A stewardess cleaned up the mess and swabbed the floor with pungent vinegar.

After a while Captain Jamieson came into the saloon to report on the storm.

'It's one of the fiercest storms I've encountered on the voyage to Australia,' he warned the passengers. 'We've grave fears for the forward mast, but we've axes ready in case we need to cut it free.'

One of the stewards ran in at this moment, his face pale with panic.

'Capt'n, sir, we're taking on water,' he yelled. 'Someone opened the portholes in their cabin and there's seawater flooding the first-class cabins and corridor. We've managed to get them shut but there's water everywhere.'

The captain turned and hurried to the door to deal with this new emergency, the sailor at his side.

'Everyone, stay here until we've dealt with the flood,' the captain ordered the passengers sternly, over his shoulder. 'I don't want anyone getting in the way.'

'What idiot would open their portholes in a storm?' Charlotte overheard Captain Jamieson mutter to the sailor.

Charlotte felt nauseous, not with seasickness but with the realisation that the first-class cabins were flooded and all her treasures were in her carpetbag on the cabin floor.

She thought of her father's book of Robbie Burns' poetry, the twin portraits of her parents in their silver frames, their books and sketching paper, and her tiny sprig of blooming heather. Most of all she worried about her carved oak treasure box. All would be irretrievably ruined by water damage.

'Nell, wait here,' Charlotte whispered. 'I will be back soon.'

'The captain said we must stay here,' murmured Nell, alarmed at the thought of Charlotte leaving her.

'All our precious things are being flooded in the cabin,' Charlotte replied. 'I have to save them.'

'Be careful, Charlotte,' Nell begged.

It was incredibly difficult to walk as the ship bucked and plunged beneath her feet.

Sophie, following behind, found it hard to fly and was lurched right through a cabin wall. She caught a quick glimpse of a woman moaning in her bunk, then was flung right through the wall again into the corridor.

Outside the saloon, the corridor was awash with seawater

sloshing back and forth. Several crew members were working with buckets and cloths to mop it up.

'Watch out, miss,' yelled one of the crew. 'You shouldn't be out here. Go back to the saloon.'

Charlotte swayed and clutched one hand to her stomach, and the other up to her mouth.

'I think I'm going to be sick,' she groaned.

The steward waved her away impatiently. They had enough mess to contend with, without another vomiting child.

Charlotte hurried to the cabin she shared with Nell, sliding and slipping on the sloping, sloshy floor. Seawater had poured under the cabin door, forming a huge puddle on the floor. The trunks and carpetbags were sitting in the midst of the puddle, completely soaked around their bases.

Charlotte started with the carpetbags, fighting the ship's unpredictable motion as she worked. She piled the most precious items on her bunk, at the back of it so they would not slide to the floor.

Thankfully the treasures were dry: the carved oak box, her parents' portraits, the book of poetry. Charlotte took a moment to gaze at each of the portraits of her parents before she packed them away. Charlotte could feel the warmth of her mother's locket, nestled inside her bodice.

The treasures were wrapped carefully in her shawl and she knotted them securely to the bunk post, under the bedclothes.

The clothes at the bottom of the carpetbags were saturated but Charlotte could do nothing about that now. She hung the carpetbags on hooks on the wall then started on the trunks. Everything at the bottom was wet, including many of the precious books.

She stacked all the books and sketch paper on the top bunk, then carefully packed them under her blankets, tucking the bedcovers in firmly to hold them securely in place. The wet books were wrapped in dry clothes and packed right at the foot of her bunk, under the blankets.

A sudden lurch sent a pile of books tottering towards the floor. Sophie grabbed them and stopped them from falling into the puddle on the floor, pushing them back on the bunk.

At last Charlotte had saved all she could. The trunks were too heavy to move, and the clothes could be dried out later. She felt exhausted, but relieved with her efforts. She picked up *Wuthering Heights* and carried it back to the saloon to read to Nell.

Nell was lying on the bench looking tired and ill.

'I am back, Nell,' whispered Charlotte gently. 'I saved all the treasures and most of the books, although a few are soaked.'

Nell looked up and smiled wanly.

'Good, Charlotte,' Nell replied listlessly. 'Sorry, I could not help – my head aches dreadfully and my body feels like lead.'

'You lie with your head on my lap, Nell, and I will read to you for a while. It will take our minds off this terrible storm.'

Charlotte read in a clear, soft voice, ignoring the moans and cries, thumps and crashes around her. Sophie and some of the other children had come closer to listen to her, and they seemed comforted by the magic of the story and her steady voice.

A particularly loud crash sounded and the very timbers of the ship shuddered as if straining apart. The ship listed dangerously to the starboard side, the floor slanting steeply. Sophie braced herself against Charlotte and Nell, stopping them from sliding.

Faint cries of alarm, shouted orders, a clanging bell and the chopping of wood were heard over the howling wind, lashing rain and smashing waves.

'The mast,' cried one woman. 'It must have gone over.'

'No,' retorted a man with gingery whiskers. 'It sounded lower. It must be the hull stoving in.'

'We're lost!' shrieked a large woman, who, ineffectually comforted by her companion, proceeded to have loud hysterics.

Charlotte continued to read aloud as calmly as she could, encouraging Nell and the other children to concentrate on her reading, rather than the chaos around them.

Another loud crash. The ship staggered and jarred, jerking to the opposite side, throwing people and objects to the floor. The ship wallowed back and forth, finally bobbing at a more natural angle. People picked themselves up, rubbing bruises and exclaiming loudly.

A soaked Captain Jamieson bustled into the saloon to report on the damage. He took in the scene with interest: the matron having hysterics, the adults animatedly discussing the potential damage and Charlotte calmly reading to her entourage of children.

'Ladies and gentlemen,' the captain began. 'The boom snapped, dragging down much of the rigging, but we've chopped it free with axes, so for the moment we're safe.

'However, the storm shows no sign of abating so it'll be

a long, rough night,' Captain Jamieson continued. 'I suggest you retire to your bunks, say some strong prayers and think of us. The crew and I'll be spending the night on deck battling the storm.'

The captain grinned ruefully at the passengers – who were uncomfortable and frightened, but warm and dry – then steeled his shoulders and strode out to face the storm.

'Come to bed, Nell,' encouraged Charlotte.

Sophie and the other children reluctantly stretched and stood up. Charlotte helped Nell stagger back to their cabin, undress and climb into the bottom bunk. Sophie flitted up to the top bunk to perch on Charlotte's pillow. She could hear and see everything from here, but was safely out of the way.

'Sorry, Nell, I will have to sleep with you tonight,' said Charlotte. 'My bunk is full of books.'

'Good,' Nell said and smiled bravely, as Charlotte tied the ribbon of Nell's nightcap over her long red curls. 'It is not so frightening if you are with me.'

'Let us say our prayers, then I will tell you one of Nanny's stories to help you sleep,' Charlotte offered, as she took off her petticoats.

'Lovely,' Nell sighed, tossing under the bedcovers, her legs curled up. 'Could you tell the story about the tailor and the water horse?'

When Charlotte had changed into her nightdress and nightcap and said her nightly prayers with Nell, she blew out the candle.

The darkness closed in all around. The ship tossed and rolled wildly. Outside, the ship creaked and screamed, tussling the storm. Charlotte lay back on the pillow, with one arm tucked under her head, staring up into the darkness.

'Once upon a time, on the Isle of Islay, there lived a laird who was very miserly,' Charlotte began. Nell snuggled down deeper under the covers, soothed by the words.

While Charlotte and Nell usually spoke with the English vowels of their parents, Charlotte automatically adopted the stronger Scottish brogue of Nanny to give the folk tale its comforting rhythm and cadence.

'Laird McAllister would ne'er pay full price for anything and was always scheming how he could cheat his crofters and retainers. One day Laird McAllister decided he needed a new pair of trews, the trousers the Scots wore many years ago.

'So he called for the village tailor, Robbie McGregor, to come and measure him up. As usual, Laird McAllister was too mean to pay for anything, but had a scheme to cheat the tailor.

'"How much for these new trews, Robbie McGregor?" the laird asked. Robbie McGregor's heart sank, for he knew that Laird McAllister would try to cheat him, and he had a wife and six wee bairns to feed.

'Robbie named a fair price for a good day's work – enough to put oatmeal bannocks and barley broth on the table that night. The laird grinned.

'"Well, that seems high, McGregor, but I need these trews by dawn," claimed Laird McAllister. "I'll pay thee double if you have them to me before the sun comes up."

'Robbie McGregor's heart leapt with joy. For that much silver, there would be braised venison for the kailpot.

'"O' course, me laird. I will work all night," Robbie crowed. "I will make ye the finest trews a laird e'er wore."

'"Not so fast," said Laird McAllister. "My only condition is ye must sew my trews inside the kirk tonight. Not one stitch must ye make before the sun sets, and not one stitch must ye make outside the hallowed kirk. If the trews are not finished by dawn, I pay thee naught."

'Robbie McGregor turned pale as a ghaistie, for he knew that a terrible beast lived under the kirk. On the stroke o' midnight a huge water horse climbed up through the trapdoor and devoured all the creatures he found.

'But Robbie McGregor was a brave and clever man, and had eight mouths to feed, so Robbie shook hands with Laird McAllister to seal the bargain.

'Robbie took the laird's measurements and hurried home. He carefully cut out the material and prepared all he would need into a neat bundle.

'Gravely he ate the delicious broth his wife had cooked, kissed his bairns and bade them farewell.

'His guid wife shook with fear when she saw him gather up his bundle, and clung to him tightly.

'"Robbie, where are ye gaeing so late, when 'tis nearly dark and time for bed?" she begged him.

'"'Tis naught, my bonnie wife," Robbie replied calmly. "Do no' fret. I have work to do for my laird by dawn, and he will pay me well for it."

'"That can mean nothing guid," his wife retorted angrily. "My laird is the meanest man who e'er walked the earth, and ne'er pays well. There must be mischief about it."

'"Aye, my love," Robbie replied. "But I must gae with all speed. My very life may depend upon it."

'So Robbie ran to the lonely kirk. It was late on a bonnie summer evening and the sun was setting. 'Twas an hour till the kirk clock struck midnight.

'Robbie dragged a heavy chest o'er the trapdoor in the kirk floor and climbed on top, with his bundle. He set out his needles and thread, the cut-out trews and scissors. From his perch, Robbie could see out the western window to the sinking red sun.

'The moment the sun sank below the rim o' the world, Robbie began to sew, his fingers flying. The seams grew straight and true, the stitches tiny. His legs cramped, his arms ached and his fingers bled, but still he sewed as fast as he could.

'The hour till midnight flew by faster than his fingers could sew, and his heart leapt with terror when he heard the first stroke o' midnight. He sewed faster, his stitches longer and not so neat, the hem a wee bit crooked. The last stroke o' midnight sounded, the trapdoor creaked beneath him, and still Robbie sewed.

'The chest moved. The chest heaved beneath him as something huge and terrible under the kirk floor fought to break free. The chest lurched and slid across the floor, but still Robbie sewed. He was on the last hem now, and his fingers whirred through the air faster than e'er.

'The last stitch was sewn as the beast hurled the chest in the air. Robbie snipped the thread with his scissors and fled as fast as his cramping legs could take him, all the way to Laird McAllister's castle on the hill. With a whinny o' rage, the water horse escaped and gave chase, galloping through the streets o' the village, his giant hooves striking sparks from the cobblestones.

'Laird McAllister's men heard the commotion and threw open the gatehouse door for Robbie just as the water horse arrived. Laird McAllister arose from his bed, shocked to hear that Robbie McGregor had arrived with a monstrous water horse close on his tail.

'"My laird," said Robbie with a bright sparkle in his eyes, "here are your new trews, sewn from first stitch to last in the kirk this very night. I have come to collect my double payment, as promised."

'Laird McAllister bluffed and dawdled but had no recourse but to pay the promised sum. Robbie bunked down in the servants' hall, well pleased with himself.

'Laird McAllister swore revenge on Robbie McGregor. He climbed up on the battlements and paced the walls, planning how to ambush Robbie in the morning on his way home. In his fury he kicked a pebble, which hurtled off the walls and bounced down to the depths below.

'The water horse was prowling around the castle walls and smelt the anger and the meanness from the laird above. In one great leap the water horse hurtled through the air, scooped up Laird McAllister and devoured him in one bite, then galloped back to his cavern under the lonely kirk.

'To this day, you can still see the trews o' Laird McAllister in the great hall of the castle on the Isle of Islay, the hems a little crooked and speckled with stains from the bloodied fingers of Robbie McGregor. And nae-one in those parts will walk near the kirk on a moonlit night, in case the great water horse gallops out and devours them too.'

Charlotte stopped and breathed deeply. It was almost a shock for Nell and Charlotte to realise that they were back in their narrow bunk, in a dark and wildly tossing cabin of a ship in a storm at sea. The story had seemed so real that the bucking motion and keening sounds had seemed like the struggles of the water horse to be free.

'Thank you, Charlotte,' whispered Nell, so faintly it was almost breathing. 'I love that story.'

'That was wonderful,' murmured Sophie, but no-one could hear her.

Nell fell asleep and was soon breathing heavily. Charlotte lay awake for what seemed like hours, cradling Nell in her arms. Charlotte felt comforted and reassured. The story of Robbie McGregor reminded her that a man or a child who was clever and brave could outwit and vanquish even the most frightening monster.

15

Nell's Illness

The next morning, the storm gradually quietened and the tired crew laboured to right the ship. The storm was over, but Nell was worse.

Nell's body burnt with fever, her head pounded with pain and her throat was raw. She vomited constantly and could not keep down even a sip of water.

'Nell, Nell, are you all right?' asked Charlotte, feeling Nell's fiery forehead.

'Mama,' called Nell weakly, thrashing free from the sheets. 'Mama?'

Charlotte set off to find some help. She begged a jug of fresh water and some cloths from a stewardess.

Nell seemed weaker when she returned and did not answer Charlotte's entreaties, but Charlotte wet the cloths and dribbled water into Nell's mouth, and bathed her face and hands.

Charlotte searched the ship urgently for the surgeon and

found him below tending to dozens of seasick travellers.

'Please, sir,' Charlotte begged, 'my sister is very ill.'

'Everyone on board this ship is very ill,' the surgeon replied impatiently, gesturing to the dozens of foul-smelling passengers who were lying prostrate, moaning or violently vomiting into buckets.

'Please, we are all alone,' Charlotte insisted. 'She has a high fever and is delirious. She is only eleven and very weak. I am frightened she might even die.'

The surgeon patted her kindly on the shoulder.

'I will come as soon as I can,' he assured her. 'Keep sponging her down with cool water to lower her temperature, and dribble small amounts of water down her throat to keep her hydrated, even if she keeps vomiting. Which cabin are you in?'

But the doctor did not come, that day or the next. Charlotte worked to nurse her, emptying the sick bucket, sponging Nell down, fetching fresh water, giving her tiny sips.

Nell lay on the bunk, so frail and thin that she looked like she might snap. Charlotte had never felt so alone in her life.

'Nell,' Charlotte begged, tears welling up, 'please do not leave me. Please do not die and leave me all alone. I could not bear it.'

Nell tossed, then sank further into her fever.

Sophie felt as though her heart would break too. She felt so helpless. Nell could so easily die on this ship in the middle of the ocean. Sophie had visions of the tiny body being wrapped in canvas and dropped over the side of the ship into a watery grave.

What could they do?

Sophie cuddled next to Nell on one side, Charlotte on the other.

'Hold on, Nell,' whispered Sophie right in her ear. 'Hold on, don't give up.'

Charlotte felt a faint stirring of hope. Suddenly she didn't feel all alone on this vast sea. She would *fight* to save Nell with every weapon she had. Charlotte took Nell's hot hand in her own and started to whisper stories to her, partly to keep the silence away and partly to remind Nell that she existed, to make her keep her tenuous hold on life.

She told Nell stories of their childhood and about their parents; she told her tales about the great Mackenzie battles and how Bonnie Prince Charlie had hidden in Castle Dungorm until the English blew it to ruins. Charlotte retold Nanny's fairytales about brownies and elves, changelings and selkies. She talked until her voice was hoarse.

And all the time, Charlotte kept sponging Nell with cool cloths, dribbling water down her throat and watching over her every breath. At last, after two days, Charlotte was exhausted and fell asleep curled beside Nell.

Then Sophie took over. Sophie stroked Nell's scorching forehead, face and hands with her cold ethereal hands. She lay beside her, cuddling Nell with her chilly ghostly body.

All the time, she whispered stories of Australia and all the wonders Charlotte and Nell would find when they arrived. Stories of the animals – the koalas, kangaroos, wombats, emus, dingoes, possums, echidnas and platypuses – the exotic flowers and trees, the people and the land.

'The platypus has a bill and webbed feet like a duck, sleek fur like a seal, and lays eggs,' murmured Sophie.

'When the first stuffed platypus was sent back to London from Australia, the scientists thought it was a practical joke – an animal stitched together from the parts of other animals.'

Nell smiled in her sleep, and settled down into a deeper sleep. Sophie kept stroking her hair, her cheeks and scorching hands all through the night.

The next morning, Nell woke up and was lucid, but very weak. She tried to smile at Charlotte through cracked lips.

'I woke up this morning and there was a girl lying beside us,' whispered Nell. 'You were on one side of me asleep, and she was on the other, stroking my hair.'

Charlotte's heart sank. Nell must still be rambling. 'Who was it, my sweet?' she asked.

'It was our guardian angel.'

Charlotte stared at the narrow space beside Nell against the wall. Sophie smiled back at Charlotte and Nell, and squeezed Nell's hand.

'See?' whispered Nell. 'She called me back, and told me not to die.'

Nell was sick for a week. Charlotte nursed her constantly, barely leaving the cabin except to fetch hot soup or fresh water. On the seventh day, while Nell was sleeping, Charlotte went up on deck to get some fresh air.

Blinking furiously, Charlotte climbed up into the strong sunshine. The first thing that struck her was the heat. The sun danced on the deep blue ocean. A stiff, warm breeze filled the sails and whipped Charlotte's red curls across her face. Children ran and played on the deck, supervised by their chatting mothers. A couple of men lounged near the railings, reading.

It was only ten days since they had left Liverpool but it felt like a different world. The sun had never shone this brightly or warmly in Scotland. The sky and sea had never been this deep, clear blue. Somewhere to the south-east was the exotic coast of Africa.

The warmth and sunshine and fresh, salty air made her feel startlingly alive. First Charlotte walked around the deck, breathing in the air and the sights, enjoying the feeling of her muscles working once more. When she tired a little, she sat down on a bench in the sunshine and soaked up the warmth, deep into her very bones.

The hair whipping across her face tickled her nose like a feather and made her smile. Charlotte gathered the unruly curls and crammed them back under her bonnet.

A feeling of hope welled up from deep inside her. Charlotte and Nell had survived. They had survived their parents dying, the deep despair of grief, the loss of their family and home. They had survived the fierce storm at sea and Nell was recovering from her terrible illness. Now the sun was shining and it was a truly beautiful day.

Sophie whispered goodbye to Charlotte, flew across the deck of the clipper and slowly circled around the masts, exploring the rigging and bulging sails. She glanced back at the activity on the deck below, then swooped up towards the sun.

Sophie felt a tickling sensation under her nose. She swatted her nose and turned over, hitching the doona over her face. The tickling started again behind her right ear; Sophie batted her ear and felt something feathery and soft.

Sophie sat up, wide awake now. Jessica was leaning over her, brandishing a long turquoise-and-iridescent-green peacock feather.

'Sophie, *wake* up,' insisted Jessica. 'All you ever want to do is sleep these holidays. It's *sooo* boring.'

Sophie felt a wave of annoyance wash over her, and a sharp retort leapt to her lips. 'You're *sooo* boring. Leave me alone.'

But she didn't actually speak the words, because then Sophie remembered the adventures of the night, and how Nell had nearly died on the ship to Australia. Little sisters could be extremely annoying sometimes, but life would be sadly empty without them.

'Morning, Jess,' Sophie said instead, and grinned. 'Did you sleep well?'

Jess looked surprised, then smiled back.

'Yes, but I've been up for *hours*, and Nonnie is taking us to the beach today,' Jess explained, jiggling up and down. 'It's the most glorious day and I bet there's good surf at Whale Beach.'

'Okay, okay,' Sophie cried. 'I'm coming.'

16

The New World

The voyage of three months seemed interminably long. The girls felt homesick and bored. At last, in August, Charlotte and Nell caught their first glimpses of the new continent, Australia, which was to be their home. The coast looked scrubby and flat and desolate, so different from the emerald misty hills of Scotland.

Black seals, dolphins and huge whales dived and played alongside the ship.

The sky seemed vast and deep, deep blue, and the sun always seemed to shine, although it was still winter in this topsy-turvy land. On August 25, 1859, they landed in Port Phillip Bay, near the town of Melbourne.

Here Charlotte and Nell transferred to a smaller coastal steamer, which transported them to Sydney in New South Wales, a voyage of two days.

Sydney town seemed busy and overcrowded, with twisting dusty tracks and a confusing jumble of slab huts, bark humpies and imposing stone houses.

The port was filled with people milling around and going about their business: soldiers in red coats, bearded bushmen in cabbage-tree hats, women in voluminous skirts, children ducking and weaving, sailors cursing and gambling, and Chinese coolies carrying buckets of water and baskets of vegetables. Scrawny dogs fossicked among the rubbish looking for scraps.

Charlotte, Nell and Sophie all stared with wondering eyes. It was so different to anywhere they had ever seen before. While Sophie had grown up in modern-day Sydney, this Sydney was completely different, except for the stunning blue vista of the harbour.

Beside the wharf, a troupe of jugglers performed, throwing burning torches into the air and nimbly catching them, turning cartwheels and walking on their hands. They ran and sprang and formed a towering human pyramid.

'Look, Charlotte,' Nell exclaimed. 'It is incredible. That boy is walking on his hands as deftly as if they were feet.'

A tall, dark man walked past them carrying a bundle of rush brooms and a bark gourd full of sweet-smelling honey. He was wearing nothing but a stained blue shirt; his thin legs were long and bare and black. Charlotte and Nell had never seen black skin before.

The Aboriginal man felt their stare and turned to look. He smiled shyly at them, revealing strong, white teeth. Charlotte and Nell smiled back. In a moment he was gone, enveloped by the crowds.

'Nell, did you see that man?' Charlotte asked in wonder. 'He must be one of the natives. He did not look like a bloodthirsty savage.'

'Perhaps – however, he was not wearing many clothes!' Nell exclaimed in shock.

The steward who was escorting them to their next steamer found them still staring at the colourful throngs of people.

'Come along, this way, misses,' he directed them.

Their journey of many weeks was still not over. From Sydney they took an overnight steamboat up the coast, where they were met at the river port of Easthaven later the next morning.

A stocky man with a thick beard covering most of his face surged forward to greet them on the wharf. He was wearing a broad-brimmed hat, blue shirt, moleskins and elastic-sided boots, and had an assortment of paraphernalia attached to his belt: a coiled stockwhip, two pistols, a knife, tobacco pouch and a clay pipe.

'Good morning,' he greeted them with a warm smile, sweeping his hat off with a flourish. 'I presume you must be Miss Charlotte and Miss Eleanor Mackenzie? I'm Edward McLaughlin, Annie's husband. Welcome to Australia.'

Charlotte and Nell stared at him in wonder, then quickly remembered their manners.

'Good morning, Mr McLaughlin,' the girls chorused shyly.

'Come along now,' invited Mr McLaughlin, picking up the two carpetbags and hefting them over his shoulders. Two porters followed behind, carrying the trunks.

'The wagon is over here. I picked up supplies while I was here to fetch you. It's a week's drive to Rosedale – a hundred and eighty odd miles away.'

Charlotte's spirits sank. *Still a week to go!* she thought

with dismay. *Will this journey never end?*

Mr McLaughlin seemed to sense the girls' despondency and smiled.

'It's a pretty drive to Rosedale,' explained Mr McLaughlin, as he led them across the road. 'Mrs McLaughlin is so looking forward to you coming. She gets lonely in the bush, surrounded by so many men, especially since our own little girls died.'

'I am sorry,' murmured Charlotte, a wave of sadness washing over her. So much death.

'Of course, you girls both know how terrible it is to lose the people you love,' replied Mr McLaughlin sympathetically. 'We try not to talk about our little girls in front of Mrs McLaughlin. She finds it too painful.'

Mr McLaughlin showed them to a wagon drawn by two bay draught horses, which was piled high with sacks, boxes and bales. Another two horses were tethered behind. The girls' trunks and carpetbags were added to the load and securely lashed on. Sophie settled on the back of the wagon. The two draught horses snorted and pawed the ground, unnerved by her invisible presence.

'Easy, boys,' soothed Mr McLaughlin.

The girls climbed up onto the hard wooden seat, followed by Mr McLaughlin. There was so much to see as they trotted out of town: wagons, buckboards and buggies, people strolling along the dusty street, boats on the river, farmers riding horses, children playing, the timber slab houses and shops, the beautiful sandstone church and fine public buildings.

It all seemed so rough and new, dusty and noisy compared to Scotland. Mr McLaughlin pointed out buildings and people of interest as they passed.

Soon they were out in the countryside, a wide, fertile valley cleared of trees and dotted with white flocks of sheep tended by shepherds. To Sophie this landscape was now wonderfully familiar, yet somehow still strange.

All day they sat up on the narrow seat being jolted and bounced over the rough track, until their very teeth felt like they might be shaken loose. Big flocks of colourful parrots swooped through the air, shrieking raucously. In the early afternoon, Mr McLaughlin pulled over near a small running stream to water the horses and change over the teams.

'Jump down and stretch your legs, girls,' Mr McLaughlin suggested, handing them a tin pannikin. 'Have a drink of water from the creek. You'll be thirsty after all that dust. Just make a bit of noise to scare off any snakes.'

The girls stomped down to the creek, stamping their boots on the ground to warn any terrifying snakes and glancing nervously around at the strange, wild bush. They washed their faces and hands in the chilly water, taking deep draughts of water to slake their thirst. It was a relief to move around after so many hours of riding in the wagon.

Sophie took the chance for a good soar, swooping above the treetops, frightening a noisy flock of rainbow lorikeets.

Their respite, however, was short. As soon as the new team was in place, Mr McLaughlin called to them to jump up on the seat once more and they set off, heading ever north-west.

'In that bag you'll find a few johnnycakes and some cheese,' Mr McLaughlin instructed. 'We'll eat while we ride along. We need to cover a few miles before we make camp tonight.'

The three of them had a picnic lunch of flat scone-like bread, called johnnycakes, hunks of crumbly cheese and some tiny pickled onions. The girls did not speak much, simply drinking in the strangeness of the scenery and the unusual birds and animals they saw along the way. Mr McLaughlin rarely spoke, except for occasionally pointing out interesting creatures.

In the late afternoon, they had left the farmland and were travelling through thick bush.

Three long-legged, comical-looking birds ran from the scrub and scampered in front of the horses, causing them to shy.

'They're emus,' Mr McLaughlin explained with a laugh, reining in the horses. 'Otherwise known as bush chickens. They cannot fly and they lay huge eggs which are quite delicious.

'We have two pet emus called Ernestina and Edgar that live around the homestead at Rosedale. We also have a tame native bear called Mala and two pet wallabies called Christabel and Joey.'

Charlotte felt a flutter of excitement in her stomach. It sounded like a fascinating place to live with all these strange and wonderful creatures.

'We have never seen a native bear,' said Nell nervously. 'Are they dangerous?'

'Mala is very tame, although you need to be careful of her claws. Our son Will loves animals and is always encouraging native birds and animals to live with us. Mrs McLaughlin draws the line at snakes, though.

'Look out for kangaroos now. They generally come out in the late afternoon. We will be making camp fairly soon.'

Towards dusk, Mr McLaughlin pulled over the horses in a small clearing off the track, near a creek.

'This is where we'll camp for the night,' Mr McLaughlin explained. 'I'll unharness the horses. Could you girls gather some fallen branches for the campfire, please? Pile them up over here.'

Charlotte and Nell were astounded. They had never been asked to do any form of work before. There had always been an army of servants to do everything for them. Slowly they set off along the banks of the creek gathering up an armful of fallen timber, looking around them in wonder.

Mr McLaughlin deftly unharnessed the four horses, hobbled them with leather-and-chain straps so they could not wander and tied a bell around each one's neck.

Next he dragged over several large branches and set to work making a campfire. He dug a small depression in the soil and surrounded it with rocks set in a circle. He snapped the wood into more manageable pieces with his hands, or using his boot.

'First we make a small pile of dried grass and leaves,' Mr McLaughlin explained, piling up a mound of tinder. 'Then we pile up the twigs like this, leaving plenty of space for the air to circulate.'

The smallest twigs were leant up together to form a structure like a tiny tent over the mound of leaves and grass. Carefully he struck a match and lit the tinder, then blew gently on the delicate flame.

The dried tinder caught alight, licking the twigs. Slowly and patiently Mr McLaughlin added larger twigs and small branches to the structure, in a crisscross pattern, until there was a merry campfire blazing.

The girls sat cross-legged on a couple of blankets by the fire, enjoying the complete novelty of camping.

Mr McLaughlin went to work, efficiently making camp and preparing dinner. First he slung some canvas on a rope between two small trees and pegged the edges to the ground to make a tent. He gave the girls a pile of rugs to make a bed, using their carpetbags for pillows. He would sleep in the open by the campfire.

'Now we'll make johnnycakes,' explained Mr McLaughlin. 'If you're going to be pioneer maids in the bush, I'll need to teach you some bush crafts.'

Nell fetched water from the creek in the quart pot. Charlotte mixed together flour, baking soda, cream of tartar and water to make a dough. Mr McLaughlin showed them how to bake the thin bread over the hot coals for ten minutes and quickly fry slices of salt beef.

This meal was washed down with a tin mug of steaming sweet black tea. Even Nell ate hungrily.

'Thank you,' Nell said. 'That was delicious.'

'My pleasure. It looks like you can do with some feeding up,' replied Mr McLaughlin. 'Don't worry, Mrs McLaughlin will see to that soon enough. Perhaps you girls could wash the dishes down at the creek while I check the load?'

'I am not sure,' said Charlotte tentatively. 'At least, we have never done that before.'

Mr McLaughlin laughed kindly. 'It's not hard. Just scrub them out with river sand until they look clean.'

Charlotte flushed in confusion, but gathered up the dishes with Nell and set off.

The sun set in a blaze of glorious colours. When all the chores were done, the girls sat by the fire, and

Mr McLaughlin told them stories about Rosedale and adventures of living in the Australian bush: floods, droughts, bushfires, shearing and lambing.

He told them about his family – his sons, Henry and Will, his wife Annie – and some of the shepherds, stockmen and characters who lived at Rosedale.

The stars arced overhead in the black velvet sky, stretching away to infinity. A haunting, otherworldly cry sounded from the trees in the bush.

'What was that?' cried Nell in alarm, glancing around nervously at the dark bush crowding in on them.

'That was the cry of a bird called the curlew,' answered Mr McLaughlin. 'Many Scottish folk would have you believe it's the sound of a banshee wailing. It sounds eerie enough.'

Nanny's words came back to Charlotte: 'Why, if you hear a banshee wailing, someone you love will die soon enough, but if you actually *see* one o' the sprites – perhaps sitting in a branch all dressed in white, combing its long, fair hair wi' a silver comb – then ye yourself are no' long for this world.'

Charlotte and Nell shivered with apprehension. Sophie felt their anxiety and tried to comfort the girls, whispering reassuring words, but they could not hear.

'Don't worry, there are no banshees in Australia,' joked Mr McLaughlin. 'There's nothing out there in the bush to harm you while I keep guard.'

'What about bushrangers or snakes?' asked Charlotte, remembering Sally the chambermaid's tales.

'I'll keep you safe, I promise,' Mr McLaughlin assured them.

At last the girls crawled into their tent, Sophie beside them. Charlotte took her carved oak box out of her carpet-bag 'pillow' and lay clutching it in her arms.

'Charlotte, it is all so strange,' Nell whispered. 'I miss home. I miss everything.'

'I know, Nell,' replied Charlotte, holding Nell's hand. 'I do too. It is just you and me now. We must look after each other and be strong.'

The girls lay for some time listening to the strange sounds of the bush around them, the fire crackling, rustling in the undergrowth, a thumping on the earth. Charlotte and Nell had never slept outside in their lives, but at last they fell into an exhausted sleep.

In the morning the girls were woken by the sound of the horse bells and a peculiar raucous laughing sound. Mr McLaughlin was leading the horses to be harnessed to the wagon. A small campfire was flickering, the quart pot was boiling and a delicious aroma of freshly baked johnnycakes wafted past their noses.

Charlotte and Nell dressed quickly and hurried to the creek to wash. Here they startled a mother kangaroo and her joey drinking at the waterhole. The animals stared at the girls with round doe-like eyes, then the mother clicked her alarm, the joey scrambled headfirst into her pouch and the mother bounded away through the scrub, her tail thumping.

Charlotte and Nell stared at each other.

'What beautiful creatures,' breathed Charlotte in wonder. 'They are the most unusual animals I've ever seen.'

'What about the emus we saw yesterday?' Nell reminded her.

They wandered back to the campfire, drawn by the delicious smell of baking bread.

'Good morning, girls,' replied Mr McLaughlin cheerily. 'Are you hungry? Did you sleep well? Did our noisy friend the laughing jackass wake you up?'

He pointed up to a sharp-beaked bird sitting in a bough over their heads that was once more making a loud kookookaka kookookaka laughing shriek.

'Good morning, Mr McLaughlin,' answered Charlotte and Nell together.

'What is it? A laughing bird?' Charlotte asked.

'We saw a mother kangaroo and baby down by the burn,' added Nell shyly.

'They are pretty animals, are they not?' replied Mr McLaughlin. 'But I will need to teach you some Australian words so you do not sound like new chums.

'A baby kangaroo is a joey. Here we have creeks, not burns or streams. We have bush instead of woods, and a field is called a paddock. A new chum, by the way, is someone straight off the boat from England, who does not know a kangaroo from a wallaby.'

'I guess we are new chums, then,' admitted Charlotte, smiling.

'You won't be for long,' Mr McLaughlin assured them. 'We will make Australian lassies of you soon enough. Now let's eat.'

Breakfast was hot johnnycakes with jam, and bush tea. Extra bread was baked for lunch. Then the camp was packed up in a matter of minutes, the campfire covered in soil and the horses harnessed, and the girls climbed up on the wagon seat ready to go.

Mr McLaughlin clicked his tongue and the horses pulled forward into the traces, plodding steadily to the north-west. A few miles down the track they came to the top of a steep riverbank.

The girls looked down in consternation. The track descended down the bank, through the deep, swiftly running waters of the wide river, then up the sharp bank on the other side.

'Hold on as tight as you can, girls,' advised Mr McLaughlin. He cracked his whip and slapped the horses on the rump with the reins. The horses leapt forward in a canter, hurtling down the bank at great speed.

Charlotte and Nell clung to the seat with all their strength, certain the wagon would be overturned on top of them. Mr McLaughlin cracked his whip again, urging the horses into a gallop.

The horses hit the water with a huge splash which drenched the passengers, then hurtled through the river, sending water splattering up over the wheels and onto the luggage on the back.

Nell screamed in fright. The horses tethered behind whinnied and complained as they found themselves dragged forward into the deep water, across the river and out the other side.

Sophie fell off the back of the wagon and had to fly to save herself, swooping back up onto the wagon on the other side.

The horses galloped up the other bank and slowed to a canter then a trot, but only paused when the horses, wagon and passengers were all safely on the top of the slope.

'Sorry about that,' apologised Mr McLaughlin. 'Are you

all right, Nell? We have to keep the speed up to get the horses through the deep water and up the other bank. The sun will dry you off soon enough. Wrap a blanket around you if you get cold.'

Nell nodded her head shakily, her face pale. Charlotte, on the other hand, felt completely exhilarated. The wild ride through the river crossing had made her heart pound and her pulse race. She grinned up at Mr McLaughlin.

'That was exciting,' she laughed.

Charlotte and Nell learnt to love the final stage of their journey through the bush and farms and villages of the countryside. They felt a liberating sense of freedom living in the outdoors, sleeping in a tent, washing in a creek and eating all their meals by a campfire.

By the end of the week they were building fires and making damper, johnnycakes, fried salt beef and bush tea with ease. On the seventh day, they started very early so they would make it to Rosedale by nightfall.

'Mrs McLaughlin will be expecting us for dinner,' Mr McLaughlin explained. 'Knowing my wife, she will have prepared a welcome-home feast for us.'

Charlotte's heart contracted with nerves at the thought of a new home, and her stomach churned. Nell went pale and silent.

'I am sure you will love Rosedale,' Mr McLaughlin assured them. 'It is a homely, welcoming place.'

17

Rosedale

Sophie and Jess were watching television after dinner, when the phone rang.

'I'll get it, Nonnie,' yelled Jess, leaping to pick up the phone.

'Hello? Oh hi, Mum . . . No, we're just watching TV. Good, yes we had a lovely day. No, she's right here. Nonnie, Mum wants to speak to you.'

Nonnie took the phone and chatted briefly, then she lowered her voice. Sophie's ears pricked up over the background noise of the television.

'No, she seems a bit better the last couple of days and she's been eating more, although she still seems pale and withdrawn. I don't think I should take her to a doctor for another few days as it doesn't seem to have developed into an illness of any kind . . . Well, see what you think on the weekend . . . All right, lovely, see you then. Bye.'

Nonnie held the phone away from her ear and called out.

'Sophie, your mother would like to speak to you.'

Sophie walked over to take the phone from Nonnie, wondering if she should just tell her mother and Nonnie of her strange nightly visits to the past. No, they would probably think she was crazy and call the doctor straightaway.

'Hi, Mum,' Sophie said.

'Hi, darling,' answered her mother. 'How are you feeling? How are the headaches? Dad and I have been worried about you. I thought perhaps I might take you to the doctor when you get home.'

'No, Mum,' Sophie replied. 'Really, I don't need to go to the doctor. I'm just tired and need a few good nights' sleep. We're having a lovely time with Nonnie. How're Will and Sammy?'

'Missing you both. Are you sure you're all right?'

'Absolutely. Okay, Mum, I have to go. I'm missing the movie.'

'All right, darling. Enjoy. Love you heaps. Bye.'

It was early evening when Mr McLaughlin turned up a dirt track consisting of two wagon ruts and wending its way into a valley, alongside a small river. Sophie perched up behind the girls on top of Nell's trunk, where she could see and hear everything.

'This is the start of our land,' Mr McLaughlin informed the girls. Tall, graceful gum trees grew along the banks, their trunks silvery and leaves greeny-grey, shivering in the breeze. The valley narrowed as they trotted along, the hills on either side rolling and rounded.

They passed a shepherd on horseback slowly herding his fleecy flock towards the sheep pens for the night. The shepherd waved and tipped his hat. The girls waved back. Sophie waved too, even though she knew the shepherd could not see.

Towards the end of the valley, they saw a cluster of buildings, smoke curling from the chimneys and cheery light spilling from the windows. They crossed the river, which was really not much more than a creek at this end of the valley. Two large dogs bounded from the house, barking a noisy welcome.

'Rosedale,' announced Mr McLaughlin, a strong note of pride in his voice. 'It was nothing but wild bushland when we came here ten years ago, and now it is one of the prettiest farms in the district.'

Sophie was as curious as Charlotte and Nell to see their new home. All three of them felt butterflies fluttering in their bellies as the horses clopped into the yard.

The dogs greeted the horses, licking one on the nose, then jumped up on the side of the wagon. They seemed to sense Sophie and barked loudly at Nell's trunk, their tails between their legs. Sophie floated up away from the wagon and hovered safely near a tree branch.

'Nicky and Tiger,' scolded Mr McLaughlin. 'Mind your manners.'

Two brown emus startled by the noise stopped pecking for grain and scampered for the scrub, stretching their long skinny legs. The dogs were immediately distracted and gave chase, barking with delight.

The noisy dogs brought a number of people out from the homestead. There was a small woman, with dark hair pinned under a lace cap, dressed in a cotton print dress with a blue shawl around her shoulders.

A boy of about fourteen stood beside her, holding a grey furry bundle in his arms, and there was a taller young man of about sixteen behind him. Charlotte guessed these were Annie, Will and Henry McLaughlin.

From the smaller kitchen building to the left came a number of servants and stockmen, including an older couple and an Aboriginal boy who looked about twelve.

Mr McLaughlin pulled up the team of horses near the gate to the garden. Annie, Will and Henry started forward to meet them. Henry, the elder son, helped the two girls clamber down, their legs stiff after the long drive.

'Welcome home, Edward dearest,' cried Annie. 'It is wonderful to have you safely back with us again.'

'Hello, Annie, my dear,' replied Mr McLaughlin. 'Good evening, Henry and Will. Here are our bonnie Scottish lassies, Charlotte and Nell.'

Annie smiled warmly, embracing the two girls in turn.

'Charlotte, Nell,' Annie cried. 'It is so wonderful to finally meet you. Welcome to our home. These are my sons, Henry and Will, and this is our pet bear, Mala.'

'How do you do?' asked Charlotte and Nell shyly, confused by all the strange faces crowding around them.

There were introductions and greetings all around. Mr and Mrs Gregory, the older couple, worked at the homestead and the young Aboriginal boy was introduced as Nathanial, usually known as Pot.

'When Pot was a tiny boy, he took to wearing a copper pot on his head, like a helmet,' explained Annie, smiling at Pot. 'It was one of the first English words he learnt to say, so we called him Pot, and somehow the nickname has stuck. Pot's parents, Mary and Billy, also work at Rosedale.'

Charlotte and Nell were intrigued by Will's native bear, which was curled up sleepily in his arms. The bear was plump, with soft grey fur, a big oval black nose and round fluffy ears.

'Would you like to hold Mala?' offered Will. 'She's quite tame, but careful of her claws, she can give you a nasty scratch if she gets a fright.'

Charlotte and Nell took turns to cuddle the furry grey koala, stroking her gently on the head. Mala snuggled down happily into their arms, closing her eyes. Sophie stroked the koala too, which Mala did not seem to mind at all.

Henry and Will went to unharness, groom and tend the horses, while Annie led Charlotte and Nell to the house, followed by the two golden dogs and Sophie.

'Leave Mala in the crook of the gum tree here,' suggested Annie, pointing to the huge eucalypt tree growing beside the house. 'She sleeps nearly all day, and will not be bothered by the dogs up there.'

The homestead was built from split timber slabs and had a deep verandah on three sides. It had a large, comfortable drawing room with a fireplace, carved cedar furniture, a piano in the corner, sketches on the wall and china knick-knacks on the mantelpiece. Other rooms in the house included the dining room, study and four bedrooms.

Annie showed the girls into one of the bedrooms at the rear of the house. It was a pretty whitewashed room with two single beds covered in pale-green quilts. The window looked out onto the yard behind the house and there was a flowerbed of roses just under the window.

A chest of drawers stood between the beds, with a jug of fresh jonquils atop it scenting the air. There was a washstand and a mirror against the opposite wall.

Sophie went to look in the mirror. It was strange because in the reflection she could see Annie, Charlotte and Nell talking, but as usual she could not see her own reflection at all. It was completely eerie.

'This will be your room, my dears,' Annie explained. 'I hope you will enjoy it. I am so very sorry about your dear mama and papa. I loved your mama like a sister.'

Charlotte blinked rapidly, tears welling up as the familiar grief hit her like a punch. She felt with her fingers for the gold locket that always hung around her neck. Nell swallowed and hung her head.

'I am so glad your uncle wrote to ask me if you could come and live with me,' Annie continued. 'We too have lost dear ones: my little daughters Annie and Rose died with scarlet fever four years ago. They would have been nearly your ages by now.

'I miss them so much. The grief gets a little easier with time. At first you simply cannot believe it could be true, then you feel so incredibly angry that they have been taken from you. But as time passes you can think of them with love and remember there can still be happiness in life.

'I hope that, in time, you can discover joy and happiness here with us,' said Annie, taking one of each of their hands and pressing it gently. 'Now, Mrs Gregory is bringing you some hot water so you can wash and change for dinner. Come to the dining room when you hear the bell.'

Mrs Gregory arrived then, carrying in a large jug of hot water and a pile of washcloths, followed by Pot carrying the two carpetbags. In a moment, the girls were left alone.

'You wash first, Nell,' suggested Charlotte. 'I will unpack a few things. I hope we have something presentable to wear for dinner. Everything seems so crushed and dusty. I will give everything a good shake.'

Charlotte unpacked her bag, taking out her precious carved wooden box, the book of Robert Burns' poetry and the portraits of her parents, which she carefully set out on top of the chest of drawers.

'They all seem so charming,' Nell said wistfully. 'Perhaps . . .' She paused and took off her gloves and bonnet, leaving the sentence trailing.

'Annie was Mama's best friend, so of course Annie and her family will be lovely,' Charlotte assured her sister. 'It will just be a little strange at first.'

Nell sighed and started stripping off her dirty travelling dress and petticoats.

Sophie decided to escape into the garden to give the girls some privacy while they washed and changed. She knew the girls did not know she was there, but it did seem like an invasion of privacy to stay in the room while they bathed.

The dinner bell rang. The two girls were now clean and fresh, wearing slightly crushed white dresses and petticoats, their hair combed and tied back. They found their way to the dining room, Sophie hovering behind.

The McLaughlins were already seated, leaving two places for Charlotte and Nell. The table was set with a white damask tablecloth, silver cutlery and pretty china, with a large blue-and-white tureen in the centre.

'Come and sit down next to me, girls,' welcomed Mr McLaughlin. 'I thought I would say a Scottish grace this evening in your honour, from your father's favourite poet.'

The girls took their seats on either side of Mr McLaughlin, who sat at the head of the table. Annie was at the opposite end, with Will and Henry seated on either side of her. Everyone bowed their heads as Mr McLaughlin said grace over the meal.

'Some hae meat and canna eat,
And some would eat that want it,
But we hae meat and, we can eat,
Sae the Lord be thankit.'

'Amen.'

Charlotte smiled to hear the familiar Scottish words.

Annie served the soup out. The boys chattered eagerly, asking questions about the journey and sharing the latest Rosedale news.

'I hope you like this soup, girls,' Annie said. 'I am sure you probably have not tried it before. It is kangaroo tail soup – my husband's favourite.'

The soup was rich and flavoursome, and they ate it hungrily. Mrs Gregory came back and forth from the kitchen to clear away the soup plates and bring in the second course: roast pork with apple sauce, crunchy crackling, mashed potatoes, brown gravy, peas and green salad. Mr McLaughlin carved the meat and shared out the crackling, the boys begging for extra servings.

The meal was absolutely delicious, especially after living

on simple camp meals of damper and salt beef for a week. Charlotte and Nell sat quietly, enjoying the food and letting the conversation wash over them, learning much about the family as they listened.

Sophie longed to enjoy the feast – it looked so good – but when she ventured to steal a tiny morsel of crackling, it tasted of nothing, even though she could smell it quite clearly. There seemed no point eating food that was tasteless.

Mrs Gregory cleared away the dirty plates and brought in the dessert, a huge peach pie with a jug of thick yellow cream, followed by cups of milky tea. Charlotte had thought she could not eat another morsel, but found herself enjoying every crumb of the pie. At last she could not eat another thing and sipped appreciatively on her tea.

'Now enough of your chatter, boys,' reproved Annie. 'I want to hear about the girls' journey. How was the voyage out on the ship? Were you very ill?'

Charlotte told the story of the great storm in the Irish Sea and how Nell had nearly died with the fever afterwards.

She told stories about crossing the equator and watching the fun as a sailor dressed as King Neptune took over the ship, held a mock court and sentenced many of the passengers and crew to a dunking in water to celebrate their first crossing of the equator. Nell gradually added in reminiscences of her own.

Henry and Will listened with great interest, as Henry had been too young to remember the journey and Will was born in Australia.

'What an adventure,' exclaimed Will. 'I wish I could make the journey back to Scotland.'

After dinner, the family retired to the drawing room to sit in front of the fire. Mr McLaughlin read a book, Henry and Will played chess, Annie sat with her needlework and the girls fetched some of their stockings to mend.

'Do you play the piano, Charlotte?' asked Annie.

'Not very well,' Charlotte confessed. 'I have not played for such a long time.'

'Do you think you might play us something?' Annie requested. 'We promise not to tease you if you make a mistake.'

So Charlotte sat at the old piano, which was a little out of tune, and softly played one of her favourite Scottish ballads. Her fingers were rusty at first, but she soon improved.

It was pleasantly warm in front of the fire, after the large meal, and Nell was soon suppressing a yawn.

'Oh, you poor wee mites must be exhausted,' Annie exclaimed. 'Why do you not go along to bed now? You boys need to get some sleep too.'

So they said their goodnights and crept off to sleep in a real bed.

18

The First Morning

The next morning, like most mornings at Rosedale, dawned fair and bright, with a clear blue sky and sunshine. The mornings and evenings were chilly, as it was early spring, but the middle of the day was quite warm.

The girls yawned and stretched, not wanting to get up, but finally curiosity got the better of them and they decided to get up and dressed so they could explore. Sophie could not wait, so swooped ahead of them to see what she could see.

The house seemed empty and quiet. Charlotte and Nell wandered out onto the verandah to see if they could see anyone. Mala was asleep in the crook of the gum tree. She yawned sleepily as Charlotte and Nell patted her.

Will was sauntering across the yard carrying a bucket of kitchen scraps, with Nicky and Tiger walking at his heels. The two dogs came gambolling over to greet the girls and happily licked their fingers. They sniffed suspiciously at Sophie but did not bark.

Charlotte thought of Flossie and wondered how she was and if she was missing them as terribly as they were missing her.

'Good morning, Charlotte. Good morning, Nell,' Will called cheerily. 'Come and help me feed the poultry and I will show you around.'

'Good morning, Will,' answered the girls, a little awkwardly. But their shyness was soon forgotten as Will showed them around, explaining everything as they went.

The homestead sat on a small rise, with a picturesque view looking back down the valley, over the creek to the steep hills beyond. The house itself was surrounded by a large fenced garden designed to keep out chickens, sheep, emus, horses and kangaroos. Mr Gregory was working in the garden, weeding and digging.

Pot, the Aboriginal boy, was helping him, carrying buckets of water from the pump to water the vegetables.

'Mother loves her garden,' explained Will. 'She says it reminds her of her home back in Scotland, though she says the plants grow much faster and stronger here, as long as they get plenty of water. We grow all our own fruit and vegetables too.'

The garden closest to the house included wide beds of roses, daisies, lavender, geraniums, camellias and spring bulbs just starting to bloom. Sophie buried her nose in the lavender to enjoy its scent.

Further to the left were the kitchen gardens, filled with neat rows of vegetables and herbs: peas, beans, carrots, cabbage, spinach, lettuce, cucumbers, melons, pumpkin, onions, potatoes, shallots, thyme, marjoram, peppermint and chamomile.

Lemon and orange, apple and peach, cherry and plum trees grew to the right, in the orchard.

'Christabel. Joey,' called Will, holding out his hand.

Will's two pet wallabies jumped over and eagerly nibbled some scraps from the girls' hands.

'What darlings,' exclaimed Nell, taking off her gloves to pat the wallabies' heads.

'They are beauties, aren't they?' Will said. 'The shepherds shot their mothers, then we found the joeys still alive in their pouches.

'Father said I could raise them as pets, so I kept them in a sugar bag hanging on the kitchen door. I fed them milk until they were old enough to fend for themselves. They can go back to the wild whenever they fancy, however they prefer to live around the house and eat the kitchen scraps.

'Gregory is furious when they break into the vegetable garden and eat his precious plants. I've had them for a couple of years now, so they are as tame as anything.'

The kitchen, laundry and storehouse were built just behind the main house, connected by a roofed path.

Outside the garden fence and behind the main house were the outbuildings: a stable, barn and carriage house, men's quarters, the dairy, fowl yards and pigsty, with the home paddock and stockyards behind these.

A number of horses were grazing in the paddock, with the two emus, Ernestina and Edward, pecking between their legs. In the stockyards five calves were locked up, bellowing loudly for their mothers.

'Mrs Gregory is milking the cows,' explained Will. 'We catch a few of the cows each evening, lock them away from their calves for the night, milk the mothers in the morning, then let them all go.'

Will showed Charlotte and Nell into the poultry yards, where there were sixty fowls, seven fluffy yellow chicks, a glossy red rooster and a couple of dozen green-and-brown ducks scratching in the soil. Will dumped half the bucket of scraps on the soil.

He gathered up a couple of large duck eggs and slid them under one of the broody hens sitting on a nest in a box inside the henhouse.

'The ducks are too silly to hatch their own eggs,' Will explained, 'so we give them to the hens to hatch. We are expecting a new batch of chicks to hatch in a couple of weeks. Now we need to gather up some eggs for our breakfast.'

Charlotte and Nell willingly hunted around the yard for some freshly laid eggs. Next they visited the pigsty and fed the pigs the remainder of the scraps, before wandering back to the kitchen.

The kitchen was a large room with a huge fire at one end and ovens set into the chimney. A long scrubbed table, which was covered in the preparations for breakfast, dominated the centre of the room.

Annie and Mrs Gregory were in the storeroom that led off the kitchen, discussing the menu and food supplies needed for the day. Annie kept the storeroom locked when it wasn't in use, carrying the key at her waist.

Through the open door, Charlotte and Nell could see shelves of jars, canisters, sacks and bags. The meat was kept outside in a meat safe, with water dripping down the hessian sides to keep the meat cool. Sophie was interested in everything, peeking inside the meat safe and the storeroom.

Mr McLaughlin and Henry had been out riding around the property, checking on the various shepherds and flocks of sheep, which were lambing. They were riding back now, ready for breakfast, both carrying odd-shaped bundles on the front of their saddles.

'Good morning, everyone,' called Mr McLaughlin as he dismounted and tied his horse to the other side of the fence. 'Nell and Charlotte, we have presents for you.'

Nell, Charlotte and Sophie rushed over to see what the odd damp bundles were wrapped in hessian sacks. They were newborn lambs.

'Sadly they are orphans,' Mr McLaughlin explained. 'Their mothers died during the night, so I thought you might like to raise them as your own pets. Will can show you how to feed them.'

Charlotte's heart leapt with anticipation. The lambs were crinkly and velvety and baaed loudly once they were released from their sacks. Will fetched two ceramic baby bottles from the kitchen, and milk from the dairy. Nell and Charlotte each fed one lamb.

First they dipped their fingers in milk and let the lambs suck the milk from their fingertips, their tails wagging madly.

'I shall call mine Polly,' decided Nell, stroking her lamb's woolly head.

'And mine shall be Lucy,' added Charlotte. 'We can tie coloured ribbons around their necks so we know which one is which.'

When the lambs seemed to be sucking lustily on their fingers, the girls tried to feed them from the bottles, dribbling the milk into their mouths, loudly encouraged by Will. When the bell rang for breakfast the girls were sticky with spilt milk, but laughing at the wobbly antics of the lambs.

Will showed them where to wash at the tub in the laundry, where a hand pump brought water up from the creek. They dried their faces and hands on a cloth, and hurried into the dining room.

Annie, Henry and Mr McLaughlin were already seated, while Mrs Gregory carried in a tray laden with food. There was porridge, ham, poached eggs, toast, preserves, tea and coffee.

The family was all busily eating when Henry noticed something unusual.

'Look, Tipsy has brought us a present,' Henry exclaimed, as a black-and-white cat slipped through the door, carrying something in its mouth.

'Not a rat, I hope,' cried Annie, looking squeamish.

'No, worse than that,' Henry replied, standing up slowly. 'A black snake!'

Everyone turned to face the cat, who was now sitting proudly displaying her gift. She held a long black snake just behind the head, its body stretched out for five feet along the floorboards, its belly gleaming a coppery red. The tail thrashed and whipped as the venomous snake struggled to get free.

Annie screamed in shock, knocking her chair over backwards. Sophie jumped. She hated snakes.

'It's all right, Annie,' assured Mr McLaughlin. 'Henry, go and get a shovel from the garden. Will, get some sacks.

Annie, take the girls out on the verandah to the drawing room. Good puss, Tipsy. Hold him tight.'

Henry and Will raced to obey their father, taking the exit through the French doors onto the verandah, with Annie, Nell, Charlotte and Sophie following behind.

'Those snakes are so dangerous,' Annie told the girls as they hurried along the verandah. 'One strike and you die a slow, painful death. We have lost two horses and one of our dogs to snakebite. It is horrible to see. Oh, I do hope Edward is careful. Fancy Tipsy bringing it right into the house like that!'

The excitement was soon over, with the snake dispatched with the shovel and carried off in a sack. Breakfast was almost cold by the time everyone gathered back in the dining room. Tipsy was given a big bowl of milk as a reward. Sophie patted Tipsy as she lapped her milk.

During breakfast, the McLaughlins discussed Nell and Charlotte's future.

'I know that your mama thought it was very important that both of you received a good education,' Annie said. 'The nearest school is Dalesford, which is too far to travel every day, so I think you should do lessons here each morning with Will.'

Will pulled a comic face at Charlotte and Nell, rolling his eyes to the ceiling. His mother smiled at him and continued.

'We thought you girls could help Will do some chores before breakfast, such as feeding the animals, then have lessons between breakfast and lunch,' added Mr McLaughlin.

'I know you probably did not do chores at home in Scotland,' apologised Annie. 'But we do not have many servants at Rosedale, so everyone helps.'

'I do not mind,' replied Nell quietly. 'I like feeding the animals.'

Annie smiled at Nell. 'After lunch you can help us in the kitchen,' she went on. 'Mrs Gregory and I usually spend the afternoon preparing meals, and making preserves and soap. It is important you learn how to cook and keep house. Then in the late afternoon, you can ride or walk. I believe your mama wrote that you like to ride?'

Charlotte and Nell nodded.

'Excellent,' replied Mr McLaughlin. 'We always have plenty of horses at Rosedale, and we have two that are used to side-saddle, from when Annie used to ride.'

Charlotte felt confused and lost. It was all so different here. The McLaughlins were kind and thoughtful, but she was not sure she wanted to slip into a completely new life.

'Thank you, Mr McLaughlin,' said Charlotte. 'But do you know how long our uncle plans for us to stay here? When do you think we might be going back to Dungorm?'

Annie and Edward McLaughlin glanced at each other with worried faces. Sophie stiffened, feeling Charlotte's tension.

'My dear,' started Annie, 'your uncle wrote to us and said that he and his wife were unable to look after you. Your aunt wished to send you to boarding school in England, however your uncle thought your mama would not have wished that.

'He asked us to look after you until you are grown up and able to make your own way in the world.'

'We must stay here until we are grown up?' repeated Charlotte in consternation. 'Until we can make our own way in the world?'

'Your uncle thought you would be happier with Annie as she was your mother's best friend,' added Mr McLaughlin.

Charlotte felt the familiar wave of anger, grief and frustration rising up.

'No, no,' argued Charlotte, tears choking her voice. 'My uncle cares nothing for our happiness. He wants to steal Dungorm from us. He is going to shut it up and use it as a hunting lodge. He burnt Papa's will. I saw him do it. There must be something we can do to stop him.'

Nell buried her face in her napkin. Sophie patted her on the shoulder, trying to comfort her.

'That is wicked,' exclaimed Will. 'Can he do that?'

Annie and Edward McLaughlin frowned at each other, Annie biting her lip.

'We don't know the true circumstances, Will,' warned Mr McLaughlin. 'It's obviously a complicated legal situation. Annie, perhaps we should consult with a lawyer to see if we can help the girls?'

'It is not a complicated legal situation,' insisted Charlotte. 'Dungorm is our home.'

Charlotte stared down at the tablecloth, her body trembling and her mind churning.

'Come on, Charlotte and Nell,' suggested Annie, rising from the table. 'You are naturally upset about everything. Why don't we go out to the kitchen? Mrs Gregory is making scones this morning so could do with some help.'

In the kitchen, Mrs Gregory was cleaning up from cooking breakfast, but was happy to show the girls how to bake scones.

'Mix the milk into the flour, Miss Nell,' said Mrs Gregory. 'Just a bit more.'

Sophie remembered baking scones with Nonnie. They always ate them hot with strawberry jam and whipped cream. The memory made her mouth water.

'*Lightly* knead the pastry now, Miss Charlotte,' warned Mrs Gregory. 'You'll be thumpin' all the life out of it at tha' rate and the scones will never rise. We'll be havin' rock cakes for tea if tha' happens.'

The weeks passed quickly as they became familiar with Rosedale and all the new people in their life.

October was a difficult month, when both Charlotte and Nell were cast into a deep well of depression. October was the month when Alexander had drowned with the wreck of the *Eliza Mackenzie* and then Eliza herself had died just a couple of weeks later, with the premature birth of her son.

The weather veered between winter and summer, from overcast, cold days when everyone huddled around the fire and the wind howled around the chimney pots, to warm, sunny days when it was hotter than Scotland in midsummer.

A few days after the anniversary of Eliza's death, Annie called the girls into the sitting room. On the floor was a large parcel wrapped in brown paper and tied up with string.

'Open it,' cried Annie, her eyes sparkling with pleasure. 'It is for you.'

Charlotte felt a thrill of anticipation. Together, Nell and Charlotte cut the string and tore open the parcel. Sophie came close and could not resist helping to tear the paper open.

Inside were several coils of coloured ribbon, and bolts of blue and green material.

'Look, girls,' announced Annie. 'Are they not pretty? We will make you some gorgeous new dresses to wear. I thought the blue for Nell and the green for Charlotte. What do you think?'

Annie held the blue bolt up against Nell.

'Perfect. It is time we added some coloured ribbon to all your white dresses now. You cannot keep mourning your mama and papa and baby brother forever.'

Charlotte felt the familiar stab of grief as she was reminded of what she had lost, mixed with a sense of warmth, in that Annie had been so kind to them.

'Thank you, Annie,' replied Charlotte with a wan smile, stroking the green fabric. 'The material is so pretty, and you are right, it will be a nice change to wear some colour.'

'I love this blue, thank you, Annie,' added Nell, draping the material over her shoulders like a cape.

'Good,' said Annie. 'We will start cutting out the dresses today. It is a long time since I made any dresses for little girls.'

So, Annie fetched her scissors and began to cut out pretty new dresses from the material, while Nell and Charlotte worked beside her, trimming their bonnets with green ribbon.

An hour later, Will came to collect Nell and Charlotte to take them riding.

'Charlotte and Nell,' called Will from the door. 'Pot and I are riding out to deliver the week's supplies to the shepherds. Would you like to come?'

Charlotte was sure Annie had suggested it, to help stop them from moping.

'Thank you, we would love to come,' replied Charlotte.

'That is, if it is all right with you, Annie?'

'Of course,' Annie assured them. 'I can finish cutting out the material myself, then you can both help me sew them this evening.'

19

The Bathing Place of the Spirits

One afternoon Will and Pot suggested that they should ride upriver, to the spring that fed Rosedale Creek. They were excused from chores for the afternoon, so had packed some picnic supplies for lunch in the saddlebags, with their tin mugs and pannikins so they could drink from the creek and boil a quart pot for tea.

It was a gorgeous ride. The valley became narrower as they rode along beside the creek, with the hills rising steeply on either side. Tall gum trees grew along the creek banks and in the gullies. A kangaroo was startled by their presence and stared at them, before bounding away into the ti-tree scrub.

'Look up here,' instructed Will, pointing up into a tall eucalypt. 'It's a family of native bears. I think this must be Mala's family.'

It took a moment for the girls to see them. In the tallest branches were two grey, furry balls, apparently asleep.

Lower down was another native bear, but this one was awake, staring at them with sleepy, glassy eyes.

'She has a baby,' whispered Pot, pointing at the lower koala. Charlotte could see a smaller bundle cuddling into the arms of its mother.

'They come down near the homestead sometimes,' explained Will. 'They come to visit Mala's gum tree, but they have to cross the stable yard to get to it.

'The male bear has a peculiar barking cry and he calls out to me when he wants me to tie up the dogs. The dogs go crazy when they see the wild native bears, although they are used to Mala now.

'That was how I came to find Mala, when she was a baby. Tiger attacked her and had his face scratched to ribbons. I managed to separate them before either of them was too badly hurt.'

They rode on for another couple of miles, until they came to a large clear pool. Further up the hillside, a spring welled up from the ground under some rocks and trickled down into the pool. The spring and pool were surrounded by soft tendrils of ferns and velvety white flannel flowers.

The four children dismounted and hobbled the horses, leaving them to graze.

Charlotte and Nell gathered twigs and fallen branches, built a fire and set a quart pot of water on to boil. They unpacked the saddlebags with their pannikins, tin mugs, tea, flour bag, sugar, butter, salt and a plaid rug to throw over the damp ground.

'Do you see this young banksia cone?' asked Pot, picking one from a nearby tree. 'My people used to use these to light fires in the old days.'

'I thought you used to make fire by rubbing softer wood into hard wood, until the friction sparked a flame,' commented Will.

'We did that too but it takes a long time,' agreed Pot. 'It's easier to light some banksia cones from a burning campfire. The cones burn for hours, so the children would carry them to the new camp spot to start a fresh fire.'

Pot bent over and pushed the banksia cone into the fire to show the girls how it slowly smouldered.

'That's clever,' commented Nell, twisting the smoking cone in her fingers. 'It is hard to believe it burns for hours.'

Charlotte made a mug of tea for everyone when the quart pot boiled, adding a pinch of tea and sugar to the hot water.

Will and Pot had fishing rods baited with worms and they hoped to catch a fish or two for lunch. Pot also had a long wooden spear, straight and strong, with a sharp barb of fencing wire on the tip.

'It is so peaceful here,' said Nell, picking some wildflowers growing on the bank. 'I think it is amazing the way the water bubbles up from deep underground.'

'This is a very sad place for my people, this spring,' commented Pot. 'It's the bathing place of the spirits.'

Charlotte and Nell squatted down beside the two boys with curiosity.

'Why is that, Pot?' Charlotte asked. 'Did one of your relatives die here?'

'Many years ago, there was a young girl of my people who used to come here to swim and play with her friend,' Pot explained.

'One day, the girl was betrothed against her will to marry

an elder of the tribe, so she ran away with her young lover to the spring up the hill. The elder was a jealous old man who followed them and killed them both in revenge. They died entwined in each other's arms.

'On moonlit nights, if you listen closely you can still hear the sound of the two spirits splashing and laughing together.'

Pot threw his line out into the water with a gentle plop.

'That is so sad, Pot,' Charlotte replied. 'I wish I could hear the sound of the two spirits laughing.'

'I would not care to at all,' shuddered Nell. 'I do not like ghosts.'

'I think our ghost is more like a guardian angel,' Charlotte replied quietly.

Will looked at her quizzically. 'Our ghost?'

Charlotte laughed awkwardly, wishing she hadn't mentioned anything. 'Oh, nothing really,' Charlotte explained, flushing with embarrassment. 'Several times at Dungorm, Nell and I thought we saw a ghost. It seemed to be a pleasant ghost.'

'A pleasant ghost?' Nell laughed. 'She was nice to *us*, but she seemed very fond of shaking the candelabras and curtains.'

'Yes, but only when we were in some kind of trouble,' Charlotte retorted, groping inside her collar for her locket. 'She scared off that horrid governess, Miss Crowe, and helped get Mama's jewellery back for us. I think she was watching over us somehow.'

'She?' asked Will curiously.

'Yes,' Charlotte answered. 'She spoke to me once – a young girl with a white gown, golden hair and bare feet.

She told me that Nell and I would come safely to Australia and that we would have good fortune here. She said it was very beautiful here, and she was right about that at least.'

Will laughed. 'Now, Charlotte. You can't expect me to believe your ghost stories.'

'Don't laugh, Will,' warned Pot. 'Sometimes the spirit people help us and sometimes the spirits are angry. There is much magic in this world, sometimes good, sometimes frightening.'

Pot suddenly leapt to his feet, snatched up his spear and threw it. The spear twanged through the air, and faster than Charlotte could gasp in shock, the spear had found its mark.

Pot threw himself after the spear, and then stood up grinning, his clothes saturated. On the end of his spear was a large silver fish wriggling wildly, its mouth gasping open and closed in surprise.

'This is good eating fish,' Pot declared proudly. 'It's big enough to make a meal for all of us.'

'That was incredible, Pot,' Charlotte exclaimed. 'I have never seen anyone catch a fish like that.'

Will threw his fishing line down in disgust. 'I didn't even have one nibble again, and I certainly didn't see that perch of Pot's.'

'You just need to practise more,' Pot said with a grin, flashing his straight white teeth.

Pot set to work with his knife, gutting the fish. He stuffed the inside with some green native herb that was growing near the spring and tossed the whole fish directly onto the glowing coals.

Into a pannikin he poured some flour from the bag, added a splash of water and worked it into a dough, which he shaped into an oval loaf. He raked out some hot coals beside the fire, placed the damper on top, then piled some more hot coals over that.

The clearing filled with the delicious aroma of baking damper and cooking fish. Pot sat back on his heels and poked the fire. At last it was ready. Pot scraped the black coals off the damper and fish, and wiped away the worst of the ash with his hands.

The four children sat on the rug on the ground eating hunks of buttered hot damper with salty fish and tea.

'Mmm,' sighed Charlotte. 'This is the best fish I've ever tasted in my life.'

'Better than Scottish salmon?' asked Will.

'Definitely,' insisted Charlotte. 'It must be the fresh air, sunshine and exercise, or maybe it is the way it is cooked on the coals straight from the pool. Anyway, thank you, Pot.'

After lunch, Pot and Will continued fishing, hoping to catch some more fish for the rest of the household.

'Boys, Nell and I are going to wash the dishes downstream a little way,' announced Charlotte.

'Good idea,' agreed Will. 'Have fun. Don't let the bunyips get you!'

'Bunyips? What are bunyips?' asked Nell.

'Bunyips live in billabongs and eat little girls,' replied Will, laughing.

'No,' said Pot. 'I've never seen one, but sometimes you hear their strange cries in the night. They're supposed to look something like a horse with flippers and horns.'

'They sound a little like the water horses in Scotland,' said Nell.

'All right, we will be careful of bunyips,' replied Charlotte with a laugh, as she gathered up a pile of dishes and cloths.

'And snakes!' added Nell.

The girls wandered downstream to another pool out of sight of the boys. Here they looked around cautiously, then started stripping off their hats, gloves, boots, stockings, petticoats and riding habits and draping them neatly on a mossy log.

Once they were down to their white chemises and drawers, they leapt into the water, shrieking with the sudden cold. Charlotte and Nell splashed and played and swam. A flock of pink-and-grey galahs were frightened by the noise and swooped away, shrieking loudly.

'What a beautiful day for a bathe,' Nell cried.

'I like taking my bath in the creek, out in the open air,' agreed Charlotte, splashing her face with a handful of water. 'It is so much more enjoyable than sitting in the tiny hip bath in the house.'

'We would never have *dreamt* of swimming in the burns or lochs at Dungorm,' said Nell, rolling over.

'For one thing, it was far too *cold* in Scotland,' Charlotte added. 'And for another, it simply would not *do*.'

Nell laughed and sank her face under the water.

At Rosedale, baths were often taken in the creek, as it was so much work to heat and lug so much water into the house. Annie alone preferred her baths hot and indoors.

There was a deep billabong a few minutes walk from the house which was lovely for swimming, especially on warm days. The household had a special signal, which was a cloth draped over a branch to warn others that someone was bathing there and required privacy.

The men and boys often finished a hard day's work by swimming together down at the creek, and Annie had suggested that the girls might like to try it too. Since then Charlotte and Nell had enjoyed bathing together regularly.

After their bathe, Charlotte and Nell rubbed themselves dry with the cloths, changed into fresh underclothes and dressed themselves once more, helping each other to tidy their unruly hair.

Nell sang as they strolled back to meet the boys.

'Sophie, please come and play with me,' called Jess, splashing Sophie with water. 'It's lovely in the water.'

Sophie was lying in the sun on her towel down by the pool in the apartment complex.

'Don't splash,' retorted Sophie, closing her eyes and turning away.

Jess retaliated by doing a bomb-dive into the pool, drenching Sophie and her towel.

'Jess! Don't be such a pest!' growled Sophie.

Nonnie lay on a banana lounge, reading a book, wearing a dark blue one-piece swimming costume, her face protected by large sunglasses and a huge straw hat. Her arms and legs were tanned a deep brown by the sun.

'Come on, Jess,' Nonnie called. 'If you don't get out now, you will be as wrinkly as a prune, and I think you might have had enough sun for one day. I don't want you going home sunburnt. You need to be careful with your fair Scottish skin.'

'I think my skin has already turned to prunes,' complained Jess, inspecting her fingers and toes.

Reluctantly Jess climbed out of the pool and sat in the shade next to Nonnie.

'I'd like to have Scottish red hair and green eyes,' said Sophie wistfully. 'It would be much more interesting than boring blonde hair and brown eyes.'

Nonnie laughed, pulling one of Sophie's tresses.

'I think you're gorgeous the way you are, both of you – one dark, one fair.'

Sophie flicked the despised hair over her shoulders and smiled.

'I wished I lived in the olden days,' mused Sophie. It would be so much fun, riding around on horseback or buggy, having amazing adventures instead of just going to school.'

Jess nodded in agreement. 'And wearing all those gorgeous clothes.'

'It does sound romantic,' agreed Nonnie. 'But hard work too. The clothes looked pretty but they must have been quite uncomfortable to wear – all those petticoats and corsets. Imagine how hot they must have been in this heat.'

Sophie and Jess glanced down at their swimming costumes and tried to imagine having to wear layers of clothes on even the hottest day.

'There was no electricity, no dishwashers or washing machines,' Nonnie continued. 'Everything had to be done by hand, even milking the cow to have milk in your tea. People really knew what it was to work in those days – unless you were wealthy and could afford servants.

'Imagine life if you were a girl from a poor family and had to earn your living as a serving maid. There weren't many options for girls to earn a living even when *I* was growing up. All the opportunities were aimed at giving the boys the best education, as they would be the breadwinners.'

Sophie wrinkled her nose, thinking of her own father, who could not earn a living at the moment. It was lucky her mum was working, or they would be much worse off. She felt the familiar ache of a headache coming on and rubbed her forehead gingerly.

'That's not very fair,' complained Jessica.

'I think you girls are very lucky growing up now,' declared Nonnie. 'You can do or be anything in life that you choose. The world is your oyster!'

Nonnie kissed each girl on top of her head, then picked up her book and began to read.

Sophie lay down on her towel, stretching her tense shoulders and concentrating on pushing her headache away. Her hand slipped inside her bag, where she had hidden Eliza's locket.

With the locket clutched loosely in her hand, Sophie gradually dozed, lulled by the monotonous sound of cicadas tik-tik-tikking in the trees and the lazy heat of the summer day.

20

Ambush

'Charlotte,' called Annie. 'Charlotte.'

Charlotte came running in from the garden, carrying a posy of freshly cut roses for the table.

'Charlotte, I have just received a letter from Mr Thompson, our lawyer,' announced Annie, waving the note. 'Edward wrote to him some weeks ago enquiring about the legal situation with your uncle and Dungorm estate. Mr Thompson says he will be in Dalesford tomorrow and is free to see us. Would you like me to organise a meeting?'

Charlotte thought for a moment, conflicting emotions running through her mind: grief, homesickness, betrayal and confusion.

'Yes, please, Annie.'

Annie reached for a pen, dipped it in the ink pot and started to write the reply.

'Unfortunately Edward will not be able to come with us,' sighed Annie. 'He is so busy with the shearing. We will just have to go by ourselves. I think you should bring any papers you have, or anything you think will help clarify the situation.'

Charlotte thought of her box of treasures. She did not have any papers, just her journal and Papa's book of poetry, but she would take them anyway.

When Sophie returned to Rosedale the next afternoon, Pot had harnessed the pair of bay draught horses and hitched them to the buggy. Another pony was standing already saddled.

As suggested by Annie, Charlotte and Nell wore their dark riding habits, but carried their best white dresses safely packed in a bag. Charlotte also carried her oak box carved with the figure of a stag outlined against the rising full moon. As always, Charlotte wore her mother's locket tucked inside her collar.

'Thank you, Pot,' said Annie, climbing up onto the buggy seat and taking the reins. 'Put the bag in the back, girls, and climb up.'

The girls scrambled up, took a seat on either side of Annie and stowed their bag in the back. Charlotte sat carefully nursing her precious treasure box in her lap.

'Giddy-up, boys,' called Annie, cracking the whip and shaking the reins. Sophie quickly zoomed onto the back of the buggy and made herself comfortable next to the bag of dresses.

It was a beautiful afternoon. The horses trotted down the valley, with Pot riding behind on one of the station ponies.

The vehicle lurched and bumped over the wheel ruts, blowing up dust, past a couple of the shepherds herding their flocks of sheep.

After about an hour, Annie steered the buggy off the track and pulled up near some trees.

'Pot, could you please mind the horses?' asked Annie. 'Come on girls, bring the bags. We need to make ourselves look presentable.'

Charlotte and Nell smiled at each other. They certainly were in no fit state to go to a meeting with a lawyer in town. Their hair was knotty and wind-blown under their bonnets. Nell had a streak of dirt on her face and their riding habits and boots were dusty.

Sophie mischievously tweaked one of Nell's tangled curls. Nell smoothed it back with her fingers.

Annie led the way down to the rivulet. She took the three dresses out of the bag, shook them carefully and draped them over a branch. Next she pulled out cloths, ribbons, a comb, a hairbrush and a small looking glass. Charlotte carried her oak box with her and carefully placed it on a rock.

The three of them washed their faces, hands and necks in the rivulet, then Annie tidied all their hair with the comb and brush. Sophie fingered Annie's fine silk dress draped over the branch, admiring its delicate lace and pretty ribbons.

The girls changed from their dusty dresses into fresh white gowns tied with new blue ribbons. They smiled at each other, enjoying the transformation in that incongruous setting.

Annie slipped on her own gown, fastening her best gold-and-ruby brooch at the throat. Charlotte helped her with the tiny buttons at the back of her gown.

'We look like we are going visiting in Edinburgh, not

gallivanting around the bush in a buggy,' joked Charlotte, holding her skirts and executing a deep curtsey.

'You both look gorgeous,' commented Annie.

The three immaculately dressed ladies climbed back into the buggy and sedately trotted the last two miles to Dalesford. The girls had not visited the local town before, so were intrigued to see the people bustling about their business, dogs running in the dusty street and barefoot children playing.

Annie pulled up outside one of the few brick buildings. Pot dismounted and tethered first his horse, then the draught horses, to the hitching post in the street. Pot stayed outside, sitting in the shade and watching the horses and buggy, while Annie led the girls inside.

They were shown into the lawyer's large office. A tall man wearing a three-piece suit rose and bowed politely as they entered.

'Good afternoon, Mr Thompson,' said Annie.

'Good afternoon, Mrs McLaughlin,' Mr Thompson said. 'Good afternoon, Miss Charlotte, Miss Eleanor. Please take a seat.'

Annie sat down on the middle chair, while Nell and Charlotte sat on either side of her, Charlotte clutching her oak box on her lap. Sophie floated over near the window.

'I have read the letter that Mr McLaughlin wrote to me, and also a letter which your uncle, Roderick Mackenzie, sent to Mr McLaughlin outlining his plans for your future,' began Mr Thompson, resuming his own seat behind the large desk.

Mr Thompson picked up the pages in front of him and flicked through them. Sophie peeked over his shoulder, reading the pages.

'I will outline the situation to you as simply as I can,' promised Mr Thompson.

'According to Scottish inheritance laws, the estate of Dungorm automatically passes to the closest male relative, which in this case is your uncle, Roderick Mackenzie, and in time it will pass to his son. If your brother Alexander had survived, the estate would have passed to him.'

Charlotte gasped, as though she had been struck. She had been so sure that the lawyer would say that Dungorm should belong to her and Nell. Her mind reeled in confusion.

'But my father's will – I saw Uncle Roderick burn it,' blurted Charlotte, clutching the box tighter.

'Are you sure it was a will? Did you read it?' asked Mr Thompson.

'Nooo,' admitted Charlotte. 'But it looked official and important.'

'It may have been a contract, a business letter or anything at all. However, whether it was a will or not makes very little difference,' continued Mr Thompson.

'A heritable estate such as Dungorm, which has been in the Mackenzie family for generations, must be inherited by the closest male relative, usually the eldest son.

'If a man, such as your father, dies without a son, the law says the estate will go to his younger brother. It is called the law of primogeniture. If your father had bought the estate himself, he could have left it to whomever he chose.'

Mr Thompson paused to let this information sink in. Nell sighed and slumped forward. Charlotte felt numb with shock and disappointment. Annie took first Nell's then Charlotte's hand and squeezed them gently.

'Well, now we know the true situation, girls,' comforted Annie.

'However, it is not all bad news, Miss Charlotte. This law relates to the actual heritable estate, but there is also your father's moveable property: all the furniture, books, jewellery and household effects.

'I will not go into all the legal terminology, but what it means is that by law, the bairns – that is you and Nell – each receive one quarter of your parents' goods and investments; the remaining half goes to your uncle.'

Nell looked at Charlotte, confused.

Mr Thompson picked up one of the letters, which was written in Uncle Roderick's flourishing handwriting. Sophie had trouble reading the swirly letters.

'Your uncle has indicated in this letter that he has sold your share of the jewellery, goods and furniture. A portion has been set aside to pay for your education and living expenses here in Australia until you grow up; the remaining money has been invested in trust until you come of age.

'This means that when you are twenty-one, you will both be wealthy young women.'

Annie nodded to Charlotte, confirming the news. Sophie started in surprise.

'But what if we did not want our goods sold?' cried Charlotte, her hands clenched around her box. 'What if we wanted to keep them? What do we want with money when we have nothing left of our parents? What of my mother's jewellery? I suppose *he* sold it to Aunt *Arabella* for a pittance. How can he do this to us?'

Nell looked upset and hung her head, twisting her hands. Mr Thompson looked grave and played with his pen.

'Roderick Mackenzie is your guardian and executor of your father's estate. He can manage your inheritance however he sees fit. I am afraid neither you nor Miss Eleanor has any say in the matter.'

Charlotte slumped, all the fight gone from her. It was final. Dungorm was gone. It was all gone.

Mr Thompson picked up the letter, weighing it in his hands, making a decision.

'There is one more thing,' added Mr Thompson. 'Your uncle mentioned the possibility that one day you, Charlotte, might return to Dungorm.'

Charlotte's pulse quickened and she sat up straight, her fingers playing with the gold locket around her neck. Perhaps there was still hope after all?

'Me? But not Nell?'

'Your uncle mentioned the possibility that when you are older you might marry your cousin, Roddy Mackenzie, and return to Dungorm as his wife.'

Charlotte thought with disgust of her horrible, bullying cousin, with his sly pinches and cruel taunts.

'Never,' insisted Charlotte, shivering violently.

'What a dreadful idea, Charlotte,' cried Nell. 'As if you ever could.'

The shock and disappointment of the lawyer's news suddenly washed over Charlotte and two huge tears rolled down her face. Annie took a linen handkerchief from her sleeve and handed it to Charlotte, patting her hand.

'There, there, Charlotte,' soothed Annie. 'Please do not cry. Everything will be fine.'

Mr Thompson picked up the letters from the desk and

handed them to Annie, who folded them and put them away in her reticule, with a nod.

'I am sorry, Miss Charlotte,' apologised the lawyer, rising to his feet. 'I know you were hoping for different news. Perhaps we should give you a moment to compose yourself?'

Mr Thompson showed Annie to the door, Nell following. Sophie stayed behind.

'Thank you, Mr Thompson, for your advice,' replied Annie, as they walked across the office. 'We will wait for you in the front room, Charlotte. Come out when you are ready.'

Charlotte sat still, tears rolling down her face. She could hear Annie and Mr Thompson chatting outside. She sat for a moment feeling totally miserable, holding her box. Sophie sat down on the chair vacated by Annie and stroked Charlotte's arm, making her shiver.

Using the gold key, Charlotte unlocked the box and emptied her 'treasures' out onto the desk: the red pebble, the swatch of tartan, the sprig of heather and the poems of Robbie Burns.

Charlotte's mother's gold locket swung free and glinted in the light. Sophie held the identical locket around her own neck.

Charlotte picked at a corner of the violet silk lining and carefully peeled it away from the base. Then she used the reverse end of the gold key – a flat, rounded loop – to slide down between the timber base and the side of the box.

The key levered up the base to reveal a hidden cavity in the bottom of the box. Sophie froze.

Two objects were hidden there: Charlotte's black leather-bound journal and a tightly wrapped wad of cloth. Charlotte unwrapped the cloth to reveal a flash of blue fire and a dazzle of white.

The Star of Serendib, Eliza's wedding ring.

Sophie gasped in surprise and delight. Eliza's ring had not been thrown in the loch or found by Aunt Arabella. It had been hidden in a secret compartment in the oak box all this time.

Charlotte held the cornflower-blue sapphire up then slipped it onto her middle finger. The ring was too loose for her finger and slipped around with its weight.

'The Star of Serendib,' Charlotte murmured to herself. 'I wonder if it is indeed a lucky talisman? It does not seem to have brought us much fortune yet.'

'I think it will, Charlotte,' whispered Sophie in answer.

Charlotte smiled as though she had heard, slipped the ring off, wrapped it and put everything away, locking the box once more. She scrubbed her face with Annie's handkerchief and stood up, her back and shoulders straight, and walked out to join the others.

'Be careful on the way home,' warned Mr Thompson. 'There is a band of bushrangers, Captain Lightning and his gang, that have been making raids on travellers in the district around Dalesford. Last week they killed a native constable while robbing the mail coach.'

'Indeed?' replied Annie, glancing at the girls with concern. 'Surely they will not still be in the district. The police must be looking high and low for them.'

'I believe so,' agreed Mr Thompson. 'Ah, here is Miss Charlotte.'

Mr Thompson showed them into the street, where Pot was waiting with the horses and buggy.

No-one talked on the ten-mile journey home, Pot jogging behind on his shaggy piebald pony. Everyone felt jaded and exhausted after the meeting with the lawyer.

The shadows were long on the ground and the air was chilly. They were still three miles from Rosedale on a lonely stretch of track. A branch cracked. Sophie felt a shiver of apprehension ripple up her spine. She swooped off the buggy to look around.

A horse sprang out from behind a boulder to the left of the track, in the path of the moving buggy, its rider levelling a pistol directly at Charlotte. He had seven pistols and a coiled stockwhip stuck in his belt, a red kerchief knotted around his neck and a felt hat jammed low over his eyes.

'Pull up, in the name of Captain Lightning,' bellowed the rider, his horse prancing.

Annie had no choice but to pull up the horses, her heart pounding.

Another three men emerged from the scrub on either side of the track. One pointed his pistol at Pot and grabbed Pot's pony by the bridle. The other two pointed pistols at Annie.

Nell screamed. Annie glanced around in horror. Charlotte gripped her box protectively, her knuckles white.

Sophie swooped towards the bushranger, hoping to disarm him.

Captain Lightning's horse went crazy as Sophie flew around him; it bucked and reared, its eyes rolling. Captain

Lightning struggled to stay on, fighting the reins, his pistol pointing in the air.

'What is the meaning of this outrage?' demanded Annie. 'How dare you point guns at my family?'

'Hand over your valuables now, or we shoot,' ordered Captain Lightning, bringing his mount under control.

Annie remembered Mr Thompson's warning about the murder of the Aboriginal tracker. She held up her hand in supplication.

'There is no need to shoot anyone,' Annie replied calmly. 'We have very little of value, as you can see.'

'Well, hand it over quickly,' insisted Captain Lightning. 'Jack, tie up the boy and if there's any nonsense, shoot him.'

Pot was dragged off his horse, struggling futilely, and tied to a tree.

Sophie flew to help him. Her transparent fingers struggled with the knots that bound him.

'Do not hurt Pot,' cried Charlotte anxiously.

Annie fumbled inside her reticule; she had only a few small coins there. She was wearing her best jewellery: a heavy gold chain bracelet, a ruby brooch at her throat and a diamond-and-gold ring on her wedding finger.

Annie handed over her coins. Her fingers fumbled as she undid the clasps of her brooch and bracelet. The wedding ring was tight on her finger and she struggled to pull it off.

Charlotte thought of her mother's locket tucked safely inside the collar of her white dress. She longed to touch it for reassurance. More frightening still, she worried about the Star of Serendib, hidden away in her oak box.

'Open that box,' demanded Captain Lightning, pointing with his pistol.

Charlotte obeyed with trembling fingers, unlocking the box and opening the lid. The bushranger picked through the items – the pebble, the heather, the book of poetry. He pocketed the silver elf bolt. Charlotte felt sick with terror. *Will he find the Star of Serendib?*

'Not the elf bolt,' Nell cried, then bit her lip.

Captain Lightning slammed the lid shut. Charlotte took back the box, keeping her eyes downcast, trying not to let her fear show.

'Now, young ladies, take off your gloves, pull up your sleeves and show me your throats,' ordered Captain Lightning.

Nell and Charlotte obeyed silently, Charlotte moving her collar slightly, trying to conceal the locket.

'Aha,' cried the bushranger, spying a glimpse of gold. 'Hand over that necklace at once, young lady.'

Charlotte grasped the locket protectively, her face pale but determined.

'Please, do not steal my locket,' begged Charlotte. 'My mother gave it to me just before she died. She asked me to wear it always.'

'That's a shame, missy,' replied Captain Lightning, holding out his hand. 'But I can't afford to let you keep it. Take it off.'

Charlotte reluctantly took her locket off, fighting back the tears. She did not want these rough bushrangers to see her cry.

Sophie had to do something. If the locket was stolen, would that mean she wouldn't have it in the modern world? Would that mean she couldn't come back to Charlotte's time any more? Perhaps she may not be able to return to her own time, to Nonnie's apartment?

Her fear made her stronger. She zoomed into Captain Lightning, pushing him away. Captain Lightning felt the sensation of a freezing shove on his body and shivered violently. His horse reared.

'Have you no shame?' cried Annie, her face flaming. 'These girls have lost everything: their mother, their father, their home, their land. That locket is the only thing Charlotte has that was her mother's. Take all *my* jewels but show the poor lassie some pity. Let her keep her mother's locket.'

The bushranger paused, guilt chasing greed across his face. 'Take it then,' he snarled.

Charlotte took the locket gratefully, hiding it in her bodice once more.

'Now lads, blindfold that boy and tie him on his pony,' ordered Captain Lightning. 'He's coming with us as a servant.'

'No,' Annie begged. 'Don't take Pot. He's just a boy and has been living with us since he was born. His parents will be distraught.'

'Good,' answered Captain Lightning. 'He'll be well trained. Don't try to follow us if you value his safety.'

Two of the bushrangers untied Pot, blindfolded him and hauled him towards the pony. The other held the horses.

Sophie saw her chance, and moved. She swirled around the horses, slapping the buggy horses on the rump and swishing up under Captain Lightning's horse.

All the horses bucked and reared, causing chaos. Captain Lightning was thrown to the ground, cursing.

The buggy horses bolted, racing for home. Charlotte and Nell clung to the buggy for their very lives. Annie stared back at Pot, then at the two girls beside her. Decision made, she cracked her whip and urged the horses to gallop faster, heading north to Rosedale.

Captain Lightning's horse kicked down on Sophie, knocking her to the ground, striking her with its hooves. She rolled away, curled up in pain, hitting her head. Consciousness faded in a jumble of rearing horses, dust, swearing and the loud crack of a pistol shot.

Sophie's head thundered with pain. She crawled out of bed and limped across the floor, leaving smudges of dust on the cream carpet. In the bathroom, she stripped off her torn nightdress, filthy with brown dust, and threw it in the washing basket.

She turned on the shower as hot as she could bear it. In the mirror she saw dark black bruises on her body in the shape of hooves. Her left shoulder was torn and bleeding.

How could the horse's hooves have hurt me? I was supposed to be an insubstantial ghost in the past. The horse's hooves should have flailed straight through me. Could it be possible I am becoming more substantial in the past than in my own world?

The thought made Sophie feel sick.

Sophie washed her hair and towelled it dry. She found Nonnie's first-aid kit and dabbed some antiseptic and a bandage on the cut shoulder, and some arnica on the bruises. She dressed and went out to the living room.

'Sophie, what have you done to your arm?' asked Jess.

'Oh, I fell,' mumbled Sophie, avoiding Jess's and Nonnie's concerned glances.

Nonnie looked at Sophie sternly.

'Sophie, did you go out anywhere last night?' asked Nonnie suspiciously. 'You weren't sneaking out to meet someone?'

Sophie was shocked, her heart pounding. What should she say? She couldn't possibly tell Nonnie the truth.

'No, Nonnie, of course not,' replied Sophie. 'Why would you think that?'

'There were dirty footprints on the carpet this morning, and you have that bruise on your arm,' said Nonnie, frowning. 'Plus you've been acting very strangely this week – not eating, not talking. You look pale and exhausted, yet you sleep so much . . . I'm really worried about you, Sophie. Do you think you could be anorexic? Is there something else you're doing –'

'No, no,' interrupted Sophie, tears welling up. 'I'm not anorexic. I'm not doing anything wrong. Please, Nonnie, believe me,' she begged. 'I think I might have been sleepwalking and fallen. I dreamt a horse was kicking me, but I *promise* you I did not go out or meet anyone.

'I just can't sleep properly any more. I've been dreaming about Charlotte Mackenzie losing her home and coming to Australia.'

Nonnie was puzzled. The strangest thing was that the dirty footprints led from Sophie's room straight to the bathroom, not from the front door. The apartment was three storeys high, so it would be impossible for Sophie to climb out the window. So how did her feet get dirty?

Jess came up to Sophie and hugged her.

'You're worrying about us losing *our* home, aren't you?' asked Jess. Sophie hugged Jess back and nodded.

Nonnie searched Sophie's face. She did not know what to think.

'I don't know what the future holds for your family, Sophie,' Nonnie said. 'But I do know that fretting like this will not help you, or your parents.'

Sophie remembered Nanny saying to Nell, 'Wha' canna be changed must be endured.'

'I know, Nonnie,' Sophie answered, smiling shakily. 'I'll try not to worry so much.'

21

Search for Pot

It was dark when the horses cantered up the last stretch of track towards Rosedale homestead.

Mr McLaughlin rode to meet them, his face creased with worry.

'Are you all right, Annie?' called Mr McLaughlin. 'I was worried.'

Annie spilled out the news of the attack and Pot's kidnapping. The bell was rung at the homestead to call in all the men. Mr McLaughlin organised the men into teams to search for Pot and the bushrangers. The horses were caught, saddled and bridled, the rifles loaded.

Someone rode to Dalesford to fetch the police. Pot's parents, Billy and Mary, were informed, Mary shrieking with grief.

Annie organised hot soup for the girls and ordered them to huddle in front of the fire, wrapped in blankets. Charlotte and Nell were miserable, worried about Pot and frightened by their experience with the bushrangers.

The search party clattered out of the stable yard into the dark, heading back to where the hold-up had taken place.

Annie, Charlotte and Nell sat in the sitting room too nervous to eat or talk. Charlotte read aloud to take their minds away from the endless waiting. At last, Annie sent them both to bed.

Many hours later, Charlotte and Nell were woken by the sound of bits jingling and saddles creaking. They jumped out of bed, threw shawls over their nightgowns and hurried out to the sitting room, where Annie was still sitting up in her chair.

'It sounds like they are back,' agreed Annie.

A few minutes later, Will, Henry and Mr McLaughlin came into the house, looking exhausted. Mr McLaughlin shook his head despondently in answer to Annie's questioning gaze.

'No sign of them,' Mr McLaughlin said. 'We looked everywhere, but it was too dark to find any tracks. They could've been just under our noses. At last we decided to come home and sleep, so we can make an early start in the morning. Tomorrow we'll take supplies, and Billy might be able to find their tracks.'

Annie stood up, tightening her shawl around her shoulders.

'Sit down, my dears,' urged Annie. 'Charlotte and I will heat you some soup and bread for supper.'

The next morning, the search party set off before dawn, carrying saddlebags of food, blankets and supplies in case they needed to camp out. Charlotte had begged to be allowed to join the search party but had been refused and told to stay home where it was safer.

Charlotte and Nell occupied themselves by feeding the animals: the poultry, the newborn chicks, the lambs, wallabies and the pigs. They read their books and helped Mrs Gregory make marmalade in the kitchen.

The day dragged by slowly. Annie, Charlotte and Nell ate by themselves that evening and there was no sign of the men. Nor the next day or the next.

At the end of the third day, well after sunset, the men finally returned, their weary ponies stumbling, with their heads hung low. Charlotte and Nell rushed out to meet them, hope surging in their hearts.

'No, we didn't find Pot,' admitted Mr McLaughlin. 'Billy discovered their tracks and we followed them for fifty miles. They must've known we were following because they took to the river and we lost them.

'We searched up and downstream but found nothing. At last the horses were tired and we were worried about everything at Rosedale, so we came home.'

Everyone looked worried and disappointed. The men set to work unsaddling the horses and giving them all a good feed. The horses rolled happily in the dust, pleased to be home once more.

Mrs Gregory set to work boiling water for hot baths and preparing a hot meal.

So life continued on much as normal, except everyone missed Pot's cheerful face around the homestead. The police came and questioned the McLaughlins about the robbery, although they seemed more concerned about the loss of Annie's jewels than the loss of Pot.

Two weeks later, at dusk, Charlotte was out picking thyme and marjoram in the garden, when she noticed a small dark figure stumbling up the track. She looked closely. The figure looked familiar.

'Pot!' shrieked Charlotte at the top of her lungs. 'Pot's back.'

Charlotte dropped her handful of herbs and raced down, over the fence and along the track towards Pot. Nell, Annie and Will followed behind, alerted by Charlotte's shouts.

Soon Pot was surrounded by an anxious, happy, boisterous crowd of well-wishers welcoming him home and asking him dozens of questions.

'Are you all right?'

'How did you escape?'

'Did the bushrangers let you go?'

'Did you walk all the way home?'

'How did you find your way back?'

Pot nodded, too tired to talk, but grinned his happy, familiar smile.

'Leave the poor boy alone,' insisted Annie. 'He looks all done in. Come inside, Pot, and we will get you some food, then you can tell us all about it. Will, run and get your father. Charlotte, fetch Mary and Billy too.'

Everyone ran to do Annie's bidding. Soon Pot was seated at the kitchen table, wrapped in a blanket with a big bowl of hot beef stew in front of him, which he stuffed in his mouth hungrily. An eager audience, including the McLaughlins, the Gregorys, Mary and Billy, Charlotte, Nell and Sophie, sat around the kitchen, waiting for him to finish and tell his tale.

At last, after his third serving of stew, Pot pushed away his bowl, which had been wiped clean with bread.

'Do you feel up to telling us, Pot?' asked Annie with concern. 'Or would you rather wait until the morning?'

'I feel much better now,' admitted Pot. 'Is there any pie, Mrs Gregory?'

Mrs Gregory obligingly cut him a huge wedge of apple pie and smothered it in golden cream. Pot wolfed that down, as though he hadn't eaten for a week. At last he finished, with a huge sigh and a rubbing of his bulging stomach.

'The bushrangers took me to their hiding place far to the south,' Pot began. Everyone listened avidly.

'We rode for three days, riding down rivers to hide our tracks. At last we stopped in a valley deep in the bush. The bushrangers untied me and ordered me to hobble and unsaddle the horses.

'We climbed up a cliff to a big cave. There were sacks of food, cooking gear, beds and weapons stored there.

'The captain made me collect wood, build fires, cook meals, wash up, cart water up the hill. They fed me nothing but scraps, and hit me if I was slow. At night I was tied up.'

Annie bristled as she heard about how Pot had been mistreated. She gently patted him on the arm.

'Captain Lightning made sure they always watched me, with a pistol. A few days later, the captain and another bloke went to town for supplies. The others became lazy, drinking rum.

'They sent me to get firewood, but didn't come with me, just watching from the cave.

'I got a big pile of firewood, collecting it till they were more interested in the rum than me. When it was getting dark, I slipped away.

'I walked and ran all night. Once I heard the bushrangers coming after me and hid in a tree till they passed. It was dark and I had a good start, though they had horses.'

Charlotte's heart pounded as she thought of Pot hiding in a tree with the bushrangers in pursuit.

'When the sun rose I hid my tracks, then slept in a hollow log. I walked only at night, until I was far away.

'The cockatoos showed me where to find water and I found grubs and bush fruit to eat. I didn't waste time fishing or hunting, and I couldn't light a fire in case they saw it.'

Mary and Billy nodded proudly, patting Pot on the back.

'For the first four days it was hard, because I didn't know the country or the way home, so I just kept heading north. Then suddenly I felt the spirits of my people. Then it was easy because the spirits guided me home. Seeing the lights of Rosedale homestead was the best sight I've seen in ages.'

Pot stopped talking and gave a great yawn.

'Well done, Pot,' cried Annie. 'Welcome home. I think now you need a good night's sleep.'

Mary and Billy ushered Pot away to their room, murmuring their goodnights. Pot received many pats on the back and hearty congratulations from the family on his way out.

'Extraordinary,' pronounced Mr McLaughlin. 'That boy found his way home with no map or compass, no food or water and no boots. He must have walked more than a hundred miles. It is a miracle he found his way here.'

'*And* he was half starved and beaten,' added Annie. 'Those bushrangers are villains.'

'With Pot's help, the police might have a much better chance of tracking down those bushrangers,' suggested Mr McLaughlin. 'I wonder if Pot can find his way back to the cave as easily as he found his way home?'

A couple of days later, when Pot had rested, another party set off on horseback, made up of Pot, Billy, Mr McLaughlin, stockmen and police constables. They were gone for over a week, but eventually returned happy and triumphant.

They had taken the bushrangers by surprise in their lair. One was captured down by the creek; the others had surrendered after a lengthy gun battle, when they realised they were outnumbered and trapped.

The police had taken the bushrangers into custody and were sending them down to Easthaven to stand trial. The police felt sure the bushrangers would be hanged for their crimes.

Mr McLaughlin returned with Pot's missing pony, the silver elf bolt and Annie's jewellery.

'Yes, but can you *please* get up now?' Jess insisted. 'Nonnie wants to do some cooking with us today. She wants us to pick oranges and lemons from the trees down in the courtyard, to make marmalade, and we are going to make scones.'

'Okay. Okay. I'll be right out.'

Sophie felt pleased. She loved cooking with Nonnie. They had the time to make things properly and cook them from scratch. Mum always seemed to be too busy these days, with Will and work, to cook anything except mince, mince and more mince.

Sophie and Jess went down into the garden of the apartment and picked four oranges and two lemons from the trees.

'Wonderful, girls,' said Nonnie with a smile, handing over a juicer. 'Let's start by juicing the lemons. Be careful to save all the seeds because we need them to make the pectin.'

Sophie and Jess squeezed the juice out of the halved lemons, setting aside the lemon seeds.

Nonnie carefully peeled the skins off the oranges with a sharp knife and scraped the white pith off the orange flesh. Jess chopped the oranges, while Sophie thinly sliced the peel. Nonnie showed Jess how to pop the lemon seeds, pith and chopped lemon peel into a clean stocking.

'We cook the bag in with the fruit to make pectin, which makes the jelly set,' Nonnie explained. 'This is how my mother taught me to make marmalade, and her mother taught her before that.'

'All the way back to Charlotte Mackenzie?' asked Sophie quickly.

'Probably,' laughed Nonnie, scraping all the chopped orange fruit and sliced peel into a saucepan. 'Now we add four cups of water and cook it all up with the bag of pith and seeds.'

The orange mixture simmered for fifty minutes. Nonnie, Sophie and Jess cleaned up the mess, then placed the clean jars in the oven to heat.

'You girls add the sugar, while I stir.'

Four cups of sugar were added to the mix while it was brought to the boil.

'We have to keep stirring or the sugar will burn,' warned Nonnie, stirring vigorously. 'Now let's taste it. If it's too sweet we add more lemon juice, if it's too bitter, it needs more sugar.'

The girls tasted the warm mixture and decided it needed a touch more sugar. When Nonnie judged the mixture was ready, she turned off the heat and left it to cool down.

'Now we test how our mixture is setting,' explained Nonnie. She tipped a teaspoon of the hot fruit mixture onto a cold saucer and placed it in the fridge. A few moments later, she tested the fruit, which was now firm like a jelly.

'Perfect,' pronounced Nonnie. She scooped the seed-and-pith bag out of the mixture and squeezed it between two teaspoons to extract all of the pectin.

The warm marmalade was finally poured into hot sterilised jars and left to cool.

'And there we have it – the finest Scotch marmalade, as made by the Mackenzie women for generations!' announced Nonnie with pleasure.

'It looks beautiful,' agreed Sophie, feeling a sense of pride in the row of jars, glowing bright orange in the sunlight.

'Can we have it on our toast tomorrow morning, Nonnie?' asked Jessica.

'Of course, and there should be plenty of jars left for you to take home to your mama,' Nonnie assured her. 'Now, do you have any cooking energy left for making scones, or should we go out?'

'Scones. Scones,' cried Jess enthusiastically.

'Scones it is, then.'

22

Mustering

In November, Mr McLaughlin invited Charlotte and Nell to come on their first cattle muster. The cattle were to be brought in from the scrub on the ridges and herded down to the stockyards.

'Stay out of the way of the stock hands and be very careful,' warned Mr McLaughlin. 'The horns of those wild young bulls are deadly.'

'It's so much fun,' cried Will. 'Sometimes the bulls charge right at your horse, and you have to be mighty fast to get out of their way. They don't like the sound of the stockwhip though, and that frightens them back into line.'

The next morning everyone woke before dawn. Charlotte and Nell dressed in their riding habits, boots, gloves and shady straw hats. Breakfast was eaten quickly and quietly, everyone too sleepy to chat. The horses were already in the yards, so were easily caught and saddled.

Nell and Charlotte saddled their ponies themselves,

with a little help from Mr McLaughlin to tighten the girths. Then they rode off through the cool half-light before dawn. The big golden dogs, Nicky and Tiger, loped along beside the horses, watching for emus or kangaroos to chase.

Sophie flew behind the horses, excited to be part of the early-morning expedition. She saw Charlotte riding side-saddle on her black pony and felt an overwhelming desire to ride a horse too, instead of skimming above the ground.

Sophie hovered close, causing the horse to shy and cavort. Sophie took a deep breath and slid onto the horse's back, behind Charlotte, holding on around her waist. Sophie rode astride, but she was weightless, so the horse cavorted once more then settled back into her usual stride, her ears flicking back and forward.

Charlotte settled the horse with a gentle stroke on her neck.

'Whoa. Easy does it, girl. Are you shying at your own shadow?'

On their left, the eastern horizon glimmered with a pearl-escent glow of pale pinks and violets, gradually washing the hills and valleys with a rosy stain. A flock of pink-and-grey galahs swooped through the sky, shrieking merrily.

'Rosedale looks so beautiful in the dawn light,' murmured Nell to Charlotte.

'It always looks gorgeous on horseback,' added Charlotte. 'I think I am even getting used to the heat.'

The red sun was now over the horizon, filling the valley with light.

'How about an early-morning gallop, girls?' asked Mr McLaughlin.

'Race you all to the creek,' yelled Will.

The valley stretched out before them, flat and cleared. The horses sensed the coming gallop and pawed the ground, their ears flickering in anticipation.

'Ready. Set. Go,' bellowed Will, kicking his heels into his horse's sides. The girls rode side-saddle so had to use a crop, as well as their left heel, to encourage their mounts to canter.

All the horses leapt forward, galloping across the valley. Charlotte's heart sang, her hair whipping across her face and the skirts of her riding habit flapping. Sophie sat right behind her, holding Charlotte tightly around the waist. Sophie's hair flew and her nightgown billowed in the breeze.

Both Charlotte and Sophie felt as one. It was one of the best feelings they could imagine, as if they were flying across the earth. A log appeared under Charlotte's horse's hooves and she flew over it, hardly changing her stride.

Everyone pulled up at the creek, elated by their ride.

'I won,' cried Will triumphantly.

'That is because you started before anyone else,' argued Charlotte, her cheeks flushed and her eyes sparkling with excitement. 'You cheated!'

'I had to, to beat Blackie,' Will admitted with a laugh. 'She flies like the wind.'

'It must be one of the best feelings in the world to gallop across an open valley,' said Charlotte with a smile.

'I love it,' agreed Nell, patting her own pony's neck.

The riders rode on in companionable silence, until Henry spied a small herd of cattle drinking at the waterhole.

'Now stay behind me, girls,' warned Mr McLaughlin. 'Henry and Will, you come in from the left, and Billy and Pot from the right.'

The cattle saw the men and horses and spooked, fleeing for the safety of the scrub. The men urged their horses into a canter to chase them and head them off, cracking their stockwhips as they rode. Tiger and Nicky jumped to work, racing after the cattle, barking loudly and nipping at their heels, harrying the cattle into a tight mob.

Charlotte and Nell cantered after, watching how the men, horses and dogs worked together to control the herd and move them where they wanted them to go. Sophie clung on tightly to Charlotte's waist, wondering if it would hurt if she fell off.

'Yah. Yah,' shouted Charlotte, urging Blackie into a gallop as a young steer made a break from the herd.

She was the closest so gave chase, dodging and wheeling through the trees. In a few moments, Charlotte had neatly gained on the steer and cut him off, heading him back to the mob.

'Well done, Charlotte,' yelled Henry in approval. 'That's how it is done.'

Charlotte flushed with pleasure. When the mob of cattle was subdued, the riders dropped to a walk, moving the cattle quietly through the scrub.

Every now and then another small herd would be discovered and rounded up into the main herd with much cracking of whips, barking, shouting and kicking up of dust.

At one waterhole, they found a calf bogged to its belly in the soft mud around the edge, struggling weakly to escape. Its mother mooed helplessly on the creek bank, trotting back and forth in anxiety.

'Down you go, lads,' called Mr McLaughlin. 'Bring those ropes, Henry.'

The ropes were carefully tied around the calf's body, behind the front legs, then fastened to the pommel of Mr McLaughlin's horse. Henry, Pot and Will jumped in the waterhole to push the struggling calf free, getting covered in slimy mud, while Billy hauled from the front.

Mr McLaughlin urged his horse forward to pull the rope, tied to the calf.

'Steady, boy,' ordered Mr McLaughlin. 'Easy does it, boys. Now heave.'

The mud sucked hungrily around the legs of the calf, refusing to yield its prey. The calf bellowed and its mother mooed in distress. The boys floundered and heaved. The horse strained and pulled, then with a loud sucking, gurgling noise, the calf was dragged free onto the bank.

The mother charged towards the calf, licking it lovingly. The calf struggled up the bank on trembling legs and collapsed next to its mother, suckling frantically.

'Hurray,' cried Nell.

'You did it,' shrieked Charlotte. 'Well done.'

The boys climbed out of the quagmire, half sinking in the deep mud. They splashed cleaner water over themselves to try to wash away the worst of the mud.

Charlotte and Nell slithered off their ponies and carried pannikins of water to wash the mud off the distressed calf, transferring most of the mud to themselves.

When the herd had been mustered, the stockmen turned the mob for home. The cattle walked quietly now in the afternoon heat, swarms of flies buzzing around the cattle, horses and riders.

Near the homestead, the cattle were herded into the narrow entrance to the stockyards. They jostled and broke away, jumping on each other's backs in panic, charging and tossing with their horns. The men rode tightly around the herd, cracking the stockwhips constantly.

'Stay right away, girls,' warned Mr McLaughlin. 'Some of those steers will cause trouble going into the yards. Watch from outside.'

Sophie swung with the girls, climbing on the stockyard fence.

When all the cattle were safely in the yards, Mr McLaughlin, Henry and Will came to lean on the fence rails, beside the girls.

'Well, a good day's work, thanks everyone,' said Mr McLaughlin, pushing his hat back and mopping his sweaty, filthy brow with a handkerchief. 'What did you think of your first muster, girls?'

Charlotte and Nell glanced at each other, grinning. They were both splattered with mud, covered from head to toe in dust and bone tired.

What would Nanny think if she could see us now? thought Charlotte. *She would be horrified.*

'I loved it,' replied Nell with shining eyes.

23

Inferno

Sophie swooped above the homestead, brushing the blue-green gum-tree tops with her bare feet. Down below she could see the horses grazing, Edgar and Ernestina the emus pecking for grain, and a flock of woolly-backed sheep clustered in the shade of the eucalypt trees.

Sophie loved the sensation of flying. It made her feel so free. She zoomed around the sheep, scattering and chasing the lambs. A strong breeze, blowing from the west, gusted and buffeted Sophie as she floated on the air currents; it whipped the tops of the gum trees and flattened the grass in the paddocks.

A spark wafted past her, glowing red hot as it fell.

Sophie breathed deeply. She could smell something different on the air today, something smoky. She banked and dived, pirouetting as she fell, then turned and headed straight into the wind.

It took a moment for Sophie to recognise what was in

front of her. A thick black cloud of smoke blanketed the western horizon, billowing and boiling.

Bushfire, thought Sophie, her mind reeling in panic. *A bushfire racing straight down the valley, towards the homestead. I must warn Charlotte and Nell!*

Charlotte and Nell were inside in the dining room, working on their lessons.

'It is so *hot*,' complained Nell, pushing back the damp curls from her forehead. 'I feel exhausted.'

'It is like an oven in here, and my brain does not work,' moaned Charlotte, throwing down her pen. 'I would love a swim.'

Sophie burst through the dining room door. How could she warn the girls?

Emotion, such as grief, anger or fear, made her stronger in the past world. Sophie concentrated as hard as she could, summoning up her fear, concentrating on making herself visible. She could feel her body thickening and becoming heavier.

'Charlotte, Charlotte,' cried Nell, grabbing Charlotte's hand. 'Look!'

Charlotte stared. A shimmery figure wearing a white gown and with bare feet and tangled fair hair stood next to the table. The figure wavered and faded, then grew sharper.

'Quick, there's a fire coming, a bushfire,' called Sophie urgently. 'You must hurry. It's coming fast.'

Charlotte and Nell leapt to their feet, all lethargy forgotten. 'It's our guardian angel,' blurted Charlotte. 'Have you come to help us again?'

'Come with me,' called Sophie, leading the way out onto

the verandah. Sophie went straight through the French doors; Charlotte had to open the doors so she and Nell could follow.

Sophie flew around to the back of the house, facing west, the girls running behind her.

Down the valley, from the thick bush on the hillsides, came a high wall of roiling, surging black smoke, fanned by the wind.

Charlotte and Nell felt their stomachs knot. They had never experienced an Australian bushfire, but had heard stories of the deadly fires that swept the countryside, killing and destroying everything in their paths.

'Annie, Annie,' screamed Charlotte.

Annie came running from the dairy, where she had been churning butter. Sophie could not maintain her visible form for very long, and faded away to invisibility.

'Annie, look,' cried Nell, pointing to the horizon. 'A bushfire.'

Annie stared in horror.

'Oh my goodness, it's heading straight towards the homestead. Why is Edward always away when these things happen? There's only the three of us here.'

Mr McLaughlin, Henry and Will were near the outlying boundary of the property with the stock hands mustering sheep. Mr and Mrs Gregory had driven the wagon into town with Pot to fetch supplies.

Annie thought quickly, sketching out a plan in her mind.

'We need to change into something more practical for fighting fires,' Annie decided, indicating their pale long skirts. 'We can borrow shirts and trousers from the boys.'

Annie, Charlotte and Nell emerged a few minutes later

wearing trousers and shirts, with elastic-sided boots, their long hair caught up under hats. Charlotte thought it felt so strange to move without the usual hot weight of her full petticoats and skirts, almost as if she was just walking around in her underwear.

She was glad there was no-one else to see her.

'Now we need to gather up all the buckets and sacks we can find,' Annie ordered. 'Look in the barn, while I search the kitchen.'

'Bring the buckets over here by the pump,' cried Annie. 'Throw the sacks in to soak in the copper. Now, Nell, you pump, while we carry buckets.'

The buckets were filled with water from the pump in the laundry, and splashed over the walls and roof of the homestead and outbuildings to soak the dry timber. Everything was flammable: the slab walls, the wooden roof shingles, the support posts and fencing.

Charlotte and Annie ran back and forth, ferrying the buckets from the pump to the homestead. The drenched hessian sacks were draped over the outside walls and roughly nailed into place.

Charlotte scrambled up on the roof and Annie passed buckets up to her, to slosh over the roof and walls.

They worked as fast as they could. Every now and again, they glanced up to see the big black cloud moving ever closer and closer. The light had grown dim and red and menacing, as smoke obscured most of the sky.

The horses in the paddock were whinnying frantically, galloping up and down the fence line, pawing the ground and snorting in fear.

The pet wallabies and emus, sensing the danger,

wriggled through the fence and bounded for the creek.

Nicky the dog paced up and down nervously, looking out towards the encroaching fire and whining nervously.

'All right, that should do it,' announced Annie. 'Now we need to catch one of the horses and hitch it to the water cart.'

Charlotte, Nell and Annie took quite some time to catch one of the frightened horses and hitch it to the old water cart, which was always kept filled and ready near the barn.

'Come on, Blackie, steady girl,' clucked Annie calmly, as she manoeuvred the water cart over to the paddock.

Together Annie and the girls tore down armfuls of green leafy branches to use as fire beaters.

'Now we need to burn a firebreak,' ordered Annie. 'Charlotte, start some flames halfway across the paddock and we will extinguish them when they have burnt right across the grass.'

Everyone ran to take their positions. The wind whipped up the flames and sent them racing through the dried grass. Sophie floated between Charlotte and the fire as though she could shield her with her filmy presence.

Annie swung the canvas hose from the water cart to control the blaze, while Nell and Charlotte beat the flames with the leafy branches to douse the flames.

It was difficult to judge the fire, to let it blaze through large areas of grass without letting it get out of control and endanger the homestead. Whenever the fire did race away out of control, Annie and Nell would pursue it, swirling the hose and beating the ground.

Now the flames of the real bushfire were clearly visible, leaping and raging forty or fifty feet into the air. The scrub and bush on the mountain behind was well alight, huge gum trees burning like gigantic flaming brands. The wind gusted fireballs of burning fuel through the air, to land in fresh patches of bush and start new infernos.

Charlotte and Nell could feel the heat in the air scorching their eyeballs, their throats, their noses, until each breath felt ragged and harsh. The baking earth seared the soles of their boots and blistered their gloved hands.

There was now a wide swathe of blackened earth covering much of the paddock. Charlotte and Nell drove the horse and water cart down to the river to refill it, over and over again. Their arms ached with lugging heavy buckets, but fear and adrenaline drove them on. They drove the cart back and parked it close to the homestead once more.

The fire had reached the edge of the bush, which was now a solid wall of fire from the earth to the sky. Swirling leaves and flying coals landed in the grass at the distant edge of the paddock, starting dozens of spot fires, which spread and joined, becoming a sea of fire. The red tide was coming straight towards them.

'We cannot do much more here,' decided Annie, wiping her black, perspiring face. 'We have a good, wide firebreak so we just have to pray it works. We should pull back to the outbuildings now.'

'What about the horses?' begged Charlotte, as she watched the herd of horses plunging and rearing in terror.

'Let the horses out,' ordered Annie. 'The horses will escape the fire if they have enough room to run. They will find shelter in the creek or work their way around behind the fire to a burnt-out patch.'

Charlotte raced to open the gate to the pastures beyond. Sophie flew behind the horses, steering them out towards freedom. Nell and Annie stamped out a new spot fire, then gathered up their buckets and sacks and retreated to the stable yard.

The hens were locked in the henhouse, which had been thoroughly doused in water, and Sophie herded the pigs and pet lambs into the barn. The cows had already been let out after the morning's milking and had taken to the distant hills.

The smoke was thick and acrid all around them, making it hard to breathe. Nell fetched a pile of cloths soaked in water, which they all wrapped around their faces, covering their mouths and noses.

No-one knew how long they had been fighting the fire. The morning had seemed interminable. The fire reached the firebreak. Everyone held their breath, wondering if it would work. For a few moments the firebreak seemed to be working. The fire paused, licking along the boundary of blackened earth, but not advancing any further.

The wind behind howled and moaned in frustration, then hurled a hundred sparks across the void. Some fell harmlessly on the burnt-out soil, but others were flung further and fell on fresh fuel. All eyes were peeled, everyone ready to race to each new spot fire and douse it with beating branches and stamping boots.

For a while they seemed to be winning the battle. Then a large patch of tinder caught alight, burning and spreading before anyone could reach it. The stout timber logs of the stockyard caught fire, spreading to the paddock fences. The fire skipped across the stable yard and licked the walls of the dairy.

'Fall back,' shouted Annie, running with an empty bucket in each hand. Buckets of water were sloshed on the walls of the dairy, dampening but not dousing the flames.

The fire took hold and roared through the timber walls of the dairy, jumping to the pigsty and racing to the chicken house.

'It has taken hold,' cried Annie despairingly. 'I want you both to go inside the house. It's too dangerous out here. I will keep fighting with the hose.'

'No, Annie,' argued Charlotte, dashing another bucket of water on the flames. 'You need us out here to help, or we could lose the house altogether.'

Annie paused, torn.

'No, Annie, please, we want to help,' begged Nell. 'It would be more frightening in the house by ourselves. Please let us stay.'

Another surge of flame silenced the argument. It was futile wasting breath on arguing when there was so much to lose. The threat to the house gave them all renewed vigour, despite aching arms, stumbling legs and raw throats. The fire was so close to the barn and the animals inside, and to the house, with everything they possessed inside.

Nell ran to hurl water over the flaming beams of the dairy. The upright posts were alight, the seasoned timber roaring. There was a sickening crunch as the support beam cracked under the weight of the roof above.

In slow motion, Charlotte saw the roof begin to fall with Nell crouched underneath.

'Run, Nell,' screamed Charlotte, racing towards her sister. Nell looked up and stumbled backwards.

Sophie swooped, zooming through the air, and pushed. Nell fell, hurtling into the dust, Sophie clutched around her. The roof collapsed, the burning beam and debris only inches from Sophie and Nell. Sophie felt winded and bruised, and her wrist stung where she had been burnt, but she had saved Nell.

'Are you all right, Nell?' screamed Charlotte, racing to help Nell to her feet.

'Yes, I am fine,' Nell said shakily, dusting off her trousers. 'Come on, pass me my bucket. We need more water.'

'Girls, that's enough,' insisted Annie. 'Nell could have been killed. Your lives are more important than mere possessions. We should let the animals out of the barn to take their chances and we will go and lie in the creek. If the men were here we would have a better chance.'

Where's our guardian angel now? thought Charlotte desperately. *Mama, Papa, don't let us lose everything now.*

Sophie felt the despair eroding Charlotte's strength.

'Don't give up now, Charlotte,' whispered Sophie. 'Don't let the fire win.'

Sophie ran her chilly fingers across Charlotte's brow and down her arm, cooling her and calming her, helping her to think.

'No, Annie,' said Nell, holding her head high. 'We have already lost one home. I could not bear to lose another.'

Charlotte took a deep breath, straightened her shoulders and threw another bucket of water on the blaze, then another, swamping a patch of flames.

Nell and Annie worked beside her with superhuman strength, hurling bucket after bucket. At last, the fire in the chicken house was vanquished.

'We are winning,' shouted Charlotte with exhilaration. 'We can save the house.'

Charlotte suddenly noticed a change. She felt something lift and stir an escaped curl at the back of her neck. There was a soft breeze blowing, cooling the slick of perspiration on her neck. It took Charlotte a moment to notice its significance.

'The wind has dropped,' called Annie in excitement. 'The breeze has swung around to the east.'

It took a few minutes for the change to affect the fire, but gradually the flames dropped, pushed back onto the burnt-out ground, away from the fresh timber.

The three firefighters ran forward once more, dousing the flames, hurling buckets of water and stamping with the sacks. Sophie urged and cheered them on. At last the outbuildings were safe and the grass fire in the paddock had burnt out, leaving a desert plain of black ash and soot.

Annie, Charlotte, Nell and Sophie stood staring at the desolation, their buckets and sacks dropped heedlessly. The telltale black scorch marks came within just a few feet of the homestead.

'Look,' called Nell, pointing. 'Look at Mala.'

Mala the koala was curled up in the crook of her eucalyptus tree, fast asleep.

'I think she slept through the whole thing,' giggled Charlotte. 'Do you think she would sleep even if her very own tree was alight?'

When a frantic Edward, Will and Henry galloped into the stable yard, followed by a group of mounted stockmen, they found the homestead transformed by an eerie silence.

In the kitchen they found three exhausted, blackened

bodies huddled around the table. The faces were so charcoaled and smudged that it was almost impossible to recognise anyone except for Nicky the dog, who was now piebald. Sophie felt exhausted and drained.

'Annie? Charlotte and Nell? Is that you?' wondered Mr McLaughlin. 'Well, bless me, Annie, are you wearing my trousers and boots? And look, the wee lassies are wearing Will's by the look of it.'

'No, they are not yours, they are Henry's, but I don't think he will be wearing them again,' explained Annie with a weary smile.

'Oh, you clever, brave darlings,' exclaimed Mr McLaughlin. 'You saved the homestead and the outbuildings all by yourselves. I was praying all the way back that you would still be alive. I was sure the house would be gone and I'd find you all half cooked in the creek.'

'The creek,' sighed Charlotte. 'What a wonderful idea. I need a swim.'

Everyone laughed, bubbling with relief and joy.

Charlotte and Nell stumbled down to the billabong, carrying cloths, soap and fresh clothes. They stripped off their filthy shirts and trousers so they were down to their underwear, and stepped gingerly into the pool. The water was warm after the hot day, and lapped around their tired bodies. Sophie splashed in beside them in her long white nightgown.

Charlotte lay back in the shallows, her hair floating under the water. The sun dropped in the west, bathing the hilltops in red-gold fire and staining the horizon with rose and crimson.

A flock of cockatoos swooped down to drink at the billabong, their white bodies and bright yellow crests flashing through the sky. A wallaby paused and watched them curiously, then hopped away into the scrub.

Charlotte and Nell lay quietly, not talking, just soaking up the beauty and peace. At last the sun sank below the horizon, firing the sky with even more brilliant hues.

Charlotte felt a warm sense of contentment steal over her. There was hardship and cruelty here in this harsh land. There were dangers and adversity. But there was also great beauty and love and friendship.

'Come on, Nell,' called Charlotte eventually. 'Let's go home.'

The sound of the phone ringing shrilly woke Sophie. The phone kept ringing, so Sophie jumped out of bed and padded out into the hallway.

''Lo?' she muttered groggily, rubbing her eyes.

'Hello, is that you, Sophie?' It was the familiar voice of her father.

'Hi, Dad,' Sophie replied warily, wondering why her father was calling.

'Hi, sweetheart. I just wondered how you're feeling. Mum was worried you hadn't been feeling well. That perhaps you'd been worrying about everything.'

Sophie paused, cradling the gold locket in her hand.

'Well, I was feeling tired and run-down, but it's been a busy year,' Sophie replied, evading the real question. 'I've had a few headaches too.'

'Have you been eating? Nonnie said you haven't felt much like eating lately.'

'No, I haven't really; it's been too hot.'

'True,' agreed her dad. 'Listen darling, I'm sorry I've been grumpy and crotchety lately. I didn't realise you were worrying so much about everything. I don't want you to worry. Mum's working hard and we have enough coming in to keep us going for a while.'

Sophie sucked in a deep breath, her stomach contracting with nerves.

'I've been ringing all the employment agencies again,' her father continued. 'They think there'll be a better chance of a job coming up for me in February, once the holidays are over and everyone starts planning for the New Year. I've sent my résumé off to a few of my old clients as well.

'We can hold off for another six months at least before we need to start thinking about selling the house. So you see, there's really nothing to worry about.'

Sophie let out a deep breath, a flutter of relief welling through her.

'That's great news, Dad,' replied Sophie. 'But you know what, Dad? It wouldn't really matter if we lost the house. At least we'd have each other, our family. It's the people that you love in your life that really count.'

There was silence on the phone for a moment.

'You're right,' replied Sophie's dad, sounding much more like his old self. 'Thank you, sweetheart. I'm so glad you're sounding better.'

'You too,' said Sophie, grinning.

'See you on the weekend. Mum is going to come and stay on Friday night and have dinner with you, then bring you both home on Saturday. Will and I will batch here by ourselves.'

'See you on Saturday. Bye, Dad.'

'Bye, darling.'

24

Christmas Joy

Christmas Day dawned hot and fair, the sun shining brightly through the windows.

Outside, the black scorched earth was veiled by a thin growth of emerald-green grass.

Charlotte and Nell woke up feeling trepidation at the thought of another Christmas. Last Christmas, in Scotland, had been miserable, just a couple of months after the deaths, with Aunt Arabella arguing with Cook about the traditional menu for the day and Uncle Roderick planning to evict half the tenants.

Then there were the bittersweet memories of the many Dungorm Christmases before that: freezing snow on the ground about the house, singing Christmas hymns in the kirk, decorating the sitting room with holly boughs, and finding the Christmas stockings hanging on the mantelpiece stuffed with oranges, figs, nuts and trinkets.

But in the centre of all those memories was, of course,

their parents filling their lives with a warm feeling of love, joy and security.

'Merry Christmas, Charlotte. Merry Christmas, Nell,' sang Will as the girls emerged from their bedroom. Charlotte wore her new green dress and Nell wore her blue one, with matching ribbons in their hair.

'Merry Christmas,' echoed Sophie. Nell and Charlotte looked around and smiled.

'Merry Christmas, Will,' chorused Nell and Charlotte in return.

Christmas morning was a busy round of prayers, breakfast and a ten-mile buggy ride to Dalesford to hear the Christmas service. Everyone returned feeling happy and excited, looking forward to a glorious Christmas dinner.

The family sat in the dining room, around the long cedar table laid with the best linen, silver and china. The servants and staff would eat later out in the kitchen.

Annie and the girls had decorated the dining room with great branches of pale yellow and pink gum blossom, its eucalypt scent filling the air.

Mala, for once, was awake and ambled around the floor on all four paws, tempted by the smell of the table decorations.

'You have surpassed yourself, Mrs Gregory,' Mr McLaughlin declared. 'This is a feast fit for royalty.'

Mrs Gregory blushed as she carried in the platter of roast duck. 'Thank you kindly, sir, and a very Merry Christmas to you all.'

Mr McLaughlin carved the large butt of roast beef, then the delicate roast duck. Annie poured the gravy, while Mrs Gregory served the roast pumpkin, potatoes and peas. When Mrs Gregory had retired to the kitchen to enjoy her own feast, Mr McLaughlin bowed his head and said grace.

'I would also like to thank the Lord for bringing Charlotte and Nell into our home,' said Mr McLaughlin, smiling broadly. 'May our Scottish lassies enjoy their first Australian Christmas and may the next year be filled with much joy and happiness for them both, and for us all. Amen and *bon appétit*.'

'Amen,' chorused everyone around the table, picking up their knives and forks.

The meal was lively, with plenty of laughter and jokes and light conversation.

'This is the best duck I've ever eaten,' declared Will.

'Absolutely, and could I please have some more?' requested Henry, passing his plate over.

'More potatoes, boys?' asked Annie. 'Mrs Gregory has made mountains.'

'Yes, please.'

After the roast beef and duck was a huge plum pudding with cream and brandy sauce, apple tart with custard and crumbly mince tarts. The meal was finished with watermelon and cups of tea.

Afterwards the family retired to the sitting room to exchange gifts wrapped in coloured paper and tied with ribbon. Mr McLaughlin received a new clay pipe, while Annie had some material for a dress. Henry and Will both received blue shirts and moleskin trousers, to replace those that had been ruined in fighting the bushfire.

Charlotte and Nell had worked hard to make gifts for their new family. They had knitted thick, warm socks for Mr McLaughlin, Henry, Edward and Pot. For Annie, they had hemmed and embroidered some linen handkerchiefs, and Charlotte had drawn a watercolour sketch of the homestead.

'Thank you, Charlotte,' said Annie. 'I love this sketch.'

Suddenly Charlotte realised that in all the pleasure of giving gifts and watching everyone open them, the only present she had received herself was a bag, embroidered by Nell.

She had only a moment's feeling of disappointment, when Annie and Mr McLaughlin grinned at each other and handed Charlotte and Nell each a parcel at the same time.

They tore open the paper to find they had received identical presents: large red neckerchiefs, very worn and stained.

'Why, thank you,' said Charlotte and Nell together in surprise. Henry and Will were almost dancing with suppressed laughter.

'Put them on, put them on,' yelled Will. 'No, not around your neck, over your *eyes*.'

Henry grabbed Nell's neckerchief and tied it over her eyes like a blindfold. Will did the same for Charlotte.

'Your *real* present is outside,' explained Mr McLaughlin, laughing. 'You mustn't peek, so we thought it best to blindfold you.'

'Come on now, girls,' Annie cried, her voice bubbling with pleasure. 'We will lead you so you do not fall.'

Charlotte and Nell were confused but obediently followed where Henry and Will led them: out onto the verandah, around the back of the house, through the stable yard.

All the while there were loud shouts of laughter and excited directions.

'Watch your step here. Step down now.'

'Now over here; watch the rose bush.'

'Out of the way, Nicky, you will trip them over.'

'Careful, boys, not so fast. They'll fall.'

'All right, we're nearly there.'

'Let's just turn them around in a circle to really confuse them.'

'No, they'll get giddy and topple over.'

'All right. You can stop now, but don't take off the blindfold until we tell you.'

The girls stopped obediently and waited, their hearts pounding. What could the surprise be?

'Keep your eyes closed,' cautioned Annie. 'Will and Henry, take off the blindfolds. Open your eyes *now*!'

The girls were standing out in the stable yard surrounded by a giggling audience made up of Henry and Will, the Gregorys, Pot and his family, and a gaggle of stock hands and shepherds.

Standing in front of them were Annie and Mr McLaughlin, and beside them were two gorgeous chestnut ponies.

'Merry Christmas!' shouted everyone.

'Your very own ponies,' cried Annie.

'Their names are Tilly and Star,' added Mr McLaughlin proudly. 'Tilly is for Charlotte and Star is for Nell.'

'Henry and I made the bridles ourselves,' sang Will. 'It took ages!'

'Billy, Pot and I made the side-saddles,' said Mr McLaughlin, grinning.

'And I sewed the saddle blankets,' finished Annie.

Charlotte was speechless. A huge lump rose in her throat, stopping her breath.

'Thank you, thank you,' cried Nell, her voice cracking a little, as she rushed across to hug first Annie, then Mr McLaughlin, then Star.

Charlotte smiled a smile from the bottom of her heart. 'Thank you so much. This is the most wonderful present I could ever receive.'

Annie hugged her, and Mr McLaughlin kissed her gently on top of her head.

'That is our pleasure, my dears,' replied Mr McLaughlin. 'You deserve them for bringing joy to my Annie. She loves having you here. And of course, for saving our home from the fire!'

Charlotte stepped forward and stroked Tilly on her velvety nose. Tilly's ears flickered back and forth, then she gently hurrumphed into Charlotte's face, just as Rosie used to do. Charlotte buried her face in Tilly's neck to wipe away the sudden tears that welled, but this time, they were tears of joy.

Sophie and Jess's mother arrived after work. She looked tired but was very happy to see them. Nonnie, Sophie and Jess had been cooking all afternoon, making a special dinner to celebrate the end of the holiday.

They had roasted rack of lamb marinated in lemon and garlic, with roasted tomatoes, baby potatoes and kumera in olive oil and sea salt, sprinkled with rosemary from the garden. Sophie and Jess had made a green salad with chopped avocado and mango, and all this was to be followed by rich chocolate mousse with chocolate slivers.

The girls had set the antique dining table with Nonnie's

best silver, crystal and china, with frangipani flowers and candles down the centre.

'Oh, doesn't the table look gorgeous,' admired their mother as she walked in. 'And it smells fantastic.'

'Here, Mum, sit down,' cried Jess. 'Sophie and I are going to wait on you and Nonnie. Would you like a glass of wine?'

'Yes, please,' sighed their mother. 'This is heavenly.'

Sophie and Jess poured a glass of golden wine for Nonnie and their mother, and a glass of pineapple juice for themselves, all served in crystal goblets.

'Well, cheers,' cried Nonnie. 'Here's to my beautiful granddaughters. I loved having you here. Thank you, girls.'

'Cheers,' chorused everyone, carefully clinking the delicate goblets together.

Nonnie served the lamb and vegetables, while Sophie passed around the salad.

'Ah, delicious, and no mince in sight,' joked their mother. 'Now, girls, we have some great news for you. It may come to nothing, but Daddy has been invited in for another interview with a company that he saw yesterday.'

'That's wonderful,' said Sophie, her eyes shining.

'Fantastic,' cried Jess.

'Excellent,' added Nonnie. 'Jack must be thrilled. Now, more lamb anyone?'

'Yes, please,' cried Sophie and Jess at the same time.

Nonnie smiled and piled their plates with lamb cutlets and roast vegetables. Nonnie and Karen glanced at each other in relief to see Sophie eating with relish.

'Don't forget to leave some room for that fantastic-looking chocolate mousse,' warned their mother. 'Now tell me, what've you been doing?'

The girls chatted happily, joking and laughing. Everyone pronounced the meal a great success, particularly the chocolate mousse.

'What are you wearing around your neck, Sophie?' asked Karen, noticing the gold locket.

'Oh!' exclaimed Sophie, flushing. 'It's the locket we found in Charlotte Mackenzie's box.'

'Yes, I remember,' her mother replied. 'I haven't seen that box for years. Why don't you show it to me?'

Sophie ran to her room and fetched the box from the chest of drawers.

Sophie opened the box and spread the objects on the table.

'This is the pebble that Charlotte picked up from the beach on her last night at Dungorm, and this is the heather that bloomed early just for Charlotte and Nell,' Sophie exclaimed. 'This is a silver elf bolt that Charlotte found on the moors and that the bushrangers stole – but she got it back.'

Karen and Nonnie glanced at each other in consternation. 'The box has a secret, too,' Sophie added. She peeled away the violet silk and inserted the end of the key to lever up the base.

'Sophie, whatever are you doing?' cried Nonnie in alarm.

'It's all right, Nonnie,' Sophie reassured her. 'It's meant to come away. There's a secret compartment in Charlotte's box, and I think there's something inside.'

Once more the bottom lifted away to reveal the secret compartment.

Sophie slipped her fingers inside and pulled out a small parcel wrapped in cloth. Sophie's hands were trembling with excitement as she unwrapped it.

A gold ring fell out onto the table, featuring a huge cornflower-blue sapphire, surrounded by dazzling diamonds. Carefully Sophie slipped it onto her middle finger. It was too big for her. The cluster of jewels caught the light, flashing blue and white and gold.

'The Star of Serendib,' announced Sophie.

'Goodness,' breathed Nonnie. 'What a treasure.'

'It's the lost treasure of Dungorm,' agreed Sophie. 'Hidden all these years in Charlotte's secret treasure box.'

'Sophie, how on earth did you know it was there?' cried her mother.

Sophie took the ring from her finger.

'I had an amazing dream about Charlotte Mackenzie and she showed me where it was,' explained Sophie with a broad smile.

Karen, Nonnie and Jess looked at Sophie in astonishment.

'Here, Nonnie – your great-great-grandmother's ring. It belonged to Eliza Mackenzie, Charlotte's mother, and now it's yours.'

Nonnie pushed the ring onto her finger, admiring the brilliance of the precious gems.

'Oooh,' sighed Nonnie. 'What a stunning ring. I'm sure it's worth a fortune. Karen, we can sell the ring and use the money to help you and Jack.'

Karen's eyes lit up.

'No, *please* don't sell it, Nonnie,' begged Sophie. 'It *mustn't* be sold. It is the good-luck talisman of the Mackenzies.'

'Is it?' asked Karen. 'I thought the Mackenzies had terrible luck – becoming orphans, losing their castle, being sent to Australia to live with strangers.'

'Yes, but they had wonderful luck too,' replied Sophie. 'They found love and joy and a new home here in Australia.'

'When one door closes, another always opens,' Nonnie said softly.

'Exactly,' replied Sophie, with a huge smile.

Acknowledgements

When I was a little girl, my grandmother Nonnie used to tell my sister and me many stories – many of them Scottish tales. My favourite, however, was how her own grandmother had come to Australia in 1858 from Scotland with her sister. The two Mackenzie girls, Ellen and Jane, were orphans, sent by their uncle away from their home on the west coast of Scotland. Nonnie used to tell us that their father had been a rich Scottish laird with a castle, but that the girls had lost everything when their father had drowned at sea, closely followed by the death of their mother.

Nonnie's mother had told her that the castle should rightfully have belonged to the girls, but the uncle had sent the sisters to Australia so he could claim their inheritance. All we have left of this Mackenzie heritage are the stories and a small gold locket. As children, we dreamt of going back to Scotland to claim our Mackenzie castle. It was only later, I learnt, that girls in those days had very few legal rights and could not have inherited the estate. *The Locket of Dreams* grew out of my own imaginings of what might have happened to my ancestors, the two Mackenzie sisters. So my first thank you must go to Nonnie for teaching my whole family a love of stories, poetry, books and all things Scottish.

The first people to read the manuscript were my family – my 10-year-old daughter, Emily; my husband, Rob and my sister, Kate. All three helped me enormously to improve the book out of sight. For all your insight, suggestions, encouragement and love – a huge thank you!

Over the last two years, my family and I travelled around Australia and overseas – including visiting the Mackenzie clan country on the west coast of Scotland, searching for our castle.

Last year, we were fortunate enough to live for three amazing weeks with a wonderful Aboriginal family in the Kimberley. The Davey family told us lots of Aboriginal stories and shared much traditional knowledge with us, including hunting, making spears, herblore and family history.

We felt very privileged and honoured to share this time with them. My character Pot is named after one of their children, and some of the scenes were inspired by stories they told us, such as Pot being guided home by the spirits. In this book, I really wanted to make a tribute to acknowledge how much early European settlers learnt from the local Aborigines and to recognise the importance of the storytelling tradition in both Scottish and Aboriginal cultures.

While the Daveys told us many traditional stories about stingrays, turtles, whales and the creation serpent, the story

Pot tells here is not from the Davey family – it is my interpretation of a story we heard in various forms in different parts of Australia. So I would like to thank the whole Davey family for welcoming us to their land and teaching us so much – particularly Frank, Maureen, Ashley and Pot, for letting me use his name in my story.

Many thanks to Looloo for lending me lots of wonderful history books for my research, especially *The Letters of Rachel Henning* – letters from an English woman who emigrated to Australia during the 1850s. Her detailed letters gave me much historical information about the lives of women and children during this period.

To Mum who, among many things, makes the best Scotch marmalade in the world, and to Dad. This book is rich with so many experiences and gifts you have both given me.

Finally to all the team at Random House, including my editors, Brandon VanOver and Vanessa Mickan-Gramazio, but especially my publisher, Zoe Walton – you are fantastic!

About the Author

At about the age of eight, Belinda Murrell began writing stirring tales of adventure, mystery and magic in hand-illustrated exercise books. As an adult, she combined two of her great loves – writing and travelling the world – and worked as a travel journalist, technical writer and public relations consultant. Now, inspired by her own three children, Belinda is a bestselling, internationally published children's author. Her titles include four picture books, her fantasy adventure series, The Sun Sword Trilogy, and her six time-slip adventures, *The Locket of Dreams*, *The Ruby Talisman*, *The Ivory Rose*, *The Forgotten Pearl*, *The River Charm* and *The Sequin Star*.

For younger readers (aged 6 to 9), Belinda has a new series, Lulu Bell, about friends, family, animals and adventures growing up in a vet hospital.

Belinda lives in Manly in a gorgeous old house overlooking the sea with her husband, Rob, her three beautiful children and her dog, Rosie. She is an Author Ambassador for Room to Read and Books in Homes.

Find out more about Belinda at her website:
www.belindamurrell.com.au

THE RUBY TALISMAN

When Tilly's aunt tells her of their ancestress who survived the French Revolution, she shows Tilly a priceless heirloom. Tilly falls asleep wearing the ruby talisman, wishing she could escape to a more adventurous life . . .

In 1789, Amelie-Mathilde is staying at the opulent palace of Versailles. Her guardians want her to marry the horrible old Chevalier to revive their fortunes. Amelie-Mathilde falls asleep holding her own ruby talisman, wishing someone would come to her rescue . . .

Tilly wakes up beside Amelie-Mathilde. The timing couldn't be worse. The Bastille has fallen and starving peasants are rioting across the country. The palace is in chaos.

Tilly knows that Amelie and her cousin Henri must escape from France if they are to survive the Revolution ahead. But with mutinous villagers, vengeful servants and threats at every turn, there seems nowhere to run. Will they ever reach England and safety?

OUT NOW!